WHITE IS FOR WITCHING

"[Oyeyemi] knows that ghost stories aren't just for kids. And *White Is for Witching* turns out to be a delightfully unconventional coming-of-age story. . . . As in Toni Morrison's *Beloved* or Chris Abani's *Song for Night*, the supernatural elements of *White Is for Witching* serve to remind the characters—and Oyeyemi's readers—of horrifying historical circumstances. . . . Oyeyemi clearly appreciates that some crimes (like slavery or genocide or, in this case, institutional racism) are so heinous that the conventions of realist fiction seem woefully inadequate to describe them. She makes us glad to suspend disbelief."
—*The New York Times Book Review*

"Profoundly chilling . . . a slow-building neo-Gothic that will leave persevering readers breathless."   —*The Boston Globe*

"Chilling . . . lyrical. . . . If you've been missing Shirley Jackson all these many years, missing the creepy character-driven goodness of *We Have Always Lived in the Castle* and *Hangsaman*, here's a writer who seems to be a direct heir to that lamented one's gothic throne."   —*The Austin Chronicle*

"Appealing from page one . . . Unconventional, intoxicating, and deeply disquieting."   —*Publishers Weekly* (starred review)

"Laced with thought-provoking story lines."   —*Booklist*

continued . . .

"Spooky and thought provoking. . . . [With] Poe-like elements. . . . The palpable aura of claustrophobic dread and menace urges the reader to conclude that the author casts the most powerful spell."
—*The Toronto Star*

"[A] remarkable, shape-shifting tale. . . . The narrative oscillates between the mundane and the supernatural, and it is this skillful blend of the fantastic and the everyday that makes it resonate so chillingly. While ghosts may skulk inside the house, the horrors lurking outside are equally alarming. . . . Yet, for all this trickery, Oyeyemi's writing is vividly emotional. . . . In the end, this isn't a fantasy about ghosts and witches. It is really about memory and belonging, love and loss."
—*New Statesman*

"Superbly atmospheric . . . [A] mesmeric exploration of alienation and loss. . . . [A] disturbing and intricate novel. The dark tones of Poe in her haunting have also the elasticity of Haruki Murakami's surreal mental landscapes."
—*The Independent* (UK)

"Oyeyemi is a writer who moves easily between the literary, the demotic, and the supernatural. . . . She is sharply amusing on the strangeness of the ordinary world. . . . Her technical skill as a novelist is remarkable, her range of reference formidable, and her use of language virtuosic."
—*The Daily Telegraph* (UK)

"A weirdly compelling mix of modern gothic, matriarchal magic, and coming-of-age tale that weaves the supernatural and mother-daughter relations deep into its fabric."
—*Financial Times*

"There is no doubt that Oyeyemi is a formidable talent."
—*The Scotsman*

"Cleverly, Oyeyemi engineers the narrative so that the novel reflects not only a teenager's solipsism but also her furious energy and capacity to attract harm. . . . The language is rich; ideas proliferate; myth and story tangle together luxuriantly."
—*The Times* (UK)

PRAISE FOR

MR. FOX

A *NEW YORK TIMES* NOTABLE BOOK

"Oyeyemi's writing is gorgeous and resonant and fresh . . . a shimmering landscape pulsating with life."
—Aimee Bender, *The New York Times Book Review*

"Cheeky and imaginative."
—*The New Yorker*

"Oyeyemi has an eye for the gently perverse, the odd detail that turns the ordinary marvelously, frighteningly strange."
—*The Boston Globe*

"Dazzling."
—*The Washington Post*

"Vibrant . . . these labyrinthine tales-within-a-tale show . . . a powerful truth: that even ideas born of our imagination matter in the real world."
—*O, The Oprah Magazine*

continued . . .

ALSO BY HELEN OYEYEMI

White Is for Witching

HELEN OYEYEMI

RIVERHEAD BOOKS
NEW YORK

RIVERHEAD BOOKS
An imprint of Penguin Random House LLC
375 Hudson Street
New York, New York 10014

First published by Nan. A Talese/Doubleday: 2009
First Riverhead trade paperback edition: February 2014
Riverhead trade paperback ISBN: 9781594633072

Printed in the United States of America
9   10   8

Book design by Kristin del Rosario

I hold my honey and I store my bread
In little jars and cabinets of my will.
I label clearly, and each latch and lid
I bid, Be firm till I return from Hell.

—GWENDOLYN BROOKS,
SELECTED POEMS

White Is for Witching

WHERE IS MIRANDA?

ORE:

Miranda Silver is in Dover, in the ground beneath her
mother's house.
Her throat is blocked with a slice of apple
(to stop her speaking words that may betray her)
her ears are filled with earth
(to keep her from hearing sounds that will confuse her)
her eyes are closed, but
her heart thrums hard like hummingbird wings.
Does she remember me at all I miss her I miss the way her
eyes are the same shade of grey no matter the strength or
weakness of the light I miss the taste of her I see her in my
sleep, a star planted seed-deep, her arms outstretched, her
fists clenched, her black dress clinging to her like mud.
She chose this as the only way to fight the soucouyant.

vampire-like monster

ELIOT:

Miri is gone.

Just gone. We'd had an argument. It was dark outside. Gusts of wind tangled in the apple trees around our
house and dropped fruit onto the roof, made it sound like
someone was tapping on the walls in the attic, Morse code
for *let me out*, or something weirder. The argument was a
stupid one that opened up a murky little mouth to take in
other things. Principally it was about this pie I'd baked for
her. She wouldn't eat any of it, and she wouldn't let me.

"Why did you use the winter apples?" She asked it over
and over. Nothing I replied could break her monotone.

She said: "You've done too much now. I can't trust you
anymore."

She shook her head and dropped to the disappointed
hiss of a primary-school teacher, or a kid trying to borrow
the authority of one: "Bad! You are *bad*."
(My sister turned seventeen in a mental health clinic; I
brought our birthday cake to her there.)

Miri's accusations, her whole manner that night scared
the shit out of me. She looked in my direction but she
couldn't seem to focus on me. She was the thinnest I'd ever
seen her. Her hands and head were the heaviest parts of her.
Her neck drooped. She hugged herself, her fingers pinning
her dress to her ribs. There was an odd smell to her, heavy
and thick. It was clear to me that she was slipping again,
down a new slide. When she said she didn't trust me, I
turned away rather than let myself get angrier.

I went up to my room. Miri didn't call after me. I don't think she came upstairs again. Or she may have, without my hearing. I'm not sure. I heard the front door slam, but I thought it was just one of the guests coming home late. I stayed where I was, knelt on my window seat, smoking, seeing shapes in the rain, listening to all the apples in the world bouncing off our roof.

That last time I saw Miri, she wasn't wearing any shoes. Five months ago I took that as security that she would come back. And now I keep coming back to that in my mind, the fact that she was barefoot. That her running away was a heat-of-the-moment thing, unplanned.

A part of me knows that we can't find her because something has happened to her.

29 BARTON ROAD:

Miranda is at *home*
(homesick, home *sick*)
Miranda can't come in today Miranda has a *condition* called pica she has eaten a great deal of chalk—she really can't help herself—she has been very ill—***Miranda has pica she can't come in*** today, she is stretched out inside a wall she is feasting on plaster she has pica

try again:

IS MIRANDA ALIVE?

ORE:

Probably not—

ELIOT:

I've been dialling her phone, the phone she lost months ago, as if she might have caught up with it somewhere. I wrote her a note and folded it in four and slipped it under her door.

I know she's not there.

But I wrote, *Miri I'm lonely.*

I dropped the words onto the paper so hard that they're doubled by the thin perforations around them.

I wouldn't have bothered trying to tell her, I wouldn't have written to her if

What I mean is, each act of speech stands on the belief that someone will hear. My note to Miri says more than just I'm lonely. Invisibly it says that I know she will see this, and that when she sees this it will turn her, turn her back, return her.

Miri I conjure you.

29 BARTON ROAD:

She has *wronged* me I will not allow her to live

The house speaks for a second time

try a different way:

What Happened to Lily Silver?

ORE:

Miranda lay beside me on the grass that circled the mill pond, her lecture notebook opened up on her stomach. Bicycles kept passing by, their wheels groaning against the wooden bridge. The sun shone through clouds swollen with the smell of wet bark, and there were bees around us.

Miranda spoke so quietly I had to move closer to her, my ear to her lips. "It's Eliot's fault," she said.

When I looked at her, she smiled brightly. Incongruous smiles were a sort of nervous thing with Miranda, a way of protecting herself from consequences, I think. Just like putting sunglasses on, or opening up an umbrella.

ELIOT:

I spent Lily's second night in Haiti on Miri's bedroom floor. Miri switched off the light and folded herself into her bed in her usual way, so that every part of her was covered and the bedsheets set around her curled body as if she was fixed in wax. I never knew how she managed to breathe. She said she slept like that so her dreams wouldn't escape.

I leaned my back against her desk, wrapped blankets around my shoulders and tried to read with a flashlight.

The weird thing started when I said to Miri, "Don't fall asleep yet." The "please" hugged the roof of my mouth and refused to go out to meet her.

Miri said, "You're scared about Lily."

I didn't answer. I tried to picture our mother in Haiti and I saw her in a tower built of guns, heaving with voodoo, creepy gods and white feathers tipped with blood.

Lily's eye transformed places. She looked at structures and they turned inside out and offered her their desolate jigsaw patterns. Once Lily pointed out a photo of hers in a magazine, a picture of a tundra with a ball of ice at noon in the sky. What was this place? My mother gave me three guesses. My best and most desperate guess was that truckloads of sand had been poured onto a simulation of the surface of the moon. "Nope," she said. "Gobi desert."

Lily was the changer who came home the same. But that last time the signs were bad. When she left, she had forgotten her watch on the telephone stand in the hallway, a brass body with thin leather arms, ticking away Haitian time, six hours behind ours. How could she have forgotten her watch? She never had before. Miri and I had debated leaving it where it was (that seemed luckier), then Miri had confiscated it for safekeeping in case one of the houseguests stole it or broke it or something.

Miri said sleepily, "The goodlady will take care of Lily. She promised."

"The goodlady?"

"She likes us."

I skipped a beat, then said: "Stay up, just for a bit more. Tell me a Herodotus story or something."

She grumbled, "*Tired.*"

A small, stiff thing coursed through the dark and sank cold claws into my head. I switched Miri's lamp on. Miri grumbled again, but the shape under her bedcovers didn't move. I got the odd feeling that her voice was coming from somewhere else. I said: "Miri . . . Lily's slipping away. We have to remember her or she'll be gone."

She opened her eyes. "What do you mean?"

"Quick, we've got to remember her. What can you remember?"

Miri's eyes narrowed and she took a long time to reply. "Lily's . . . hair," she said, finally. "The near-blackness of it, and the wave in it, near the bottom, where the brush keeps getting stuck."

"We need more than that. What else do we know? What else is real about her?"

"Eliot. Please."

"Miri, you'd better fucking stay awake. I mean it. Stay awake or Lily will die."

Shrill singing between my ears.

"Why are you saying this? It's not true," Miri said. "The goodlady—"

"No. There is no such thing, Miri. Grow up."

She slid up out of the covers, gasping, her face mottled pink and white as if she had come from a place of burning. She rested her head against her bedstead.

"Don't say that. There *is* such a thing."

She was about to cry. There was a change in the shadows and I twisted around, looking into the corners where the lamplight cracked. Miri is the older twin. Maybe she has seen things that craned their necks to look at her and then withdrew before I was born, thinking that to consider one of us is to consider both.

"Come on, don't be a baby. Just remember something."

"Lily smells of the ghosts of roses," Miri murmured. "Lily is so small she fits under Dad's chin. Lily . . ."

"Stay awake," I warned, and lay down with ice in my chest. I fell asleep to the sound of Miri listing things. "Lily loves the shape of cartoon teardrops. Lily never knew her mother, and she doesn't care. Lily's favourite films have a lot of tap dancing and a little bit of story. Lily slides towards the colour red like it's a magnet . . ."

In the morning Miri was still sitting up, her arms stiff on the bedspread before her, gone so deep into sleep that she seemed part of the wall behind her, a girl-shaped texture rising from the plaster in an unrepeated pattern. Her braid was unravelling. Her lips were pinched, her forehead lined with effort. I think in her dreams she was listing things. She tumbled awake and blurted, *"Lily can't stand Pachelbel's Canon!"* I would have laughed if she hadn't said it with such terror.

Later—when Dad told us what the voice in the phone had told him—prim, slender Miri folded her hands on the lap of her dress. She looked down and, for a moment, appeared to be smiling. She wasn't smiling. She wasn't in control of her face.

29 BARTON ROAD:

The twins were sixteen and a half when their mother died. She was shot in Port-au-Prince; gunfire sprayed into the queue at a voting station. Her camera remained intact throughout. Also, the lens was unstained. To protect it from dust and flies, Lily had covered it with a square of checked cloth and an elastic band, rustic jam-jar style.

That day two bullets were for her; they found her and leapt into her lung. She fell amidst milling feet. Someone leant against her and *pushed* her aside, outside, out of life. She pushed back, sweat standing out on her skin in droplets as if she had been rained on. But her opponent had great wings, lined with clouds of feathers that brushed her, cooled her, pricked her. The shadow of them darkened her sight. She tried to lift her head and see into the crowd. The other two she had been standing with, the newspaper journalists, her eyes couldn't find them. They had long gone. She dribbled blood, could not let it go, closed her eyes only for the length of time it took to drink it up again. The brokenness in her chest was not clean. It was not a straight line or a single throb. She couldn't see it but it consumed her.

Stupid, stupid; Lily had been warned not to go to Haiti. I warned her.

the house speaks again

Why do people go to these places, these places that are not for them?

It must be that they believe in their night vision. They believe themselves able to draw images up out of the dark.

But black wells only yield black water.

PART ONE

Curiouser

Luc Dufresne

is not tall. He is pale and the sun fails on his skin. He used to write restaurant reviews, plying a thesaurus for other facets to the words "juicy" and "rich." He met Lily at a magazine Christmas party; a room set up like a chessboard, at its centre a fir tree gravely decorated with white ribbons and jet globes. They were the only people standing by the tree with both hands in their pockets. For hours Lily addressed Luc as "Mike," to see what he had to say about it. He didn't correct her; neither did he seem charmed, puzzled, or annoyed, reactions Lily had had before. When she finally asked him about it, he said, "I didn't think you were doing it on purpose. But then I didn't think you'd made a mistake. I don't know what I thought. I suppose I thought you were calling me Mike because Mike was my name, if you see what I mean."

He wooed his wife with peach tarts he'd learnt from his pastry-maker father. The peaches fused into the dough with their skins intact, bittered and sweetened by burnt sugar. He won his wife with modern jazz clouded with cello and xylophone notes.

His fingers are ruined by too close and careless contact with heat; the parts that touch each other when the hand is held out straight and flat, the skin there is stretched, speckled and shiny. Lily had never seen such hands. To her they seemed the most wonderful in all the world. Those hands on her, their strong and broken course over her, his thumbs on her hip bones.

One night she said to him, "I love you, do you love me?" She said it as lightly as such a thing can be said without it being a joke. Immediately he replied, "Yes I love you, and you are beautiful," pronouncing his words with a hint of impatience because they had been waiting in him a long time.

He seems always to be waiting, his long face quiet, a dark glimmer in his heavy-lidded eyes. Waiting for the mix in the pot or the oven to be ready. Waiting for blame (when, at twelve, Miranda's condition became chronic he thought that somehow he was responsible; he'd let her haunt the kitchen too much, licking spoons. He forgot that he had allowed Eliot to do the same.) Waiting, now, for the day Lily died to be over, but for some reason that day will not stop.

Meanwhile he has the bed-and-breakfast to run, he has cooking to oversee, peach tarts to make for the guests who know to ask for them. The peach tarts are work he doesn't yet know how to do without feeling Lily. He has baked two batches of them since she died. Twice it was just him and the cook, the Kurdish woman, in the kitchen and he has bowed his head over his perfectly layered circles of pastry, covered his face and moaned with such appalled, amazed pain, as if he has been opened in a place that he never even knew existed. "Oh," he has said, unable to hold it in. "Oh." Luc is very ugly when he cries; his grief is turned entirely inward and has nothing of the child's appeal for help. The Kurdish woman clicked her tongue and moved her hands and her head; her distress was at his distress and he didn't notice her. The first time he cried like that she tried to touch her fat hand to his, but he said, "Don't—don't," in a voice that shook her.

Nobody knew what to say to Luc. His children were closest to knowing, but Miranda was mad and when she saw him those first few weeks after Lily's death, she wasn't sure who he was. Eliot noticed Luc more, as an eye does when something is removed from a picture and the image is reduced to its flaw, the line where the whole is disrupted.

I find Luc interesting. He really has no idea what to do now, and because he is not mine I don't care about him. I do, however, take great delight in the power of a push, a false burst of light at the bottom of a cliff, just one little encouragement to the end. Sometimes it seems too easy to toy with him. Other times . . . I don't know. But he is always so close by that it doesn't matter so much.

M y father is very brief. All in the most likeable manner possible—he gets this look of discomfort whenever someone tries to discuss something with him at length. He looks as if he would very much like to spare you the effort. He used to go through horrors with Miri on the subject of her day at school, his replies cautious and neutral in case he appeared to be disapproving of something that was a good thing. Miri would chatter and chatter about our teacher having been unfair or the disappearance of her pencils. "Ah," Dad would say, and, "Right." And, "Really?"

If I was going on a trip or something it was a simple matter of handing him a letter or an itinerary and saying, "Dad, it's £300," or whatever it was. He'd scan the paper and say, "Fine," or he'd say, "Here's the thing; can't afford that this term. Are you now resentful?"

Are you now resentful is always a genuine question from him. We never, ever said yes. It was my dad's idea to open Lily's house as a bed-and-breakfast. Lily's grandma, our GrandAnna, had raised Lily herself, and when she died she left Lily the house in Dover. I heard my dad on the phone to someone about it: "Seven bedrooms, four bathrooms and God's own 1940s kitchen . . ."

Lily wanted to put the Dover house up to let and use the

money to pay the rent on our flat in London, which, Dad said, made no sense at all. But: "Why on earth would I want to live in Dover again? I spent my childhood in a state of inertia."

Dad spent about six months working on Lily. The facts, figures and written proposals he'd prepared for the bank left her completely unmoved; she always tried to ignore things she didn't understand rather than be intimidated by them. But apparently it was the bed linen that changed her mind. Cool blue silk and cotton patchwork. When Dad laid the stitched pillowcase and duvet out for her on the sofa, the colours reminded her of something she'd never seen. She said to us, "Imagine everyone in the house—even people we don't know—all wrapped up safe in blue, like fishes. What fun . . ."

Miri and I were ten; Dad spent some time with a big map, planning a scenic route, and then he drove the moving van himself. Miri and I fidgeted at first, then settled when we saw cliffs bruising the skyline and smelt birds and wet salt on the air.

Our new house had two big brown grids of windows with a row of brick in between each grid. No windows for the attic. From the outside the windows didn't look as if they could be opened, they didn't look as if they were there to let air or light in, they were funny square eyes, friendly, tired. The roof was a solid triangle with a fat rectangular chimney behind it. Lily bounced out of the van first and I scrambled out of the other side and crooked my arm so as to escort her to the door. The house is raised from the road and laid along the top of a brick staircase, surrounded by thick hedge with pink flowers fighting through it. "Careful on the steps," Lily said. The steps leading up to the house bulge with fist-sized lumps of grey-white flint, each piece a knife to cut your knee open should you slip. Opposite our house there is a churchyard, a low mound of green divided into two. The graves beneath it are unmarked. Lily took my arm and held Miri's hand and when we got up to the front door she rubbed the crescent moon–shaped door knocker and laughed a little bit and said, "Hello, hello again."

The first thing Lily showed us inside was the dusty marble fireplace. It was so big that Miri could crawl into the place where the wood was supposed to sit. She tried to make crackling, fire-like noises.

(when we were ten I always knew the meaning of the sounds she made, even when they were unsuccessful)

but ended up choking on a puff of dust that bolted down the chimney. Next Lily showed us the little ration-book larder behind the kitchen; the shelves were wonky and the room had a floor so crazily checked that none of us could walk in a straight line in there. I remember how brilliant I thought it all was; there was nothing for it but to jump in the air and yell and kick and make kung-fu noises.

Miri and I conferred and decided that we liked the tallness of the house, the way the walls shoot up and up with the certainty of stone, "Like we're in a castle," Miri put it. We liked the steep, winding staircase with the gnarled banister. We especially liked the ramshackle lift and the way you could see its working through a hole worn into the bottom in the back left corner. We liked that the passageways on each floor were wide enough for the two of us to stand beside each other with our arms and legs spread, touching but not touching. I climbed one of the apple trees and surveyed the garden, the patches of wild flowers that crumpled in the shade, the Andersen shelter half-hidden by red camellia shrubs. I was well pleased. "Wicked house," I said. "*Magic*," said Miri, from somewhere below.

We thought it would be hard to make friends because of the way people came out and stared at us in the moving van as it passed through the streets. But Miri is good at making friends, and I am good at tagging along on expeditions and acting as if the whole thing was my idea in the first place. Miri was very pleased with Martin Jones's curly hair; the boy's head was like a sheep's. He became our first friend in the area and he brought most of the rest.

Actually, when we were sixteen Miri gave me the task of telling Martin that he didn't stand a chance with her. Miri called me into her room, fixed me with a look of dread and whispered, "He asked me out and now I just can't *look at him* anymore." I refused point-blank to be her messenger or to have anything to do with any of it, but she said, "Then I'll write him a letter." I cringed and said, "Don't do that."

Martin and a couple of others came around to smoke and watch what promised to be "strange and unusual porn." Women with horses, women with lizards, women with women *plus* horses and lizards. I pretended to be leaner than I was and at one point mentioned aloud one of the "actors'" resemblance to Miri's boyfriend. The others groaned.

"What the fuck—"

"Er, no—"

"Too gay, Silver."

Martin didn't say anything himself, but I knew that he was gutted and I didn't let him pay for his share of the weed; he put a note down and when he wasn't looking I screwed it up and threw it into his coat pocket with a sense of relief so huge it was disabling. I wrote something in my diary about it a few days later, about our teenage years being a realm of the emotionally baroque. I wasn't even lean when I wrote that.

So Martin was the first friend, but the other kids he brought liked the house too.

For a few months after we moved in it was just Lily, Miri, Dad and me in the house, no guests. Decorating happened, the kitchen got updated; Lily went away to Mexico and came back with a pair of shrivelled corn-husk dolls that she put on a shelf in her studio when Miri and I rejected them. During that time there was no better place in the neighbourhood for hide-and-seek, or for Robin Hood versus Sheriff of Nottingham swordstick fighting in the back garden. There was no better place to play Hitler Resistance Force, a game I made up so I could be Churchill. My first kiss was in the Andersen shelter, more a percussion of heads, faces, mouths than anything else. We were thirteen. Emma's the sort of girl who likes boys who have unpredictable moods and write poetry and imagine things, so I played up to that. We were in the shelter because she was supposed to be a Nazi double agent giving me secret information. For some reason whilst kissing her my main preoccupation was not hurting her or bruising her. I tried not to hold her too hard. Her hair and skin were so soft.

There is another shelter inside the house. It is beneath the sitting room with the fireplace; it is under a trapdoor set in the floor. The room is dim and long and deep; a room for sleeping in. Sleeping and not much else. I tried to revise for exams in there and ended up curled up on my side on the floor, snoring.

What took getting used to in Dover were the gulls and their croaky sobs, and the sense of climbing upstairs when walking on some roads and downstairs when walking on others. The house, the garden, moving. The whole thing was like a dream; for weeks Miri and I couldn't believe it and wandered around the place with pangs in our stomachs, preemptive homesickness ready for the time when Dad and Lily would announce it was only a holiday and it was time to leave. Aside from our great-grandmother dying, we knew that it was Dad that had made it all happen, and we revered him as a wizard.

Miri's room was darker than mine, even before she took to keeping her curtains drawn at all times and Lily started calling her room "the psychomantium." That first day, Miri found something on the floor of that room she'd picked as hers. I didn't see what it was, but it was very small, and I thought that it must have cut her or something because just after she dropped it into her pocket she sucked thoughtfully at her finger. It took me about an hour of my best teasing and insults to get the secret out of her; finally she sighed and showed me. It was a ball of chalk.

Dad had been a waiter, then a trainee chef, then a food critic, and each job had bored him to the point of existential crisis. This thing with the house was plan B. Or C, or D or X. Without the guests and the maintenance and the folders of forms and bills, Dad would just sit. It's almost as if Lily knew, years and years in advance, that she was leaving us. As if she was gifting him something to be later, after her. That's not true, and it's not possible, but . . . the way she indulged him so completely. She gave him her house; Lily and Miri and I just lived in it. The capital man is the sum of his possessions.

When Lily died, and here I am telling it exactly as it was, Dad got even more control of the house. Lily's dying meant he didn't have to ask anyone about anything. There was no longer anyone who needed convincing that it was absolutely necessary to replace the old lift shaft; he just had it replaced, three months after the funeral. He dropped me off at the clinic and said to me, "I can't stay long with you and Miri." At that time Miri would only speak to me, and I knew it bothered him the way Miri sat back in her chair and looked at him without saying anything, with that empty smile on her lips. But the other reason Dad couldn't stay was that he had to get back and keep an eye on the work on the lift.

Without saying a word I kept daring him. *Fall apart, fall apart.* If I could have seen a button to press, I would have. *Miri and I don't need you to be strong, we need you to crack a little now.*

PICA

is a medical term for a particular kind of disordered eating. It's an appetite for non-food items, things that don't nourish. The word itself is pronounced *pie*-kah, a word like a song about a bird and food. Miri said it tiredly to herself and to me. "Pie-kah, pie-kah, I've got pie-kah." Lily told all our teachers at primary school and all the dinner ladies knew. When we went to secondary school Lily wrote it down on a form as a special concern. Pie-kah meant that Miri counted bites of food and smiled with breathless relief when she had met her quota. Counting bites was Lily's idea, and Miri accepted it gladly. "That's a good idea," she said, nodding, nodding. Whenever Miri talked about her pica with Lily she seemed so grown up about it, a shaky balance of humility and dignity. Dad was relieved that Miri didn't mean to be rebellious. I might remember Miri's special pastries as more elaborate than they really were, but Dad made some astonishing things for her. Flaky cones smothered in honey and coconut and chocolate and whatever else he could think of. He did a lot of soft foods, too, soups, and jellies with (eye) balls of peeled fruit staring out of them. What Miri did was, she crammed chalk into her mouth under her covers. She hid the packaging at the bottom of her bag and threw it away when we got to school. But then there'd be cramps that twisted her body, pushed her off her seat and lay her on the floor, helplessly pedalling her legs. Once, as if she knew that I was thinking of sampling her chalk to see what the big wow was, she smiled sweetly, sadly, patronisingly, and said to me, "Don't start, you'll get stuck."

It runs in the family. Anna Good had it in 1938; a year before she became Anna Silver. She ruined her work stockings and skirt with crouching in the mud searching for acorn husks that would splinter down her throat. She ate leaves by the handful and chipped her teeth on the pebbles she scooped out of the brown water when she went walking on the promenade. *The house is Andrew's,* she told herself; *I have no part in it.*

One evening she pattered around inside me, sipping something strong that wedged colour into her cheeks, and she dragged all my windows open, putting her glass down to struggle with the stiffer latches. I cried and cried for an hour or so, unable to bear the sound of my voice, so shrill and pleading, but unable to stop the will of the wind wheeling through me, cold in my insides. That was the first and last time I've heard my own voice. I suppose I am frightening. But Anna Good couldn't hear me. When she closed me up again it was only because she was too cold. Most nights she went with the moon, and when it was round she stayed in my biggest bedroom and wouldn't answer the thing that asked her to let it out

(let you out from where?

let me out from the small, the hot, the take me out of the fire i am ready i am hard like the stones you ate, bitter like those husks)

the moonlight striped her, marked out places where the whispering thing would slip through and she would unfold. When Andrew went to war the sirens shrieked at night and the sky was full of squat balloons that flamed and ate bombs and would not move with the breeze, these balloons and nothing else, not even stars.

Anna Good you are long gone now, except when I resurrect you to play in my pupper show, but you forgive since when I make you appear it is not really you, and besides you know that my reasons are sound. Anna Good it was not your pica that made you into a witch. I will tell you the truth because you are no trouble to me at all. Indeed you are a mother of mine, you gave me a kind of life, mine, the kind of alive that I am.

Anna Good there was another woman, long before you, but related. This woman was thought an animal. Her way

was to slash at her flesh with the blind, frenzied concentration that a starved person might use to get at food that is
buried. Her way was to drink off her blood, then bite and
suck at the bobbled stubs of her meat. Her appetite was only
for herself. This woman was deemed mad and then turned
out and after that she was not spoken of. I do not know the
year, or even how I know this.

But Miranda . . . you are listening too.

Miranda.

Look at me.

Will you not?

It is useful, instructive, comforting to know that you are
not alone in your history.

So I have done you good

and now,

some harm. ꙮ

When Miranda

finally discharged herself from the clinic, Eliot and her father came to collect her. They looked at her strangely. She didn't know what it could be; she was more normal then she had been in months. She sat in the back of the car and looked very seriously at her suitcase while her brother and father looked at her, looked away, looked at her again. She passed a hand over her hair, which lay meek and wispy against her neck. Her hair had been bobbed out of necessity at first. Miranda had been admitted to the clinic because one morning Eliot had found her wordless and thoughtful. It had been a long night, a perfect full moon tugging the sky around it into clumsy wrinkles. Miranda had been bleeding slightly from the scalp and her wrists were bound together with extreme dexterity and thin braids of her own hair.

It had been six months since then but her hair had been kept short. She didn't know why, she couldn't remember having expressed a preference. There was much that she was unable to remember. Especially unclear were the days immediately after she and Eliot had had the news of Lily's death. She remembered going into school and everyone being very sorry for her loss, but Eliot said that he had gone to school and she had stayed at home. The incident with the hair was completely lost; it seemed that when she'd left herself she'd left completely and it was not worth trying to fetch the images back, pointless trying to identify what exactly it was that had made her snap.

The two doctors who had been "working with" her at the clinic had mistook her resignation for stubbornness and constantly hovered on the edge of pressing her to remember. She objected mildly, with a sense of wasting her father's money. The clinic was a private clinic. Her room at the clinic had its own phone line and plush curtains and in the common room people checked their e-mail and played snooker. She had agreed to be admitted to an adolescent psychiatric unit because no-one at home knew how to help her feel comfortable.

She had had such a strong feeling that she needed to talk to someone who would tell her some secret that would make everything alright. She had been unable to think who it was. She had sat awake long hours downstairs, looking into the empty white arch of the fireplace, her hands on her rib cage. Who was it that needed to talk to her, that she needed to talk to? She had gone through lists of people it could be. She could only think of people that it couldn't be. It wasn't Lily, it wasn't her father, it wasn't Eliot, it wasn't any of the poets whose words stuck spikes in her, not even Rumi. It wasn't God. She did not think it was someone who was alive. She did not think it was anyone who existed, this messenger. So, the morning after the bad night she went with her father to see a doctor, a different doctor from the one who had, through no fault of his own, been unable to help her with her pica. She had signed a form, her name near her father's, and admitted herself to the clinic.

Whenever she tried to think about the long night before the bad morning on which Eliot had found her, nothing came to mind. The sedatives had done their work and she'd gone away and now she was coming home again. Exactly as if she'd been put in an envelope and posted abroad, then returned to sender. Even if alive the package doesn't, can't, note events, only the sensation of travel. All Miranda had been left with was a suspicion that she had spent much of her first night at the clinic clapping. She thought there might have been a bout of bringing her hands together over and over after the lights in the room went out, her body held in frightened rigidity because if she dared stop clapping then a bad thing would come.

She hadn't told Eliot about it when he came to visit; instead she had taken to asking him whether he thought it would rain. He had said yes every time.

Eliot was wearing his reading glasses now; he'd climbed

into the car with a hardback about the history of doubt. The way he held it on his lap as their father drove, she could tell he was unsure of the ensuing protocol; no one was saying anything, so there was no reason for him not to continue reading. But at the same time, if he started reading it would be a confrontational act somehow. His pockets weren't big enough to put the book out of sight, either. Eventually he pushed his glasses up to the top of his head and looked out of the window. To make conversation, Miranda said, "Why are you reading that book? Are you in doubt about something?"

Eliot yawned, as he did when uncomfortable. "I told Cambridge that I'd read it and now I've got to make it true."

She said, "You're applying to Cambridge?"

Uncertainty worked his mouth. She thought she had wobbled in her seat, then realised she hadn't moved at all; the thought *don't go* had flashed through her like a swarm of pins. Eliot was one of those boys that made girls go quiet. He was so beautiful that it seemed certain he was arrogant or insensitive or stupid. He'd taken Luc's contrast of fair skin and dark hair and he'd taken Lily's curls and lively wide-set eyes. His bone structure was scary and unnatural and flawless. Besides that he was her knight.

The first week Miranda and Eliot had moved to Dover, they'd played King Arthur's Court with Martin, Emma and Emma's older brother, Mark. Martin was Merlin, Miranda was Morgan Le Fay, Emma was Nimue, the

Damosel of the Lake, and Mark was King Arthur. Eliot said he didn't care which knight he was—they were all badasses. He'd pulled the green ribbon down through Miranda's ponytail, tied it around his sleeve and he'd said to her, "I'm your knight." Miranda pushed him. He took a single step back and scowled. Miranda said loudly, "I'm Morgan Le Fay—I've got spells and I can stick up for myself."

He'd said, "I know, but just in case." Eliot at ten was slight and earnest, his face all eyes. He'd been quick to feel and quick to anger, and when he was angry he would smile very deliberately and with incredible sweetness before walking away. He didn't care that the others heard what he said and sniggered, but Miranda cared. That's why she'd thought, but hadn't said, *I'm your knight too.*

Now she looked at him, at the awkward length of him, so carefully arranged to fit the space in the front of the car. The sleeves of his jumper and coat were rolled up to his elbows and he was goose-bumping under the cold. He would get into Cambridge, of course he would go.

She said plaintively, "Is it too late to apply?"

She felt Luc and Eliot not looking at each other.

"I didn't know you even wanted to go there. If you want you can apply next year," Luc offered.

Miranda waited, then said, "But what will I do for a whole year?"

Neither of them answered her. She supposed the answer

was, Get better. The thought of a slow and measured crawl back to health filled her with black sand. She said, "I want to try."

Eliot twisted around in his seat. "Look, Miri, it's not . . . you can't just . . . you need to really think hard about it. There are all these different colleges and you've got to pick a college, a course, everything."

Miranda spun the combination locks of her suitcase. "Well, what course are *you* applying to? What college are *you* applying to?" She looked at him and waited, she refused to pick up the thread of any other conversation.

Luc didn't make a sound, but he looked into the rearview mirror and she saw the groan on his face. Eliot breathed out through his nostrils. His glance was disbelieving, sent her way to check that she was serious. "What the fuck," he said. Finally, in tones of outrage, he told her. Miranda noted the name of the college on the back of her hand so she wouldn't forget. Eliot said something about her having to write a personal statement. Suddenly she wanted to make him angrier; it took everything she had to stay quiet and not ask him to help her write her application.

Eliot passed her a newspaper, *The Dover Post,* rolled up. It took her a second to get her eyes focused, then she read of the stabbing of the fourth Kosovan refugee in three weeks. Three had died in hospital. Her gaze could only touch the page very lightly before it skittered away. She said, "Someone is going around stabbing these people?" She didn't want to say "refugees." She didn't want to say "Kosovans." She didn't know why. Or maybe it seemed feeble somehow, like making a list of things that were a shame, grouped in order of quantity—*shame number seventy-three (73): loss of four (4) Kosovans.*

The main picture was of a boy a little older than her. He was wearing a denim jacket that looked too snug across his shoulders. His eyes were nervous blurs. He was dead. His face was so smooth; he was old enough to shave but young enough to still be excited about shaving and thus meticulous.

She was not sure how to pronounce his name, not even in her head would the sound make any sense. She had to look away to stop herself from making up more stories about him. Also because from the page he said, Look away, look away from me, what can you do, nothing so don't. The article commented on the silence of the local refugee community. No one was naming names, or even suggesting any. Eliot told Miranda that it was a sign of the community closing to protect its own. "It's refugees killing other refugees, man. I know you can't believe it, I don't want to believe it either, but, you know what . . . it's far too simplistic to assume that just because they're escaping similar troubles and are from the same geographic location, that it's all love and harmony when they get over here. There are a bunch of differences between these people that precede their status in this country. Some of them really hate each other. I've seen kids openly spit at each other because of differences in language and what speaking a certain language means."

Miranda slumped in her seat. What Eliot was saying made sense but it didn't. There was an untruth to it that made her tired. "Like, some Armenians who speak only Armenian consider Armenians who speak Turkish to be Turks and synonymous with the very oppression that exiled them—"

Luc made a face.

"You sound like you're quoting from some sort of textbook. Far too general. Besides, why would you suddenly recover a sense of solidarity and try to protect a killer when the police come around?"

"Because they're even more hostile to the police than they are to each other? Because the truth is too good for the police? Because the police are a symbol of the country that's fucking them over and assigning them marginal status?" Eliot suggested.

Luc shook his head. "One moment, Eliot. Put the sociological exercise aside. Since we're talking about family here. *Family.* And say you knew who had hurt someone in your family and you also knew that the police have the power to stop and punish it. You really wouldn't say anything?"

Miranda shook her head, then nodded, unsure which movement was appropriate. She handed the newspaper back to Eliot and went back to spinning combinations in her suitcase lock. Eliot and Luc continued to argue, Luc trying hard to sound amiable, Eliot trying hard to sound impassioned.

The car stopped at a traffic light, the last one before home. There were some girls sitting on the bicycle railings outside the corner shop, chewing gum, kicking out at each other, talking and squealing. Miranda couldn't hear their hoop earrings jangling from where she was, but she felt the vibrations. These girls were Kosovan girls; when they weren't together they were impassive, tough, their hair gelled into stiff fans with curls slicked down over their foreheads. You saw them in the supermarket holding doubled-up carrier bags open, ready to fill with shopping, standing and gazing inscrutably into middle distance while their mothers fumbled through the folds of their big shawls, looking for food vouchers to pay with. One of these girls was in Miranda's English literature class, and her voice, soft and uncertain, belied her eyes. As the car moved past, one of the girls in the group bounced her gaze off Miranda's, then looked again, harder. She climbed down off the railings and strode over to the roadside with two other girls behind her. They were mouthing and pointing at her. Miranda didn't know what to do, so she closed her eyes. Eliot was quiet and Luc whistled and tapped his fingers on the steering wheel. A jolt as the traffic light changed. She opened her eyes and saw the girls, a little behind, running. Luc said, "Are those girls running after us?"

Miranda couldn't think what they wanted with her, those girls. She blurted, "Drive faster—"

Eliot laughed. "It's alright," he said. "They've given up."

The girls had stopped and were a street behind, each of them bent over, holding their sides. The girl who had first noticed her was still looking, though. Miranda couldn't see her expression.

She had thought that coming home would hurt, but actually she was fine. There were lights shining from the house windows that didn't have their curtains drawn, harsh yellow scattered between the top and bottom floors, two on top and three on the bottom, like a smile.

Azwer, the gardener, and Ezma, the housekeeper, came to meet Miranda at the door; their foreheads were wrinkled and their eyes were watering with emotion. Ezma squeezed Miranda's hands and Azwer said, "Good, it's good." What was good; the quality of the repair that had been done at the clinic?

Ezma turned her attention back to a woman who was writing a cheque against the telephone table. The woman's hair was full of shiny star-shaped hair clips. She was an American. She bit on the end of her pen and said dreamily, "You should grow blueberries out in the back. I think blueberries bless a place, and are great in pie. If you crush oyster shells and spread them on the soil, it'll make the earth much richer and better for growing things in."

Ezma smiled at the woman. "We don't serve oysters," she said.

Miranda took her suitcase up in the lift, feeling like a guest. She missed being able to see to the bottom of the

shaft, the mysterious dustiness of it. She went into her room
and there was a stack of cards on her bed, cards filled with
hugs and kisses from girls at school. She wondered what
Eliot had told them, and whether it was worth returning to
school with an assumed limp and only the vaguest expla-
nation of her absence: something about having fallen out of
one of the trees at the back and having broken her whole
body, "You know . . . just *everything*."

Miranda's room smelt of musty petals, and she could
hear Eliot avoiding her, helping Azwer to shovel snow outside. The dull click of spades on gravelled ice.

In a psychomantium glass topples darkness. Things
appear as they really are, people appear as they really are.
Visions are called from a point inside the mirror, from a
point inside the mind.

Miranda looked in.

She looked with the most particular care and she saw
Lily Silver standing there in her room, smiling sadly.

It took half a minute, too long a terror, to realise that
she was only looking at herself. Wasn't she? It was the hair-
cut and the fact that she had grown thinner and her eyes
had grown bigger in her head. She had been eating exactly
what she liked, and she didn't like the usual things.

Still, Lily seemed to gaze and gaze at her and say, Oh,
Miri. You fell asleep. How could you?

Miranda turned away from the mirror. "I don't like this
blame culture," she whispered. "I don't like it at all."

She checked Lily's watch. It was midnight in Haiti. The

ticking of the watch grew very loud; she wished it would not tick so loudly. She fumbled across the room to put on a CD, but she had taken it out and put it back in, pressed play three times before she realised there was nothing wrong with it, it played every time she pressed the button. There was Ella Fitzgerald, whispering *a tisket a tasket*. She gritted her teeth. She needed the sound of the watch stopped; she couldn't hear the music for the sound of the watch. She knelt on the floor and slammed her wrist against it.

Tick, tick

(break it *break* it)

tick, tick

It was the pain that made her realise what she was doing. She undid the watch clasp, inspected it for damage, then put it on the table and rubbed her swollen wrist. Then she felt for her pills, cursing her hand for trembling so much. She put her steady hand over her trembling hand, to no effect. She lay down and didn't want to shut her eyes. With the curtains drawn it could almost be night. But she heard someone talking to Luc downstairs, she heard the clatter of cutlery, she heard the whir of

the lift

broke down in the night. No one knew what time. The timing became important when Azwer and Ezma couldn't find their older daughter in the morning.

Luc had had the attic converted into two large, low

rooms. Azwer and Ezma slept in one, while Deme and her little sister, Suryaz, slept in a double bed in the second room. Deme was ten and Suryaz was seven. The two of them went about with their hands joined, smiling and full of secrets so simple that they were given up if asked after. Deme and Suryaz hopped more than they walked; it was always as if they had just left the site of some mirth particular to them. They babbled in prettily accented voices. The combination of their near-identical manes of curly hair and their mother's tendency to zip them into similarly patterned dresses meant that Suryaz had an air of having been formed without detail. Deme was the oldest, so you looked at her first.

Both girls admitted that they had spent the day before playing around with the lift, pressing buttons for three floors all at once, holding the Door Open button until the lift zinged with confusion. That was reason enough for the lift to later get confused and try to travel unbidden from first floor to second, grinding to a halt between the two. But why was Deme standing in the corner of the lift when Luc, Azwer and the technician pried the doors open? She was standing, not sitting or kneeling. They found her in the back left corner, where there once had been a hole in the floor, and she was standing on tiptoe, so close to the Alarm button, looking at it in fact, her eyes wide as if all night she had been sinking and all night a stubborn thing in her had kept her on her feet.

"I tucked her into bed with Suryaz," Ezma kept repeating. "I did, didn't I," she said to Suryaz, who looked and looked and then shrugged. Ezma hissed at her, but Suryaz would say nothing. At first Deme wouldn't talk either, then when Ezma shouted at her, Deme spat a large piece of Suryaz's Lego out into her hand and tried her best to answer the questions that everyone levelled at her, even Eliot, who tugged her ponytail and teased her about her "midnight journey." The only reply Deme ventured was that she didn't know.

"Why did you get into the lift so late, when everyone was sleeping?"

"I don't know."

"Deme, where is your sense? Why didn't you just ring the alarm?"

"I don't know."

Miranda asked, "Deme are you alright?"

Deme and Suryaz leant on each other and Suryaz said, "Thank you, she is alright."

Miranda, Luc and Eliot slept on the third floor; above the guests but below the housekeepers. Miranda told Eliot: "I heard someone crying last night. But I thought I was just remembering the clinic."

Or herself, she had thought she was hearing herself.

Later in the morning Miranda opened her wardrobe and found it full of clammy ghosts that hovered around her body when she put them on. The cold trickled down in the gaps between the material and her chest. Scarecrow girl. She felt proud and nauseous, chosen and moulded by hands that froze. She drifted downstairs to find her father, who was stalking around a newly vacated guest room with a checklist. Winter had licked every window in the house and left them smeared with fog. "Nothing fits me anymore," she said, turning in a slow circle before him, hoping for his horror. "I'll need some new clothes."

Her father took her in coolly.

"That is true," he said.

Together they searched the dressing table and desk drawers in his bedroom until they found a gilt-coloured card with the address of a boutique in Notting Hill printed on it. It was a boutique that Lily had liked for dresses, so Luc told Ezma and Azwer that he would be out for the afternoon and drove Miranda into London.

Dress shopping took longer than she had expected. It took the whole afternoon. Luc refused Miranda every dress she tried on. Each time he shook his head she gauged the extent of his dislike for the dress by checking whether he had raised one eyebrow or both.

"What's wrong with this one?" she'd ask. Mid-length sleeves, a demure hemline, a keyhole collar.

"You know you already have one just like that."

"But—"

Distress showed dimly in his eyes. "Let me see the next one, please."

They moved with increasing disheartenment from shop
to shop, hands in their coat pockets, looking at the floor
more than they looked at the clothes, and finally, knowing
that her only condition was that her dresses be black, he
swiftly selected dresses off the racks for her to try, with the
reasoning that he was more likely to approve an outfit if he'd
chosen it.

She was embarrassed; other shoppers were trying to
guess at their relationship. He looked younger than he was.
She took every opportunity to say "Father" to him, and
hated herself for sounding like such a fool, *Father-Father-
Father.*

When she tried on the last dress in the pile he'd built
up, she was sure he would like it. He had to. It didn't look
like anything she already had, the skirt flared wonderfully,
and there was the sweet ribbon bow at the waist. It was a
dress to be worn by the sort of girl who'd check that no one
was looking, then skip down a quiet street instead of walking, just so the fun of it was hers alone. She looked around
the corner of the fitting-room door and saw her father standing with his hands in his pockets, his tie removed and folded
into a pocket of his crumpled suit, where part of it unfurled
like a yellow-and-blue-striped tongue. A woman who had
come shopping alone seemed to be asking his advice on the
dress she'd tried on. He nodded and smiled, his eyes crinkling at the corners, before giving the woman's dress a
thumbs-up, which made Miranda laugh because her father

only gave things a thumbs-up when he thought they were stupid and populist. The woman touched his arm and said thank you.

Miranda put a hand over her face and looked through her fingers, the world in pieces, her father's legs gone, the woman's torso vanished. Now they looked like broken dolls, their jaws clacking, breeze blowing through their hollows. Lily had taken her to a doll hospital in New York once. Neat rooms with bright, hard-looking wallpaper tacked precisely into each corner like plastic, chests of drawers with lace cloths on top, the smell of potpourri lined with sawdust. Only the repaired dolls were on view
(Father, let's go to the doll hospital and get you repaired) she didn't know where the thought had come from, she probably had to be careful because she had been mad.

Miranda dropped her hand and came out of the fitting room, passing the woman who had been talking to her father as the woman returned to her cubicle. One of them smiled with all her teeth, and the other looked blank.

When her father saw her, he rubbed his eyes and leaned his elbow on one of the racks. He bit his knuckle and stared at her knees until she was compelled to cross and uncross them, dancing an impromptu Charleston. He didn't smile.

"Not this one either?" she asked. "But this is the last one."

"It's not the dresses," he said.

"What is it then?"

He raised his head. "You're . . . so thin."

She turned to a mirror and looked at herself quickly. "I'm not that thin."

"Miranda. No one who is well looks the way you look at the moment."

"I'm alright," she said.

"You are not alright. None of these dresses will do. They will not do at all. Nothing that fits you now will do, do you understand?"

"I suppose so, but what am I going to do about clothes, then?"

He looked around. Was his cue written on the walls?

"You will have to eat. You will wear your other clothes until they fit. It will be good for you."

Miranda nodded and her reflection nodded, so that was twice. She crossed her hands over her stomach, as if that would stop her from retching. She blushed because the light in the fitting rooms was stark and hot, like being stared at. (I'm not that thin, I'm not that thin)

She smoothed the pleated skirt of the dress she had on. She liked it. He had chosen the perfect dress for her. Or, at least, for the girl she wanted to be.

"That's just gorgeous on you," the shop assistant said, stopping in front of Miranda. She clasped her hands to her chest and shaped her mouth into a lipsticked "ooh." When neither Miranda nor Luc replied her, her smile faltered and she said "Alrighty then," and walked back into the main shop.

"You haven't even looked at the price yet. It might be reasonable," Miranda tried, once the shop assistant was completely out of earshot.

Luc lightly touched Miranda's shoulder.

"Getting healthy won't be so bad," he said. "I'll try to make it delicious, I promise."

She nodded again, everything paralysed but her head and neck. *You are being silly,* she told herself desperately, but the words had no effect. Because she didn't move to face him, her father kissed the top of her head, the point of the triangle where her parting dissolved into the rest of her hair. She felt the kiss on her actual skull, the skin of her scalp crinkling between his lips as they broke through. She endured it because he didn't know what this kiss did to her, how could he know?

He held her coat for her so she could put her arms into it. He buttoned her coat up for her and walked her out of the shop. He smiled and said goodbye for both of them. When he suggested having dinner in town she said, lightly, without looking at him, "Sorry, Father, I really can't."

They drove into Dover through the dark. Eventually Luc put on a CD and Hildegarde von Bingen's canticles of ecstasy spilt misty cries out through the car windows. Miranda concentrated on keeping her mouth completely closed.

A houseguest met them at the front door. He was holding a candle fixed to a saucer with its own wax, red on white. His name was Terry, Miranda was almost sure. "Hello there, Luc. There's been a power cut," he said, grinning. "Me and some of the others found some Famous Five books and we've been reading those and telling ghost stories for the past couple of hours. What larks . . ."

Luc shook the hand that wasn't holding the saucer, said warmly that he was very glad it hadn't been too much of an inconvenience and strode into the midst of the group of houseguests who had come out to offer theories and suggestions. Before Luc could call her, Ezma arrived suddenly at the centre, as if ejected from the floor. Her hair had tumbled out of its tidy coronets. Her face was grey.

"You'd better get an electrician, Mr. Dufresne," she said. "Azwer has looked at the fuse box, but obviously he is no expert at these things."

Miranda went to see if Deme and Suryaz were alright.

"Who is it?" the girls said together, when she knocked on the attic door.

"It's me," she said.

They wouldn't answer after

that

evening, Emma and I broke up. Her parents were out and her house was full of music, music and every light in every room was on. She even had fairy lights twined around table legs. "Hello, Eliot . . ." She pulled me in through the front door, wrapped my arms around her waist and led me from room to room, dancing ahead of me. She was wearing a short black dress and when she turned to face me I saw she was wearing lipstick. I had never seen her wearing lipstick, but knew better than to say so in case she did that mysterious alchemy some girls do and transformed the comment into my accusing her of having gained weight.

"You look good," I said, and kissed her. The music upstairs ('90s R&B from the sound of it) was different from that downstairs (Alanis Morissette), and it was unnerving somehow, like a discordant echo, as if the music upstairs was creeping up on me and if I turned around Mariah Carey would abruptly trill in my face.

"Is Miranda back?" Emma asked. I twirled her and caught her, partly because it was so inappropriate to do that while Morissette was whining unhappily.

"How did you know?"

Emma put her arms around my neck and tried to make me slow dance.

"Because you look nervous," she said.

"Yeah. Well. It's hard to know what to expect, isn't it."

She said solemnly: "Would you like a beer?"

I nodded, and she went into the kitchen. The room was so bright that I couldn't look at anything for long.

What is all this?

I called out: "Emma, are you alright?"

She came back with a glass of red wine, a can of beer, and a pair of scissors.

"Yeah I'm fine. Why?" she asked.

I sat on the sofa. I looked at the scissors, which she laid

on the coffee table with the handles wide open. I drank some beer. She climbed onto my lap, drawing her bare legs against mine, leaning into me so I could feel the curve of her.

"No," she said. "Don't touch me."

She breathed against my mouth but she wouldn't let me kiss her. I said "Emma" without meaning to. The glass of wine she was drinking from now was clearly not her first.

She yawned and, from nowhere, offered me a cigarette. I couldn't think about a cigarette; I leant back and just looked at her. She smoked one without me. "Look," she said. She showed me the cigarette she was smoking. It was red and white. "Red tips," she said. "An idea from the forties, you know. For the glamorous girl who doesn't want to leave lipstick marks on her cigarette."

"Oh," I said, stupidly.

She slid slowly down my lap and onto the floor. I didn't make a sound. It was a matter of principle. She walked around the sofa, smoking her red-tipped cigarette, then she picked up the scissors and handed them to me.

"What am I meant to do with these?"

She said, "Wait a sec, I need this for courage," and took a long drag on her cigarette before putting it out. Then knelt on the sofa beside me and gathered the dark mass of her hair up into a ponytail, the hair band tied round at the neck. She hesitated, then, without taking her eyes off me, pulled the hair band up a little higher, a little tighter. She turned her back on me.

"There, where the hair band is."

"Why?"

"I said cut it right here, Eliot." She touched the hair band.

"No."

I put the scissors down, but she picked them up and tried to force them back into my hand.

"Do it yourself," I said. "I'm off."

By the time I stood up, her ponytail had fallen onto the sofa in a silent fan. She turned around and mussed her hair, ran her fingers through the ragged ends, the ragged ends, her eyes were huge.

"You're sick," I said.

"Am I?" She reached for her lighter and cigarette box and lit up again.

She blew smoke in my face and I drifted towards the door with my best absentminded smile, as if I had been on my way out anyway, as if I'd been ready to leave her from the moment I came. Emma is an only child, and she was drunk besides.

I didn't go straight home. I walked around the park opposite our house, kicking at the railings, trying to think what to do. I couldn't blank Emma altogether, because that would look weird, also I couldn't risk her saying anything to any of our other friends.

Everyone would believe her because at the back of their minds, everyone thinks that twin brothers and sisters grow up magnetized towards each other, the prince at the foot of

Rapunzel's tower before the tower is even built, the lover you can get at all the fucking time, the one who is you but a girl, or you but a boy, whose bed you know as well as your own. How could you endure that without falling in love? The question is, were they born in love with each other, these twins, or did it blossom? At any rate it's already happened, the onlookers agree. It must have. Ask them when they fell. The brother and sister say no, no, it's nothing like that, but what they mean is they can't remember when.

Lily's photo studio was a small extension to the house, a lump that had grown on its side when it was young. It had its own tiled triangular window frame; from the outside it looked like a cuckoo clock. A thick piece of twine crossed the length of the room, hung low so that Lily could reach up and pluck down a photograph. Steel pegs dangled and didn't shine; like the capped steel tanks at either end of the room they drew dark into their outlines and almost disappeared. The cupboards had jugs in them, and a few pint bottles full of pale fluids. The jugs weren't dusty yet; Miranda dreaded the day when they would become so. She tried to put a shield up in her mind against it, a collection of bright things to do with Lily that would blaze through the dust when it came down.

When Eliot came home that evening, he took the key to Lily's studio off its hook in the kitchen.

Miranda asked him, "What are you going to do in there?"

He said, "Homework."

She tried to follow him in, but he suddenly and silently pushed the door against her until she squealed with pain; the pressure of the door between them threatened to throw her arm out of its socket.

"Eliot!" she said through the gap.

"Get back from the door," he said calmly.

"I want to talk to you."

"Later."

She thumped her fist against the door, then opened her hand so that it was just her palm, soft on the wood.

He laughed. "Get your scrawny arm out of the door, Miri."

"*You* said stay awake or she'll die. Why did you say that? How could you say that?"

He opened the door fully. Behind him the light strips glowed red. He was looking at her through the skin of his eyelids. She didn't like his eyes, she wanted to cover them with her hands, turn the lights out so she couldn't see them. This was more than weed; he must have taken something else besides. He was looking at her but his eyes were closed: "You didn't have to believe me."

She stepped inside and slapped him. Then she laughed until she hiccupped, because she hadn't known she meant to do it. The studio door clicked closed behind her. She could see her slap had been hard because there was her handprint on his face, a flushed shadow. He didn't blink, but he slapped her back, and she fell onto a counter, scraping all her weight along her wrist as the glass in the cupboard rattled. When the throb died she walked up to him and dug her nails deep into his cheek, her other hand dragging his head back by the hair.

She wasn't angry, she was just being deontological. He had to be paid out for the pain in her wrist. It was strange that she could hold him like this for even a second. She felt weak, but her will was cold. And there was a sort of wonder in seeing tears so close, in actually watching them form in his eyes. They scrabbled around on the floorboards, trying, for some reason, to hold each other flat in the shadows. She banged her head, or he banged her head, against a corner of the counter, and she let go of him and they rolled slowly away from each other. She was drowning in a flood of colour she had never seen before, she was scared it was blood from her brain. She heard Eliot breathing. She knew where he was, around the other side of the counter, out of her sight. "Miri," he said. "Miranda. Are you alright?"

She didn't answer. Let him worry.

"I'm sorry," he said. He said it as if he was choking.

She could see under the counter, a strip about two inches thick. It looked sticky, as if developing fluids had dripped through to the floor and collected there. And there was a slip of paper, or

a photograph gone astray.

She wasn't sure if she could reach it, but Miranda reached
an arm under the counter. If her fingers touched the photograph it was hers. If it was out of her reach then it belonged
to the room.

She could hear Eliot moving. "Stay there," she said. Her
fingertips clutched the paper and she drew her arm out.
With the slip in her hand, she rose to her knees at the same
time Eliot did. They regarded each other across the counter
from the nose up, wary grey gaze meeting its wet counter-
part.

Lily and Luc had agreed that she and Eliot would take
Lily's surname if they were born grey-eyed, and Luc's surname if they were born brown-eyed. Miranda and Eliot's
names were really just a matter of grey or brown, a choice
between colours.

What would Miranda Dufresne have said now, how would
she have made things better? She knew what Miranda
Dufresne would have looked like. She would have had very
straight black hair in a bob, she would have been a thin,
already tall girl towering on heels, buttoned into a dark suit.
She would have been born grown-up.

Miranda looked down at herself, touched her hair, started,
then smiled nervously. Maybe the thing she needed to do
was imagine what Miranda *Silver* would have looked like.
What if she dyed her hair blond, she wondered, knowing

that her skin was too pale to support it. Her thoughts were like ice floes, and she became too large for them—she couldn't move from thought to thought without breaking them. One day she might get better and be pretty, rather than a sicklier version of Eliot.

Out of his line of sight she was holding a piece of A4 paper, a secret easily unfolded. It was a drawing on brown, crackly paper, a drawing of a perfect person. Miranda sat down. (How excellent a body, that
Stands without a bone)

A perfect person has no joints. The arms, emerging from short sleeves, are unmarked by the ripple of skin that shows where the limbs bend. A perfect person's portrait is lifelike despite their strange clothes, a black dress that fastens without buttons or a zip, just a straight line across the material to show that it was not pulled on over the head. It was still possible to believe that the person drawn was a real person despite the great almond-shaped eyes set deep into the head, deep and open, unable to blink. Eyes without eyelids or eyelashes. The pose of the perfect person was so natural, the colouring so lifelike that the omission of joints and eyelids seemed deliberate, so that the thing was art, or honesty.

idea of the perfect person

The perfect person was a girl. Bobbed dark hair, black dress, pearls she was too young for, mouth, nose and chin familiar . . . Miranda's, almost. Look, look, remember. This sight might not come again. The perfect person had beautifully shaped hands, but no fingernails. A swanlike neck that met the jaw at a devastating but impossible angle. Me, but perfect. She quickly corrected herself. Before Lily died, Miranda's hair had been long enough to sit on. *Me after the clinic, but perfect. Lily did you know? How did you know?* Miranda turned the picture over and ran her hand over the back of it; in one, yes, two, three, four places the paper was rougher, once adhesive, now matted with fine hairs and specks of dust. Lily Silver, the lonely girl on the third floor, had kept herself company with pictures of people, no one she'd ever seen, she'd said. Miranda turned the page over again, and it was blank. So this was what happened when she hit her head.⌐

E liot collapsed onto the floor beside her. She put her head on his shoulder and he moved his head so that he was combing her hair with his chin. "That was really stupid," she said, at the same as he said, "That was ridiculous."

Without raising her head, she ran her fingers over the marks she'd made on his face, kissed each of her fingers and her thumb and touched them to each scratch. Just to be sure she touched his eyelids.

"Did you take something?"

"What?"

"Your eyes . . . I don't know, maybe you smoked something."

"No more than usual." He crossed his heart.

"What do you really do in here?"

"What d'you think?"

"Develop photos, I suppose. Since when, though?"

He shrugged. She took some chalk out of the pocket of her dress. When she offered him a stick of it he looked surprised, but took it and stuck it in his mouth, pretended to smoke it like a cigar while she ate.

Azwer gave his notice the day of Eliot's and Miranda's Cambridge interviews. He stopped Luc as he was on his way out to meet the twins by the car. Azwer said, "My wife and daughters are afraid. If we stay they will only become more afraid, and then something bad will happen." His heavy eyebrows lowered and he made some small, involuntary gesture with his hand that was recognisably superstitious, as if the words "God forbid" had flowed into his body.

Luc said, "Two weeks is too short notice for me to find replacements for you and Ezma. And we've had the lift looked at."

Azwer said quickly, heatedly, "Mr. Dufresne, it's not just the lift—"

Luc put his car keys down on the hall table, and tension pulled him taller. "Then what?"

Azwer kept his eyes fixed on Luc.

Luc looked at Miranda, then lowered his voice and said to Azwer, "Do you need more pay?"

Azwer spread his hands. "We cannot stay."

Azwer and Ezma didn't have papers; as far as the

government was concerned, Luc was running the Silver House alone. Luc said, "Azwer, listen. Think about it. Where will you work? Where will you go?"

Azwer shrugged. "To London."

Luc said, "I see," in tones that patently signalled that he didn't.

He took Miranda by the shoulders and turned her in the direction of the door.

She didn't look like a promising interview candidate at all, she knew. All the colour in her face was in her lips, and her dress was still far too big. The back of it gaped around her shoulder blades as if the dress had been designed for someone who had wings. She would have to talk fast and come to surprising conclusions and smile a lot so no one would notice.

Miranda's first interview was an hour and a half after Eliot's, so she wandered in and out of the entrances to the college's stone stairwells. She wondered how Eliot's interview had gone and where he was, but she couldn't find her phone; she must have left it somewhere. Cambridge was subdued; it wasn't just the frost and the puffy felt sky, it was the abundance of massive, old stone. And then the bells, which pealed their deep songs at mysterious intervals. Miranda felt as if she was being pressed to the ground beneath a great grey finger. She had a pocketful of onyx chips (properties of onyx: it helps you hold your emotions steady;

side effects of onyx: it is the sooty hand that strangles all your feeling out of you) and she used her teeth to carve tiny, acrid flakes of onyx onto her tongue. She knew how to do it so that it looked as if she was simply biting her nails.

She collided with another girl on her way back into the waiting area outside the interview room. They both held their heads and moaned.

"Oh Lord! You must have the hardest head in all creation," the girl said.

Miranda waited until she could look at the girl without it hurting, then lifted her gaze. The girl was black, all long legs and platform trainers, clad in grey school uniform. Her head was covered with tiny plaits that had coloured elastic bands tied around the ends, and her eyes were dark and large like drops of rich ink.

There was an awkward silence. Then Miranda held the door open and said, "Let's try again, you first," before she remembered that she had been the one going in. The other girl had been leaving.

"Look . . . what's the time?" the girl said.

Miranda said, "I don't know," and looked around for a clock.

The girl looked at the watch on Miranda's wrist.

"It doesn't work," Miranda said, rather than explain about Haitian time. "How have your interviews gone?"

"They haven't. I mean I haven't been called yet. I'm not doing it after all. Fuck it. I only wanted to know the time because there's a train I might be able to catch if I leave right now," the girl blurted.

"You're . . . not going to your interviews?"

"No! I can't be bothered."

The girl's hands were shaking. Miranda tried not to stare.

"Er . . . listen, it will be very demoralizing for me if you leave."

The girl looked Miranda up and down and quietly advised her that she probably had nothing to worry about.

Miranda frowned. "What are you saying? Do I just walk in and say a secret password?"

"I don't know," the girl said. "Do you?"

Miranda pushed the question aside with her hand. "It would be a shame not to bother. After you applied and everything. And . . . where do you live?"

"Faversham."

"Right. So you came all the way up from Faversham—"

"Indeed!" the girl said. "Look . . . what's your name?"

"Miranda."

"I'm Ore. Look, Miranda. I've already been through all that 'you've already applied and here you are' stuff in my head. But hear ye, hear ye: only one person from my school's got in here in the last five years, that's a very discouraging pie chart to draw, plus I've been thinking about my personal statement and there are at least seventeen lies in there and I can't keep track of them all. Plus I just realised I'm *stupid*, an actual dunce. I got a C for GCSE maths. It's very likely that I've only been called to interview so they can laugh at me. Anyway thanks for listening, I'm off."

"Well, I think it's a terrible waste," Miranda said, following Ore down the staircase. "And how will you ever know unless you try?"

Ore took Miranda's hands between both of hers and shook them. "Good luck," she said. "All the best. Really. I think it's really nice of you to bother."

Miranda could see how hard Ore was trying to take full breaths, to be calm. The only thing was to use a strategy of Lily's.

"I," said Miranda, "will give you a *prize* if you stay and do your interviews."

Ore perched herself on the stair rail and closed her eyes.

"Well," she said, after a moment, "I've never won a prize."

They walked back upstairs together, arm in shaky arm. Ore wouldn't let Miranda talk because, she said, she needed silence to get her lies in order.

Miranda thought about Ore throughout her interview, even when it descended into a semi-aggressive debate over her assertion that Thackeray's Becky Sharp would easily beat Brontë's Cathy in a fistfight. The only criticism she would have accepted was that she was giving patriarchy precedence over the female consciousness explored in the Gothic. But since that criticism wasn't offered, she stood her ground. She didn't remember her interviewers after the fact of her interviews—the professors didn't have features, they were learnedness dressed up as people and housed in armchairs.

"Well? Where's my prize?" Ore said, when Miranda came out. There were two others waiting outside now, a boy and a girl, both wearing blazers and silently reading thick books. They looked up when Ore spoke.

"How did it go?" Miranda asked.

"Wonderful. Really unbelievably good." Cheerfully, Ore mimed stabbing herself. "If I don't get that prize, the day might as well not have happened at all."

She held her hand out expectantly.

"Alright, here it is," said Miranda, and laid Ore's purse on her palm. "You wouldn't have got very far without it anyway," she said. "Would you?"

Ore skipped a beat, then said: "I hope you get in. It'll keep you off the streets, at least."

She demanded the time of the boy nearest her and rushed down the college steps. The nervousness in her brought an otherwise gawky frame together in concentration—she delayed reaching out to push doors to the very last second, moving towards them as if, Miranda thought, they would slip aside for her or she would pass through them.

Since Azwer and Ezma were leaving, Miranda felt she should give their daughters something. Suryaz and Deme would each need a talisman, an object that smelt lovely, or that felt kind to the hand; such things are little suitcases to put sad feelings in so that they can go away by themselves.

Miranda didn't have to go back to school until after the Christmas holidays, so for Suryaz she spent five nights under her bedroom lamp, making a cloth doll with a seed pearl smile and rose petals for eyes. She slept sparingly and unwillingly. Rest seized her and kept her until she twitched awake two or three hours later.

When Suryaz and Deme came home in the afternoons and sat down in the kitchen for their after-school snacks, Miranda mustered the energy to shuffle downstairs. She poked her head around the kitchen door for a brief but fond sighting of Suryaz, who was invariably a creature of jam, all sticky mouth and gooey ringlets. She thought, Soon I will have something to give you, and you don't know it yet. Each night Miranda worked on the doll and then she spent the day in bed, half dreaming of her needle in a circle of white. On the night that Suryaz's doll was finished, she took her big bottle of attar of roses, unplugged its glass stopper and filled a bowl, then swam Suryaz's doll in it. When the doll was slack and fat with liquid, she removed it and dropped it on the floor, where it lay beside her with arms and legs spread until the morning, by which time it had dried out.

Deme was harder to think of a gift for—Deme who'd stood on tiptoe in a box in the night, looking at the Alarm button. Deme wouldn't want a thing that flopped charmingly and had nothing to tell her. When Azwer and Ezma began loading things into Luc's car, Miranda went to find Deme.

"Please come and choose a going-away present for yourself. Anything I have that you like," she said, feeling shy now under the younger girl's glossy stare. The girls had become steely since the lift broke down; they seemed full of resolutions not to smile anymore. Deme wouldn't come without Suryaz, so the three of them stood in Miranda's room, peering around in the gloom. Miranda covered the face of Lily's watch with her hand and thought to herself, be giving. She watched Deme's eyes move from her books to the sticks of chalk that she kept in a Marlboro cigarette box.

"Never smoke," she told Deme, firmly. Deme put her hand out and pointed at a hairbrush that Lily had given Miranda. It was bone backed, with tiny skulls carved into it. Some of the skulls faced each other and were blended together at the jaw. Miranda had only recently realised that these were the skulls that were kissing. Deme chose that hairbrush, and Miranda wrapped it up in a silk scarf and gave it to her gladly. Suryaz stood by, rocking her new doll in the big pocket of her dress.

Suryaz bowed her head and her curls swung before her closed eyes, her face scrunched as if she was about to describe something and was trying to remember it with exactness and close attention. But she only seemed able to say, "Oh Miranda. Be careful."

And Deme urged, "It is true. You're nice, and you haven't been well. Do be careful."

Ezma called her daughters from the floor below. Suryaz said something to Deme in Azeri. Deme replied to her in

Azeri, then turned a sweet smile on Miranda and dropped a square of lined writing paper onto Miranda's pillow.

Miranda shook hands with Suryaz. Deme shook hands with Miranda. Each said goodbye.

Miranda stretched, then sat for a while after the noise of their departure had died in her ears. She was feeling fragile and had missed her morning dose, so she took more pills than was customary for her and washed them down with vinegar. She poured rose attar onto her tongue to mask the sourness her drink brought. She knelt down with her neck bowed as though for an axe and ran her perfume-wettened fingers through her hair.

Then she opened Suryaz and Deme's letter. It was written in a round and extra neat hand that was unmarred by the splotches the fountain-pen nib had made in several places. The letter read:

Dear Miranda Silver,

This house is bigger than you know! There are extra floors, with lots of people on them. They are looking people. They look at you, and they never move. We do not like them. We do not like this house, and we are glad to be going away.

This is the end of our letter.

Yours sincerely,
Deme and Suryaz Kosarzadeh

Miranda folded the letter several times and put it in her pocket. She tried to smile, and managed, but not for long. She took the letter out and read it again. She was thinking things, but she couldn't understand her thoughts. It wasn't necessarily about Suryaz and Deme. It was more about the exhaustion of having finished Suryaz's doll, of having worked her eyes and her nerves for someone different and distant, someone who had lived in a different house from her when she'd thought they were all living in the same house, safe as little fishes in folds of the deep blue sea. Miranda went down through the trapdoor and curled up in a corner of the indoor bomb shelter. She cried with her face turned into the wall. Lily had told her and Eliot that this house, with their great-grandmother inside it, had escaped the effects of a bomb in 1942, that the houses a short distance away had been torn apart, their roofs whirling away to reveal cakes of brick with savage bites taken out of them. The house was lucky. Or storing its collapse.

To live here without Lily . . . Miranda found that the sadness was far far bigger than her, and it was forcing her back. The wall she leant against had a damp, high temperature to it, like tears on skin.

Christmas was dismal. We went to Paris as usual, to stay with our grandparents (Dad's parents, I mean) on the Île Saint-Louis. There was too much food. There's always too much food at Christmas, but this time it kept getting stuck in my throat and each bite turned into this choice between eating and breathing, as if you should ever have to choose.

We sat around the table and Miri and I didn't even try to join in with the conversation that Sylvie, Dad and The Paul were having. I stared at the huge holly and mistletoe wreaths on the wall, and Miri accidentally counted her bites of turkey aloud. "Nine," she breathed out, and dropped her knife and fork onto her plate with a clatter, and after that no one could think of anything to say for a while.

Miri and I call our grandfather The Paul. He is very wrinkled, quite stooped, smiles amiably and is generally a most excellent and easygoing being. I aim to reach that state of grace by the time I'm his age, calmly putting my tackle box in order or reading the newspaper with seemingly unmitigated attention while my wife gets at me about something. Our grandmother, Sylvie, is not known as The Sylvie. She is the girl who fell in love with a boy who worked in a bakery and had married him by the time his patisserie P. M. Dufresne had become so notable that fashionable magazines recommended it.

Miri told me that Sylvie had once showed her a pristine 1969 copy of French *Vogue*, with a small piece about P. M. Dufresne. Alongside the piece was a photograph of some intimidatingly fashionable creatures tripping gaily in through the shop door. Sylvie only let Miri see the piece for a couple of seconds, then whisked it away, saying, "Sticky fingers. Besides, you are not able to understand it."

Sylvie is still vexed because we all tried to learn French
but had to stop because Lily couldn't get the hang of it and
would substitute any word she couldn't recall with "*l'oignon*"
and then she'd wave her hands and laugh. When Dad got
annoyed with her (which he did quietly, but curtly) her face
fell a million feet and she'd call herself an ignoramus until
we couldn't take it anymore and demanded that the lessons
stop. But I doubt it was just the thing with the French
lessons that came between Lily and Sylvie; there's also the
fact of Sylvie being impeccable. Lily was a bunch of crumpled pockets and Sylvie is a black dress, perfumed scarves,
iron posture and whatever else turns a person into an atmo-
sphere. Sylvie doesn't look capable of getting involved with
a messy pastry.

Miri was like a mini-Sylvie, but she hadn't always been.
I can't remember when she stopped wearing jeans and jumpers and skirts and started with the black and the severe
outlines (why did she start?) but I do remember Lily finding
the change hilarious for months, and I also remember being
embarrassed to have to be seen outdoors with Miri until I
realised that no one seemed to think that her dress sense
was odd. Aside from infrequent comments
("Cheer up, love," or "It's not Hallo'ween"),
no one wondered why a teenager was dressed up as a chic
governess. Sylvie approved of Miri, even at the same time
as she was confused by her. "It's style at least," she said, and
took off her rope of pearls and looped them around Miri's
neck. "Perhaps when you are my age you will have to turn

to short skirts and mini-dresses, just for something different." Then Sylvie turned to me. "You dress exactly as if you don't care, but there is some artfulness to it; your colours balance each other."

"Ah," I said, not wanting to disappoint her and not wanting to lie to her. "Where is this from?" she said, plucking at my T-shirt. I looked down at the shirt. I didn't know where it was from. I wasn't even sure it was mine. Maybe it was my dad's or something. Or Lily had bought it. Clothing just appeared in my room and I put it on. Now that Sylvie noticed I recognised the miracle of it. I read my T-shirt, which said, PLANET HOLLYWOOD.

"It's a secret," I said finally. "Can't tell everyone where I get my garms from, or there'd be too many look-alikes."

Sylvie smiled. She and The Paul had been to visit us in Dover, and she knew that the place was full of Eliot look-alikes, and that I was one of the look-alikes, a copy of some original anonymous guy. I like that; attention makes me twitchy.

Lily had perfected a way of talking to me with her gaze elsewhere but her head slightly turned towards me so that I knew her words were for me. Dad has what I think of as only child darkside syndrome; he does everything as if he is being watched.

On Boxing Day I came down early in the morning. I had heard someone moving around downstairs and thought it might be The Paul. Instead I found my dad, sitting in The

Paul's baking pantry, on a chair that propped the door half open. He had his back to me, and you'd think that would make him warier, more sensitive to the presence of someone standing behind him, but it didn't. I stood and watched him, thinking, *I'll watch until he notices.* It took me a moment to realise what he was doing. He'd made one hand into a fist and was flipping his wedding ring onto it with his other hand, as if picking heads or tails, over and over.

I watched, and when I got tired of watching I said, "What are you doing?"

He turned around and seemed unsurprised to find me there. "Nothing. I might bake something. I don't know."

"Okay," I said, and got myself some water. I went back to bed but couldn't sleep anymore. I was lying on a hardback biography of T.S. Eliot, but that wasn't the reason. After about half an hour I sat up again, and Lily was in the rocking chair by the window, Lily smiling with glad eyes as if she had something funny to tell me. Lily in the chair, I mean Miranda was, Miri in a black T-shirt that scraped the tops of her thighs, Miri holding the rockers still with her bare feet. When I jumped, she laughed. I half expected her to say, "Again, do it again!"

I sat down on the end of my bed, facing her, and said, "Good morning."

Miri didn't use lipstick, she used something in a little pot that was applied with a fingertip. Miri said, "I miss her. So much that sometimes I'm scared I'll bring her back."

The red on her mouth was so strong; maybe it was just the early morning but I'd never seen a red as startling, as odd. Maybe she'd bitten her lip.

"She liked you best," Miri said, softly.

I shook my head but couldn't speak. We both considered the lawn outside the window, Sylvie and The Paul's tidy lawn. I did not have a thought, not even a painful one. A large and colourless umbrella had opened up inside my brain. All I did know was that after that initial shock of thinking that Lily had come back I had felt a cool, small relief, a moment of adjusting to Lily's ghost so that I could be . . . not unsatisfied with the quality of her being there. I can only explain it in comparison to something mundane— my adjustment to Lily's ghost was sort of like when you're insanely thirsty, but for some reason you can't get the cap on your water bottle to open properly so you tussle at it with your teeth and hands until you can get a trickle of water to come through. A little water at a time, and you're trying to be less thirsty and more patient so that the water can be enough. The thing with having seen Lily was just like that, a practical inner adjustment to meet a need. *At least she is there,* I'd thought, *even if she is just a ghost and doesn't speak, at least she is*

there

was a bird on the windowsill later in the afternoon. I looked up from *Thus Spake Zarathustra* and saw it standing motionless. Its feathers were brown and grey; in some places bands of one colour crossed the other. The bird was small enough to stand on the palm of my hand, which it did without alarm after about twenty minutes of me rushing at it and growling, opening and closing the window with a bang in my attempts to scare it into flying away. The bird and I looked each other over. Why wouldn't it fly? That's what birds are meant to do. Slowly, carefully, expecting it to flee at any moment, I took the bird into my hand and downstairs with me, where the others marvelled at it and fed it toasted brioche crumbs.

After breakfast, Sylvie and Dad stayed in and baked, and Miri and I went out for a walk along the Seine with The Paul. I took the bird with us, holding my jacket slightly open for the bird, which I felt shuddering slightly in the inside pocket, a brittle shape with life in it, like a flute playing itself. The Paul was in between Miri and me, and Miri supported him by coquettishly slipping her arm through his. Her high heels slipped on the ice. This happened a lot, but she refused to go out without her heels so she'd adapted to it, fully bending her knees each time she slipped so that she staggered with elegance. The trees were laced with ice and only a few other people were out. When they passed us, they gave friendly nods. I made observations aloud, for the bird's benefit. "Lovely weather," I said, and "Fit girl," I told the bird, when one walked past. I also said, "I hope you don't shit in my pocket." The bird raised its beak and its eyes like wet black marbles, and it seemed to listen to me. Either that or it was trying to get a feeling for the sky and when it might fly again. The Paul said sympathetically, "Poor boy. Your old grandparents have bored you eccentric. I understand. A fellow's got to amuse himself."

Just before we left for home I tried once more to make the bird fly. I opened the window of my room at Sylvie and The Paul's house and I set the bird's dumpy body on the sill, pushed it with a finger, but it only shook itself a little and stayed with its back to me, tail feathers ruffled, a defiant loner against the sunset and against the world. I reinstated it in the inside pocket of my jacket.

Miri spent most of the train journey to Calais trying to flirt with the bird, but it ignored her, snuggled deeper into my pocket and seemed to melt into hibernation—even its claws softened. The other people sitting around us seemed worried by the bird; they kept looking at the top of its head, which was all that was visible, as if they expected it to suddenly rise and start zooming around the train carriage, buzzing like a huge fly with a beak. But the bird relaxed until we'd docked at Dover, where it suddenly chirruped, struggled from my pocket to my shoulder, and threw itself at the air, singing madly. Then it was gone.

Miri squeezed my arm. "What a lazy thing that bird was," she said. "Outrageous. Don't you see? It was *using* you to get across the Channel."

Dad was ahead of us, weighed down with Miri's bag and his own. He looked back and said, "Good job you hadn't given it a name."

There was a stack of bills for Dad on the doormat when we got in. Also there was a letter postmarked Cambridge. It was for Miri. She held it and looked at me, scared. "I won't open it until yours comes," she said.

I spoke even though my lips felt frozen. Not really frozen, actually. Intensely lethargic. My lips couldn't be bothered to form words. "Come on," I said. "We applied to the same college for the same subject."

I took the letter out of her hands and opened it for her. She had been offered a place. I kissed her cheek and said congratulations. She opened her mouth and put one hand on her chest, the other to her cheek. She didn't say anything. I don't think she cared about the offer. She was just trying to feel this for me.

Dad read the letter, then put an arm around Miri's waist and drew her to him. He kissed her forehead. "My clever, darling girl," he said. Miri smiled at last. When Dad looked at me, I looked at the wall. I wanted to leave, but told myself, stand still, stand still. The floor below, the ceiling above. I stood there until they felt uncomfortable.

THE GOODLADY

"is very beautiful, Miranda, but very strict. Everything she does is necessary, and she makes no exception to any rule. She's what I had instead of a mother, much stricter than any mother. She's like tradition, it's very serious when she's disobeyed. She's in our blood. And she's told me that if I can't get you to eat, she will. You must eat real food, and you must eat as much as you can manage, or you might end up with the goodlady for your mother. Wouldn't you rather have me?"

"Of course. Always you, always. How can you even ask me that?"

Lily wasn't even an hour into her final trip abroad when Miranda fell into conversation with the goodlady herself. There was an essay due for key skills. The topic was suicide, and the essay was to be a discussion of the ethics of ending one's own life. Was suicide wrong, right, or a value-free choice? Was it even a choice in some cases? And so on.

Eliot was writing his own answer to the question next door in his room. Both Miranda and Eliot understood that they were expected to argue that suicide was wrong. Their school was that sort of school. Eliot would probably argue in favour of suicide. He'd write that suicide was a terrible, wonderful thing, a gift from the intellect to the body. Miranda wanted to give the correct answer. She would say that suicide was wrong, wrong, not a good idea at all, terrible in fact. She just had to hope that such an answer would emerge as the result of proper consideration and would thus be conscionably correct.

She sat at her desk in the psychomantium, pushing her feet in and out of her shoes and sighing as though stricken. She had no idea where to begin. She thought about her mother, gone away again, and she thought about her renewed promise to eat full meals, and she thought about her mother's forgotten watch. A sharp pain arrived in her stomach and stayed small, like a sting. If she stayed healthy she would live for decades, and there were so many meals left to eat. But she had to keep going, otherwise Eliot would never forgive her. He hated her pica, she knew. She would eat for Eliot, not for Lily, who couldn't really care all that much if she was always on her way to somewhere else.

Miranda's hair poured over her face and onto her paper and pen, and she pushed it back so that it all fell to the base of her chair. She turned to a new page in her notebook and began writing questions. Beneath the questions she wrote answers, in a hand as different from the one the questions were written in as possible.

Goodlady, are you really good?

yes

Even when no one is looking?

of course

But do you understand your nature?

my nature?

Did you choose to be good, or were you so created?

i chose to be created

Is that really an answer?

yes

Miranda's elbow slipped against the pages of her book, and the paper cut her. The room rolled like a dice. No matter how much she pretended bravery Miranda couldn't stand the sight of blood. She reared back, a hand to her elbow, too late—a bead of blood fell and grew into a large full stop in the middle of her open page, an ending to a sentence she hadn't written yet. She went in search of cotton wool and a plaster, and when she came back the stain was even bigger— she feared it might smother the page, the entire book.

You are not good, she accused.

The answer she wrote unnerved her because the handwriting was truly different from her own. It was handwriting she'd seen before in Christmas and birthday cards, shaky but elegant, the *g*'s and the *y*'s straight legged rather than curled.

neither are you

Miranda tapped her pen against her teeth, read over what she'd written. She ripped the red spotted page out of her book and threw it away. But the page was the reason for the certainty in Miranda's voice the next night, when she told her brother that the goodlady would take care of Lily. How could she doubt the goodlady? The goodlady was Lily's creation. Besides, she thought, the blood is the life.

Our great-grandmother, GrandAnna, the one who left the house to Lily, was named Anna Good. There's a cupboard in the attic full of her things, or at least the things that Lily didn't give to charity shops. The cupboard was a treasure trove for Miri—Miri found things in there I couldn't even see until she brought them out—white kid gloves, silver hair ornaments, fans. One day I found a sheaf of newspaper cuttings from the '40s in there—pages of *The Dover Post* collected without a theme until I noticed, halfway through the pile and checking back, that each page had the same number in its corner—25. Page 25 always had a patriotic cartoon on it, all on the theme of plucky Brits defeating the enemy by maintaining the home front—a stout housewife planting her own potatoes and taking a moment to smack a potato that looked just like Hitler on the head with her trowel, that sort of thing. They were drawn by an artist who worked in curved lines and harsh scribbles to indicate shade. The biggest cartoon took up a quarter of the

page: *Be careful what you say—you never know who's listening.*
Two sweet-faced teenage girls talked avidly on a bus, while
behind them, two men grinned with their teeth and leaned
closer to the girls, closer, closer, more as if they were about
to devour the girls than eavesdrop on their conversation.
One man was a fat soldier covered in swastikas, the other
was slit-eyed, uniformed, with a moustache that fell to his
knees. You don't have to be that close to someone to listen
in on their conversation. You don't have to be licking the
person's neck. The horrible hyperbole of it—it was a brilliant
cartoon. None of the page 25s collected in GrandAnna's
folder were dated later than 1943. They had begun in 1940.
Three years worth of cartoons. And it was on the biggest
and best cartoon that I made out the signature: Andrew
Silver. My great-grandfather, whose RAF plane had gone
down somewhere over Africa before the war was even halfway through.

GrandAnna's hair was very white and came down over
her shoulders in a great mass. Lily used to have a photo of
GrandAnna, Miri and me in her purse, from when we went
to visit GrandAnna on our seventh birthday. In the photo
Miri is on Anna's lap and has her arms around Anna's neck
with the sober confidence of someone adored. GrandAnna
and Miri are looking at the camera, at Lily the photographer, and they are very poised. I am beside GrandAnna,
leaning an elbow on the back of her chair and looking at
her with an apprehensive expression.

The room under the trapdoor downstairs was her

bedroom. "After the war she was scared of bombs for the rest of her life. It was the noise, she said. She couldn't sleep anywhere else," Lily told us. It was the Christmas before Lily died and she was sitting on my bedroom floor with handmade notepaper spread across her knees. She had a tinsel flower tucked behind her ear and she was writing thank-you notes for our Christmas presents. She liked to do it and we liked her doing it.

"Where did you sleep, then? Not down there?" I asked.

The psychomantium used to be Lily's room. There was a dressing table in there, and a velvet, high-backed chair, faint smudges on the walls where posters had been, and a mirror that crawled across the wall in a wooden frame. When I go into Miri's room all I can see, all I can think of is that enormous mirror, like a lake on the wall. Sometimes I talk to her reflection instead of her, and she doesn't seem to find anything strange in that. As a child, Lily had had the whole floor to herself.

"Weren't you scared?" Miri had asked.

Lily shook her head. "I liked it. I collected pictures and I drew pictures and I looked at the pictures by myself. And because no one else ever saw them, the pictures were perfect and true. They were alive."

Miri and I looked at each other. "Alive," we said. "Alive like how?" I added.

Lily laughed. "Alive like they were alive. They talked and moved and told me who I was. I'll never forget."

"What did they say to you?" I can't remember which of us asked that.

"Lily Silver, you are more precious than gold," Lily chanted, and she looked a little bit different, the lines of her face were finer, she looked like a drawing herself. Miri yawned.

"Is that all they said?"

"Yes."

"Booooooooooring."

Lily gave me a handful of notes to sign; I scrawled my name and passed them to Miri.

"It was all I needed. I'm not even sure if they spoke out loud. I was very lonely. Nobody's fault, though. I hate blame culture."

I didn't say anything, but I knew what I thought; it was her mother's fault for abandoning her. Babies get me down, but I'd seen photos of Lily as a baby and she looked robust and fun. There was a consciousness in her eyes that made her pudgy helplessness seem sarcastic. She looked as if she could easily have been adapted into an accomplice for many practical jokes. And she'd only been a year old. Our grandma Jennifer was pretty, an indifferent student (we'd seen her photographs and report cards bound with pink ribbon) and she'd run off with someone dashing and foreign, a different dashing and foreign someone than whoever Lily's dad had been.

Miri and I wanted to know what they looked like, the

people that Lily drew. Lily laid five stamps on her palm, licked them all in one go, and flicked them onto envelopes. "People," she said. "Just . . . people. No one I'd ever seen. People I made up. They looked the way I felt they should look. I stuck them on my walls. In fact I left them there when I went to college; when I brought you two back to visit your GrandAnna here, I sort of expected the pictures to be still there."

"We used to visit? Here?"

"We did, and your dad too. Then when you were three, your GrandAnna had a crack-up. A . . . well, a really big crack-up, and she had to go into a home. You wouldn't remember," Lily said.

"I remember," my sister said. This was news. I stared at her but she didn't look up from the cards on the floor in front of her. She dotted the *i*'s in her name with sharp hearts.

Lily stretched her legs out in front of her and cricked her neck. "Oh yes? What do you remember, my Miranda?"

"GrandAnna's crack-up. It was like the heraldic pelican," Miri said. She put her pen in her mouth, the inky end on her tongue, then hastily removed it when Lily narrowed her eyes.

"Oh was it . . . was it like *the heraldic pelican?*" I said.

Lily tugged my earlobe. "Let your sister speak."

"It was," said Miri. "The bird that pecks itself to death to feed its children. She tried to give us her blood but we didn't want it."

I looked at Lily. "I did say you wouldn't remember," Lily said, calmly. "I can't think where you got that from."

Miri turned to me. "She rubbed it on our lips, Eliot, but you wiped it off."

"Er . . . I think I'd definitely remember that," I said.

"Miranda," Lily said, and we knew she was getting annoyed because the music in her voice was stronger. "I did say you wouldn't remember. You were three. You can't remember everything."

"Her whole hand was covered with blood, and she had her hand over her face and we could see her looking through her fingers, and she got down between our beds and—"

"There is nothing . . . mysterious and gothic about a crack-up. If anything it's just . . . sad." Lily was so angry she was almost singing, her temper changing the stress she put on her words. "There is no need to make up stories about it."

"Lily couldn't stop her," Miri said.

"Leave your GrandAnna alone." Lily sounded as if she was unable to believe that she had to say it. Miri's first proper meeting with our GrandAnna was at the home; I was there and I don't remember her any other way. When I think of her I see a white-haired woman kneeling on the carpet with us, motioning to the sunlight outside the window of her room and saying with desperate smiles, "Come and play, please come and play, children."

I remember once I raised my voice at Miri and our Grand-Anna jumped and burst into tears that seemed to come straight from her heart, as if it was her I'd shouted at and not Miri. I found that so strange that I shut up for the rest of the visit. GrandAnna had a heart attack a few days afterwards, and she died.

Miri looked at me narrowly and I went and sat in a corner because we thought it was my fault; I'd done it with my shouting.

And I don't remember Miri saying anything about the goodlady before that.

I am here, reading with you. I am reading this over your shoulder. I make your home home, I'm the Braille on your wallpaper that only your fingers can read—I tell you where you are. Don't turn to look at me. I am only tangible when you don't look.

Luc knows this feeling, from an early visit he made here with Lily and the twins. He knew that I was nothing like that flat of theirs in London. One day he came in from the back garden and stood in the sitting-room doorway, smiling while his wife sat on the floor knitting a tiny jacket for one of Miranda's dolls and using a socked foot to wheel Eliot's spare trains across the carpet so he could have train races. It was summer, Lily had tied streamers to the ceiling fan and her freckled shoulders were covered with sun cream. And the twins had four years of life between them, Eliot in a pink T-shirt that hugged his potbelly and Miranda in a dark-blue dress and a little sailor's hat. There was a thing that Lily, Eliot and Miranda tended to do when they were together and he joined him. They pretended he wasn't there at first. He knew that on some level it was intended for his benefit, so he could look at his rosy little English family as if they were in a portrait. When he said hello they'd come alive to him, but first he had to say it.

Before Luc could speak this time, Eliot wobbled over to Lily, wearing a look of grim determination peculiar to children who have only just learned to walk, reached out and yanked her hair hard. Lily didn't stop knitting, but she eyed Eliot sternly and said: "Eliot, you are hurting me."

Eliot didn't answer, and he didn't let go of her hair. He sat down hard, trying to drag Lily's forehead to the floor.

Luc didn't know why he couldn't move. I knew why; it was because I'd leant all my weight, every wall and corridor, on his shoulders. He was lucky I allowed him to stand.

Miranda, on one of the armchairs with her lap full of Barbie dolls and her thumb in her mouth, emptied the dolls onto the floor and crossed the room faster than a thought to grab a handful of Lily's hair too, wrenching at her head from the other side. Lily's fingers tightened around the knitting needles, and she let out a long breath. "Eliot," she said, then: "Miranda!"

She raised her hand to the back of Eliot's neck and pinched him hard. She did the same to Miranda, dug her fingers into the skin. It looked practised.

The twins let go of their mother immediately.

All three of them laughed, and their eyes were full of tears.

Luc walked away and went out again, let himself in through the front door this time, noisily this time.

"Hello!" he called, before he even reached the sitting room this time.

"Hello!" they all called back.

Good mother, good father, good children, all watched over by me.

Miranda avoided dinner on New Year's Eve by pretending to be asleep when Luc called her. She was ready for him when he came looking for her. She lay on her back and offered her face to him, knowing how she looked, knowing that he saw the dark smudges that wheeled around her eyes. He didn't try to wake her anymore.

When Luc had gone she locked the door and searched a drawer at the top of her wardrobe for the last remaining strip of a blue plastic spatula she had been working on for two months. Come slowly, Eden . . .

She put the Crests' greatest hits album into her CD player and skipped through to "Flower of Love."

Plastic was usually very satisfying. A fifty-millimetre wad of it was tough to chew away from the main body of the strip, but with steady labour, sucking and biting, it curved between the teeth like an extension of the gum, and the thick, bittersweet oils in it streamed down her throat for hours, so long she sometimes forgot and thought her body was producing it, like saliva.

She changes all the time

It was 6:00 AM in Haiti when she decided on a midnight feast. She touched the knob at the top of her spine, knowing that if the dress she wore fitted her at all she would not have been able to reach it. She knew that the meal she'd missed would wait in the oven long after Luc had called her to the kitchen and scraped the food off the plates and into the bin. Luc was asleep now, in the round bed, surrounded by the blankets, rugs, wall hangings, prints and figurines that Lily brought back from her photography jobs by the armful. It must have been like being locked into a small, cheerful museum for the night. In the morning she'd surprise him with an empty plate. But first a walk, to get up an appetite.

She left her room and knocked on Eliot's door, to see if he was back from wherever he'd gone for the night. He didn't answer. She peeked inside his room. He wasn't in there, but his lights were on and his window was wide open, the wind whisked leaves around his room in bristles, like a broom. She went back to her psychomantium and played some more CDs at low volume. She had not slept for a while, a matter of days, though she could not think how many. She didn't want to do anything but dance. If Eliot had been there she would have got him to dance with her. Somehow he had the knack of the tuneful wail, *oo-wee-ooo*, the elbow sway, the fist over the heart, though he had done it mainly for Lily's entertainment. Miranda checked the time again, watchfully going through the hours between here and Haiti. So. It was 5:00 AM. *Eliot where are you walking?*

The lift from the ground floor to the first floor, then from first to second, second to third, then from the third floor to the empty attic. She peered up and down the broad passageways and tiptoed past the bedroom doors, feeling like dust, as if she was everywhere at once. She could pull herself tight and then explode and choke everyone in the house. She had never breathed so well or seen so clearly. She could hear one person snoring with the tidy rumble of an engine. In another room, someone murmured to herself or into the phone. Next door to that person a couple quietly crushed each other with sighs and words and their bodies. The fifth and biggest guest room was unoccupied, so nothing from there. A scream came to her, the word "Fire!" but she did not let it leave her, and she didn't ring an alarm. How dare people sleep, how dare they lie so blankly in the dark?

In the dining room she looked glumly at the plate on the table before her. Beef stew and potatoes, the meat drowned in wine and limp onions, she saw brown fat running over white. She took a knife and divided the plate, pushing food aside so that there was a clear line in the middle of the plate, a greasy path of sanity. The light overhead was the deep orange of church candles. She would eat all the meat first, then vegetables. She started with a knife and fork, but soon resorted to bending over her plate with her hands planted on the table, desperately hauling food up into her mouth as if in the final seconds of an all-you-can-eat contest. She thought, There is no way that taking this stuff into my body is doing me any good. Sauce ran across her nose and cheeks and there were tears in her plate. Tears improved the flavour of the vegetables. Perhaps that was in a cookbook somewhere—a Gaelic one, probably, for a people who saw the kind of spirit that did nothing but weep and bode ill.

When she paused to chew, she bumped noses with someone who lifted their head from her plate at the same time. She smelt the beef and potatoes, reheated by the breath from their lips. She started and jumped up from her chair. There was no one else at the table.

"Who's there?" she said, ridiculously, because the kitchen was empty. She grabbed some kitchen towel, wiped her face, then walked around the dining table and put her hand on the back of the chair that had been opposite her. After a moment she sat down in it and drew her plate towards her again.

All the vegetables had disappeared. She had eaten the meat first, as she had told herself she would, but someone else had eaten the vegetables. There was the line she'd drawn in the middle of the plate, and there was a residue of gravy on her side, and then on the other side there was . . . nothing. As clean as if the plate had been washed.

The girl sitting across from her smiled. Her teeth were jagged. She had been there since Miranda had walked into

the dining room, but because she looked exactly like
Miranda she had not been noticed. After all, she might have
been a reflection in the window. The difference was the
teeth, and when she showed her teeth she became noticed.
She was not quite three dimensional, this girl. And so white.
There couldn't be any blood in her. She was perfect. Miranda
but perfect. She was purer than crystal, so pure that she
dissolved and Miranda couldn't see her anymore but still
felt her there.

The front door slammed. The noise of it was like language, and, obedient to it, Miranda put her coat on, her
scarf, her shoes.

The street outside was strewn with bits of houses, whole
window frames lying halfway across shattered sheets of glass,
as if trying to shield them. She climbed over a raft of shin-
gled slate, picked her way through heaps of bricks that
released smoke carefully, almost grudgingly. There were pale
people all along the street, the perfect people Lily had drawn.
They were spaced out carefully, like an army of tin soldiers,
and they watched Miranda without moving or smiling. She
called out to them and, though they said nothing, she felt
safe. They didn't have eyelids because you missed things
when you blinked. They didn't need gas masks because they
didn't breathe. One of them had a pipe in his mouth, or
rather, the pipe was part of his mouth; Lily had been a cruel
artist. When Miranda came to Bridge Street she walked
faster, rubble or no rubble, because of what was behind her

—she saw the moon turn away

and the trees thrashing to save their roots

dogs in every house around that still stood, their barking distant as if from inside a single locked safe, the metal syncopating the sound of fear, saying dance, dance, don't look around, dance

which she did, kicking and yelling like the first day in her GrandAnna's house, only she was going so fast, where, why?

(Because plastic is not satisfying this night

As for beef, as for *his* Frenchie beef and fucking potatoes, ha ha)

Across the cliffs, Dover Castle was black. The sun was rising and the sea was changing colour, but the castle stayed within its lines, hunched in a black mess of shapes, and the vast bank of chalk it stood on seemed to stir in the water as if fighting the darkness that tried to climb down it.

Miranda knelt, her hands holding tight to the safety bars. Someone floated facedown at the foot of the cliff. The sea refused to take the body far from the shore and contented itself with tossing the corpse back and forth between its gentler waves.

We died this morning, she thought, then saw a scrap of colour. The body wore green. Whoever was floating, it was not her.

Sleep came at last, so miraculously and completely that she walked home through the empty streets unawake, her steps guided by the slightness of her shadow.

. . .

She didn't realise she was asleep until a tapping on her door woke her.

"Yes?" Miranda said.

Her father came in, squinting, pretending he couldn't see her in the dark of her room.

"Morning, Miri."

"Morning," she said, holding the question mark back with effort. She was no longer sure what the time was, or how to calculate. Also she thought she had locked her door.

"I'm about to interview someone to replace Ezma, but someone else is about to check out," Luc began apologetically.

Miranda waved a hand. "Take their money, take the room key, print out a receipt," she recited.

Luc nodded. "And check the room, please. So I know what needs doing."

Miranda got out of bed to show her intention of moving soon. When he left, she sat down again. Her knees felt weak.

The woman Luc was interviewing was a black woman, short and round, with a placid gaze. An orange head wrap and an orange gown that made her formless, a vapour sinking through the sofa. She had a big, grey-black bird printed on each sleeve at the elbow; one was visible every time she lifted her teacup to her mouth. The birds had iron feathers and claws as long as their beaks, but they hid their heads behind their wings. She was wearing sandals despite the cold, and her toenails were painted bright orange. Her eyelids were daubed with a green that dotted her gown in emerald specks but turned khaki coloured on her skin. The woman spoke to Luc, unhurriedly and with a heavy African accent.

Miranda couldn't take her eyes off the scars across the woman's cheekbone, four horizontal stripes that cut a little farther along her face at each stage, like arrows at different stages of flight. They were smooth now but the cuts would have had to be made again and again on the same spot to make them hold. It took all she had not to ask the woman if she could still feel it. Miranda pressed the keys of the newly vacated room into Luc's hand and the form with pencilled ticks beside items that needed tidying and replacing. Towels, sheets and so on.

"Thanks, Miri." Luc looked at the woman who sat beside him on the sofa, then back at Miri. "This is Sade," he told Miranda, then: "Sade, this is my daughter, Miranda."

The introduction meant that Sade must be the one who was getting the job. Miranda, Luc and Sade got caught in a triangle of gazing. Luc cleared his throat and stood. "Sade, let me show you the house," he said.

They started at the bottom and climbed up. Sade stopped in one of the guest rooms, her hand on the windowsill. "It's so quiet," she said.

All three of them listened without speaking. Now that she'd said it, it was true. The sounds in the other rooms were muted into vibrations. Someone closed a door, someone else ran down the stairs and you didn't really hear these things, you felt them.

<u>JENNIFER SILVER</u>

lived quite long. She didn't die until 1994. A reason why Lily
never felt motherless was that her mother was there with her,
a door and a curtain away. It is a pity that Lily never understood this in a literal sense, but the concealment was necessary. Jennifer really meant to abandon her daughter, and how
could I allow that? Jennifer was going to walk away from
Anna and Lily in broad daylight. Anna was playing with her
granddaughter, lying on her back in trapdoor-room with baby
Lily on her stomach, cooing at her and comparing curl for
curl. Jennifer had convinced herself that she hated them both,
the child and the crone. She was modern and couldn't coun-
tenance being held by four walls just because she'd had a baby
at a young age. She was going to Milan with her Italian
photographer boyfriend, and he would make her face famous.
Anna and Lily could have each other, for all she cared.

One blessing born from Lily's never knowing her mother is that Lily never knew how selfish her mother was. Jennifer was nineteen years old and thought a lot of herself and how she looked; her smooth ponytail, the crowded patterns on her silk shifts, the shine of her go-go boots. She had a tiny replica of a yew tree that she used to hold her earrings, Perspex hoops dangling off the branches. Each month or so the little tree had to be replaced because she'd gnawed it to an aged apple core. The earring tree was the last thing Jennifer put in her bag. It had to go on top of all her other things so that it wouldn't get damaged. Jennifer had catlike eyes that she made stranger with kohl. Her gaze was cold and self-reflective

—am I pretty? Yes

—am I pretty?

—Yes—am I pretty?

Maybe she was not really like that. It's just that I would prefer you to think that what happened to her was justified. I opened up for her. That is to say, I unlocked a door in her bedroom that she had not seen before, a door in the wall behind her dressing table.

She exclaimed, but not overmuch. She wasn't particularly clever. She picked up her bag and went exploring. When she was safely down the new passageway, I closed the door behind her. It was the best sort of winter morning, cold but bright. That was the only sort of light Jennifer saw after that—it came through great windows and she couldn't find her way away from them and out of me. Not that she tried hard. She was dazed.

I am not sure if she was lonely. She smiled to herself, and played little games of dress-up with herself, pulling clothes out of her bag and repacking them, switching earrings and examining herself in window glass when night fell. When her little earring tree was gone, she bit at her fingers until I brought her branches from the garden. For years and years, yes. Her hair greyed quickly, but she didn't notice. When her shift dresses grew too dirty and tattered to play dress-up with, I let Jennifer back into the main part, where Lily and Anna lived. Lily was a teenager by then. I had to be very careful, and quick, letting Jennifer in. Jennifer thought that Lily's room still belonged to her. She ignored the new pictures and posters and tried Lily's clothes on. She marvelled at them. She loved them. "When on earth did I buy this?" she'd ask herself, stroking the sleeves of a suede jacket, unbuttoning and rebuttoning a pin-striped waistcoat.

Don't feel sorry for Jennifer. Why should you? She lived long and relatively well, and she was kept safe from those fears and doubts peculiar to her times. She was safe from the war that sickened what it touched from miles away, the new kind of image that lashed the conscience to the nerves, the pictures of Phnom Penh burning with a kind of pagan festivity, the young bones in the mud at Choeung Ek, the Cambodians and yellow-skinned priests sprawled in graves dug poorly and in great fear, graves they dug for themselves. It is true that Jennifer Silver never did leave home, but she had longed for an unusual life, and she certainly had that.

B elieve it, ~~don't believe it, as you will. Of course~~ there is the idea that Anna caught ~~Jennifer and tried to~~ stop her from leaving, that the two fought, that Jennifer strangled to death in a circle made of Anna's fingers. But that is unrealistic for a number of reasons. And besides, without a corpse there is no proof of what may have come

before

Lily died Eliot and Miranda had gone to school separately, Eliot coasting away on his bike each morning, leaving Miranda to inch sedately schoolwards in heels so high and thin that they would have got jammed in bicycle pedals. But Eliot walked Miranda to school on her first day back. As usual he had a half-pint bottle of full-fat milk sticking out of his blazer pocket. It bobbed as he walked. For some reason Eliot and all the boys he knew at school drank copious amounts of milk straight from the bottle. When they finished their first bottle, they'd all be at the cornershop at breaktime, buying more. No matter which one of the boys you asked why, he'd only knock his forehead with his knuckles and say, without smiling, "For the bones."

Miranda asked if she could try some of the milk. Eliot

obliged her without comment and nodded sagely when she wrinkled her nose and said, "It's just milk."

At assembly she realised she'd forgotten her hymnal at home. She looked around helplessly as the head of the sixth form approached. Appealing to him would have no effect. On Monday mornings he handed out detentions to people who weren't holding small books covered in red leather, and that was all. Help came unexpectedly; a hymnal landed in her lap and she hurriedly opened it and sang loudly until the teacher had passed. When she searched the row of girls for her saviour, Emma Roberts, safe in an area that had already been patrolled, smiled at her and held up a little note that said: *Welcome back*. Emma's hair was almost as short as Miranda's; it made her look much less substantial than she had before; the heavy gold hearts she wore in her ears seemed to weigh her down. Miranda suddenly realised that Eliot wasn't sitting beside Emma. She decided that he must have bunked assembly. Everyone knew that Eliot and Emma always sat together—they'd so comfortably and easily brought their mutual crush from the playground to lower school and from lower school to sixth form. You couldn't picture Eliot with his arm around the back of anyone else's chair, or Emma throwing fries like darts at any other boy. Eliot could be tricky, but Emma made him simpler for everyone. Miranda saw him now, two rows ahead, beside Martin. She didn't look at Emma again for the rest of assembly, not even when the headmaster read aloud a list of upper sixth formers who'd had Oxford and Cambridge

offers and she desperately needed someone vaguely friendly
to lock eyes with. All the girls on Miranda's row eyed her
with great curiosity, and, when Tijana's name was called,
the same was done to Tijana in the row in front. Miranda
looked at the back of Tijana's head and felt worried. Tijana
had been part of the pack of girls who had chased their car
after she was released from the clinic. Tijana, sitting cross-
legged in her chair, popped up the collar of her school shirt.
The headmaster stood on the varnished stage, with a large
portrait of the queen behind him and a marble crucifix to
the right of him, and he started clapping. It took everyone
a second to follow his lead. Miranda reddened and was glad
that she'd chosen a more low-key lipstick that day, a dark
pink that matched the inside of her mouth. She was okay
intelligence-wise, but she knew that she wasn't as clever as
Eliot. One of the teachers had said that Oxbridge looked
for teachability. So it must be that she was more teachable
than Eliot. She could picture Tijana at Cambridge, though,
grey hood pulled up over her head as she moved through
the stone arches with calm eyes.

When the bell rang for lunch, Miranda unchained
Eliot's bike and rode downhill and then uphill again, feeling the wheels cling to the earth's descent as shops shot by,
and the dour water that split Bridge Street. A couple of
white gulls raced her, their wings flapping about her head.
The only way she could ride a bike in shoes like hers was
fast, legs pumping in a way that outwitted the conspiracy
of pegs and holes. She stopped when the ground jutted and

sent her body leaning back, protesting the steepness. She
got off the bike and drew it along behind her. She heard and
smelt the water at the bottom of the cliffs, but it felt like a
long time before she'd walked long enough to glimpse the
sea crashing and breaking against the shore, foam eating
into stone. England and France had been part of the same
landmass, her father had told her, until prised apart by
floods and erosion.

She was not sure what time it was; when she looked at
the sun she could understand that it had changed position
but she did not dare to say how much. There were cruise ships
coming in, vast white curved blocks like severed feet shuffling
across the water. She waved halfhearted welcome. She felt
the wind lift her hair above her head. In daylight the water
was so blue that the colour seemed like a lie and she leant
over, hoping for a moment of shift that would allow her to
understand what was beneath the sea. Was this where the
goodlady lived? That was how you caught a magical creature,
you found out where it lived and you laid traps for it.

Her hands were pinned behind her and she was knocked
down by a deft kick to the back of her knee. All this was
done in complete silence. She lay and frowned into the grass,
began to get up and was stopped by the fact of a knife held
near her face. It was so sharp. Where it cut, her flesh would
hang neatly but separated, like soft dominoes.

"Oh God," said Miranda. "Come on. Really?"

A girl she recognised but had never spoken to was
crouched by her, holding the knife. She was one of the

Kosovan girls. The girl hissed at her. "Why don't you stay away from our boys?"

Miranda said, "May I get up, please?" She was lying on her front and it was hurting her neck to have to look up so steadily.

"No, you certainly may not," the girl said, mimicking Miranda's accent. Then she grew serious again. "Did you hear me? I said, why don't you stay away from our boys?"

"I don't know what you're talking about."

Another girl came into view, looking so much like the first girl that Miranda thought she might be hallucinating.

"We saw you," the second girl said. "You and Amir, you and Farouk, you and Agim, you and whoever. Then they end up getting stabbed."

Miranda thought about screaming. But she'd never been one for raising her voice, and an unpractised scream would just dissolve into seawater.

Instead she said, "Listen, I really don't know what or whom you are talking about. You have mistaken me for someone else."

Tijana appeared behind the first two girls.

Miranda said, "Tijana—"

"Agim is my *cousin*." She said it flatly, and she said it in such a way that Miranda understood that these girls really and truly meant to hurt her. She struggled to her feet, and the girls were around in a tight circle, their arms linked. Their hair, which looked so rigid, was soft and greasy and synthetically perfumed. Miranda gagged, and they rocked her,

the three of them, rocked her close enough to the cliff edge
to make her stutter, "Don't, please don't."

"Agim is my cousin," Tijana repeated.

"Who is Agim?" Miranda asked, desperately.

Silence and adamant eyes.

"I've been away for months," Miranda babbled. "Doing
my lessons in bed. I've been . . . away. If you're talking about
the stabbings I've no idea . . ."

Tijana looked into Miranda's eyes and seemed, for the
first time, unsure.

"She's lying, man. It's her," one of the other girls said,
then, to Miranda, "Now you tell us how the fuck you're
involved with this or I cut you."

"Hold on," Tijana said. "Maybe she means it. It may be.
She wasn't at school for months."

Miranda took a close look at the back of her mind while
the other two girls considered. She thought she might faint.
Whoever Agim was, she didn't want him to come. Because
if these girls thought she was someone else, then Agim
would too. She had to get away. The girls lessened their grip
on her while they argued, and Miranda stepped out of her
shoes. Miranda bent over and retched and when they
jumped clear, she ran.

She pushed and kicked Eliot's bike so that it rattled far
ahead of her until the way was smooth enough for her to
scramble onto it, nearly tipping it over, and she pedalled
harder even than her heart was thumping. She didn't know
where she was going; she had forgotten the way home. She

weaved through Market Square, narrowly avoiding riding straight into the fountain, then she passed through side streets that branched off the high street, slowing and remembering herself once she was sure she'd lost Tijana and the other girls. She made her way home and sat on the flint steps, freezing and mourning her beautiful, black pointy-toed court shoes, whose leather would be destroyed by the inquisitive tongues of the sheep that wandered on the cliffs.

When she finally went into the house, there were three cardboard boxes on the staircase that led up from the ground floor. Sade, the new housekeeper, and her father were argu-ing and laughing in the dining room.

"Sade. First of all let me tell you that you can't put pep-per in the baked beans, you really can't."

"Why not? They don't taste of anything."

Miranda looked inside one of the boxes, not knowing what she expected to see—garish prints, a Bible, a huge cross—but the box was packed solid with books. Dickens and the Brontës, even. She picked a couple of them up— each had a huge white *S* slashed across the title page.

Two houseguests picked their way around the first of the boxes on their way downstairs. They were a black couple from London who had enthused about their love of British history while Miranda had swayed, glassy-eyed and dead on her feet, and drawn red circles around the Cinque Ports on a map of Kent for them.

In order to avoid a repeat occurrence, she sidestepped into the sitting room and looked through the old newspapers for the issue of *The Dover Post* that Eliot had handed her when Luc had brought her back from the clinic. There was Tijana's cousin's name, Agim Hajdari. He'd sustained serious wounds but had recovered. He'd been found curled up in a ball between a wall and a tree on Priory Lodge road, arms crossed over himself. As if to hold his insides in, Miranda thought.

After some time she noticed Eliot had come home. He was standing in the sitting-room doorway with his arms crossed.

"I'm sorry I took your bike! But I think it was fated. Some girls tried to kill me," she said, as soon as she saw him. "And the bike revealed itself as my trusty getaway steed."

By the time she'd explained properly, he was pacing the room worriedly. "We have to sort this out," he said. "These girls sound deluded enough to keep coming after you, especially if . . . anything else happens."

"What shall I do?" Miranda asked.

"Two choices. Number one—Martin and I go after these girls and beat them with sticks—okay, you're not keen, fair enough—number two, we talk to Tijana tomorrow and meet this cousin of hers and get him to tell them that you've got nothing to do with all of this."

He stopped and looked at her carefully.

"Because you haven't got anything to do with this," he reminded her. "I mean, what? The very idea of it is . . ."

Miranda crumpled the sheets of newspaper on her lap.

"I am very concerned," she said, in a small voice, "that this will not end well. They seemed convinced that they'd seen me before."

Eliot pulled her to her feet. "There is no way, Miri," he said. "No way in the world." Grey eyes convince so well, burying the person they look at in truth like flung pebbles. But Miranda could never do that with her eyes; convince. Anyway she was never sure about anything.

"Come and have some dinner," he said.

"In a minute," she said. "Go. I'll see you in there."

"The new housekeeper is interesting," he said, on his way out of the room. "She asked Dad if he had any shirts he didn't want, and now she's slashing his old shirts by hand in the kitchen. I think she's, er, making something. Arts and crafts."

"I don't like her," Miranda said. Then, confused, she said, "Oh, I do."

Eliot rolled his eyes. "You don't have to make an immediate decision about it."

That night it rained and a disconsolate wowowowow came down the chimney and flew around the rooms. Miri, Eliot and Luc watched TV and read in Luc's room. Eliot lay under Miranda's elbows, reading *Moby-Dick* while she used his back to prop up her collected works of Poe.

"What do you think of Poe?"

"He's awful. He was obviously . . . what's the term . . . 'disappointed in love' at some point. He probably never smiled again. The pages are just bursting with his longing for women to suffer. If he ever met me he'd probably punch me on the nose."

"I think Poe's quite good, actually. The whole casual horror thing. Like someone standing next to you and screaming their head off and you asking them what the fuck and them stopping for a moment to say 'Oh you know, I'm just afraid of Death' and then they keep on with the screaming."

"Hm," said Miranda. "I'd rather they talked to someone about this fear."

"A psychiatrist couldn't put up with all the screaming." Eliot had marked his place in his book with his finger, and now he stirred restlessly, impatient to get back to it.

"Oh, not a psychiatrist, a priest. Priests can put up with screaming."

"A priest," said Eliot, "would not say anything constructive to someone who was scared of death. A priest would say 'Death is great! You get to go to heaven!'"

"True. But they'd put up with the screaming," Miranda insisted. "A psychiatrist would sedate you and act as if it wasn't normal to be so scared. In a situation of Poe's kind I would always, always go to a priest before I went to a psychiatrist. I'd be out of that House of Usher like a shot and off looking for Father Joe. And I'd have gotten rid of Ligeia with holy water."

"Would you now," Eliot muttered, and Luc, lolling in his armchair with the newspaper spread across his lap, looked up and said, "Easy to see the solution when you're not in the story, isn't it."

Miranda had found a pen somewhere. She fixed it into Eliot's hair. She wrapped four strands around it and it stayed.

"Thanks," Eliot said, sounding as if he meant it.

"How's *Moby-Dick*?" Miranda asked.

After a few seconds, Eliot admitted, "I don't . . . get it. Dad, did you get it?"

Luc put his paper down, cleared his throat, changed the TV channel.

"Yes, I understood it. It is about many things."

Miranda and Eliot waited, but Luc didn't elaborate. Eliot sniggered, and the pen fell out of his hair. It was getting to 1:00 AM and Miranda knew that soon Luc would kick her and Eliot out, and Eliot would go to bed and then it would be her and Poe until morning.

"Father," she said, "my sleep's bad again. Please give me something to do, or give me something to make me sleep, or give me death."

Luc raised an admonishing finger. "I lie in bed until I fall asleep, no matter what; I lie there until I have no choice but to sleep," he began.

"Tried that," Miranda said.

There was an especial horror in lying with her eyes closed and her thoughts coming too quickly and strongly to be deciphered. At such times she saw herself twice, the girl lying down and the woman in the trapdoor room sitting directly beneath the fireplace, delicately wiping her beautiful mouth again and again.

"Hot milk and honey, Nytol, a nice long warm bath . . . ?" Luc ticked the options off on his fingers.

"Tried that, tried that, tried that."

"I have heard," Eliot murmured, "that marijuana is a good sleep aid."

Luc snapped his fingers. "I can give you some work. I was going to give it to Eliot, but . . ."

He went to his desk and sorted through the envelopes on it. He handed her one. A friend of his had started working for an advertising agency, his job was to get feedback on television advertisements they'd filmed before they were sent for approval to the companies who had commissioned the product advertisements. Things like crisps, contact lenses, house and car insurance. There were sheets to fill in for each advert she watched. She had never realised that anyone cared so much; besides there were some terrible adverts on TV. "I'll do it," she said, picking up the pen that had dropped out of Eliot's hair.

After Luc and Eliot had gone to bed, she watched as many adverts as she could and scribbled notes, poking at her eyelids with her pen so that she could pay better attention to the dancing life-sized tadpoles that, to her surprise, made her feel like buying the soft drink they were promoting. A pungent smell of stewing meat crept out of the kitchen, getting bolder and bolder until it was wadded up behind the bones of Miranda's face. Sade was cooking vigorously, her curly perm trapped in a hairnet. She jiggled from countertop to countertop, chopping chillies, crushing garlic, tossing handfuls of spice into pots. The smell made Miranda realise how hungry she was; not for the sharp-toothed fireworks that Sade was lighting in Luc's pot. Not for chalk, not for plastic . . .

Uneasily, Miranda came into the light. She did not feel steady on her feet. She thought she had better sit down and tried to sit on the wall nearest her, forgetting that it was horizontal and high instead of vertical and low.

Sade took her arm and led her to a kitchen stool, then, when Miranda was unable to climb onto it, Sade lifted her onto the stool herself.

"They're calling you, aren't they?" Sade asked her.

Miranda found it easy to look into Sade's eyes. The pupils were simple, and the whites were slightly yellow.

"Who?"

Sade brought Miranda some water and a small plate of fried, crispy batter. The pieces looked like broken doughnuts, but Miranda could see shreds of chilli puffed up inside them like a red rash.

"Your old ones," she said. "I know it's hard."

She shrugged and took a piece herself when Miranda waved the plate away.

"No, nothing like that. I'm not sure what you mean, actually. Everything is fine," Miranda said. Her lips missed her glass and she spilled water down her front and into her lap, then put the glass down on the nearest counter. The water was so cold on her skin that it felt dry. "Please tell me more about old ones calling," she said.

Sade looked so alarmed that Miranda thought the topic must be the utmost taboo. Then she saw herself on the floor. Water makes a mirror of any surface. She'd sucked her cheeks in so far that the rest of her face emerged in a series of interconnected caves. Her eyes were small, wild globes. The skull was temporary, the skull collected the badness together and taught it discipline, that was all. Miranda wanted to say, *That is not my face*. No, it wasn't hers, she had to get away from it, peel it back. Or she had to leave and take this face with her, defuse it somewhere else. Eliot and Luc, she had to protect them.

Sade turned Miranda's head away from the terrible face.

"Thank you," Miranda said, limply. "Thanks."

(I'm very hungry)

Sade offered her the plate of fritters again, then, after some hesitation, a handful of peanut shells. As Miranda nibbled at peanut shells, Sade pulled up a stool and sat herself on it. She began plaiting strips of Luc's old shirt and dragging them through a saucer of red fat on the counter beside her. Every now and again she looked about her, checking on her cooking projects. Miranda watched.

"What are you making?"

"Juju."

"What's that?"

She pulled her finger through a knot.

"Company."

The figure Sade was making looked like two hanged men holding fast to each other. She spun black thread around a hook, breaking the thread with a sharp jerk of her arm when the hook was completely covered. She spoke without looking at Miranda, she spoke as if to herself. "Something is wrong."

"That is true," Miranda said, for want of any other comment. She was the something wrong. It was she who had fallen asleep and lost Lily's life. Now sleep wouldn't come anymore. Sade's talisman was a thing worked against her.

During one English lesson Martin sat next to her. She was surprised; they hadn't spoken properly since he'd asked her to the cinema months before and she'd said, rashly and unconvincingly, that she didn't like films because they hurt her eyes. When put on the spot she became terrible.

At the end of the lesson, he put his arm around the back of her chair.

"It's Friday!" he said.

"Yes," said Miranda. "It is."

She wondered when it was coming, the stupid thing she was going to say to him.

"Coming to the pub tonight?" he asked. "We haven't seen you for ages."

He kicked the back of Emma's chair and Emma turned around. "Yeah, come," she said.

"We're underage," Miranda said. Ah, there it was, the stupid thing. Luckily they laughed.

"She doesn't want to come," Eliot called from across the room.

"Yes I do," she said, because she hadn't been asked before.

She had no idea what people wore to the pub. She had better wear what she always wore. Later she hopped in and out of the shower, sent a hot iron skating over her black linen dress with the pouch pockets, brushed her wet hair and painted her lips with a bright red dot in the centre that grew outwards and dulled as it did. She threw rose attar over herself in a hasty splash, as if it were a liquid jacket. Then she stood, shivered, and sneezed. She would drink the juice of grapes, she told herself. From a glass. And be comfortable, and be liked, like Eliot.

Their group sat at a corner table, the girls all strawberry lip gloss, halter-neck tops and bare legs, the boys wearing so much gel that their hair didn't move when blown on at close quarters (Miranda experimented surreptitiously when they had their heads turned). Everyone was touching each other, heads on shoulders, arms around waists, and all she could smell was skin and smoke. She could hardly see—the world was fogged over.

Emma was kind, asking her neutral questions about music and TV from her precarious position on the lap of a boy called Josh. But it soon became clear that Miranda didn't watch TV, and had no opinion on any record released after 1969. Eliot sighed, got up and added a song to the jukebox selection, then went to play snooker. A few of the others got up and followed him about like ducklings. Martin stayed and spoke to her and she thought, Help, I will die, and struggled out of the corner, asking if anyone wanted anything from the bar. It was as if she hadn't spoken. Finally: "You're alright," Emma said. Josh kissed her shoulder, and she squirmed and giggled.

Miranda went and sat down at the bar. She asked for peanuts and made a circle with them in an ashtray. A vaguely familiar boy turned to her and said: "Miranda. How are you doing?"

It took her a moment to place him. Jalil. They had had once done a presentation to their class on *Lamia*. She had liked the air of fey tragedy about him, his wide eyes and artfully mussed hair. Once she knew who he was, she smiled at him.

"I'm fine," she said.

"You're feeling better now, yeah?"

"Weren't you in my English class?"

"I dropped English. For economics." He groaned and stared into his pint. "So neekish to be talking about his. Change the subject."

"What is your opinion on curses?"

"What?"

"For example, do they really persist unto the third generation?"

As if watching a slide show, she saw a series of gashes on arms and faces. They emerged so naturally and normally that she wasn't sure whether she was seeing them in conjunction with her view of the smoky room, or whether the gashes were all she could see. They were of different shapes and sizes. They were healing over, the new skin shuddering over the blood like intricate lace. She was fascinated. She was falling asleep. To wake herself up, she reached for the circle of flesh beneath Lily's wristwatch and pinched it.

Unexpectedly, he smiled. "Can I buy you a drink?"

She shook her head. He offered to show her a strange thing he could do instead. With an expression of the utmost gravity, he planted his hand on the table and swivelled his wrist 360 degrees without changing the position of his hand. All this without audible sign, as if his bones were oiled. Miranda squeaked obligingly. He relaxed, looked pleased and sat back on his stool. She noticed his jacket was hooded.

"Pull your hood up," she said.

He looked around the room. "Why?

"I just want to see."

Half smiling, waiting for the joke to catch up with him, he pulled his hood up. Its shape around his head was lumpen. It was obviously the first time he'd ever pulled this hood up over his head. He looked at her and said, "Anything else?"

Would he let her? She kissed him, gently, tentatively at first, her hand cupping his face, her fingers inside the heavy cotton of his hood. When he opened his mouth for her tongue, she drew him up and closer to her, pushing his hood back and using his hair like a leash until she could bring him no closer. Someone in the group she had left shouted, "Get a room, will you?"

She took Jalil's hand and held it, pretending, for a minute, to be in love. She looked attentively at him. Open pores grained his skin, and the shade of its brown varied from forehead to neck. He didn't know what to make of her staring and stirred uncomfortably. She was holding the hand he'd have used to lift his pint. When she said she was going home, he offered to walk her back.

"It's fine," she said, and got off her stool.

"But it's dark," Jalil protested.

"It's fine," Miranda said again. She was already walking away. Jalil wrapped an arm around her waist and tried, awkwardly, to kiss her goodbye, but she stepped away politely. She didn't want to anymore.

I'd written to lots of media training schemes and independent film companies trying to get a placement for the summer, for the majority of my year out, if possible. I didn't particularly want to travel; there was nowhere I wanted to go. But I couldn't stay. So I'd applied to things in as many different places as possible and hoped that ultimately wherever I had to go, it would be because of work. As long as English was spoken there, wherever it was, I'd go. One morning a couple of weeks into the new year I got lots of letters back and sat on the staircase, shuffling through them, looking for something encouraging. Most of them were "no"s.

Emma texted me: *Jean de Bergieres—they searched for her in the oven(!) and found her in the attic . . .*

I texted back: *And what did they do when they found her?*

Her: *Raped her—seven of them.*

Me: *O no!*

Her: *Breathe. This was in 14thC France. Church had outlawed brothels and locals were desperate.*

Me: *Actually just about to commit a couple of v brutal crimes. Wld be helpful to see them put into historical context first.*

Her: *I miss you. Also miss my hair. Can we forget drunk pre-Christmas stupidness (mine)?*

One of the houseguests wandered out of the dining room and said to me, "Something's burning . . . ?"

As soon as she said it, I smelt it. In fact I'd been sitting in a cloud of smoke; ridges of it drifted around my head as I moved, like a blurred fingerprint.

"Shit." A pan had been left on the stove, with the gas burning. It was like . . . "*Fuck*. Fuck *me*." I hadn't known oil and bacon could do that. It must have been a different kind of oil. Flame rose from the blackened pan, almost solid, like a ragged soufflé.

For a second I couldn't do anything but stare and swear powerfully and brace myself for the smoke alarm to go off. The smoke alarm didn't go off. One of the guests, a different one from the one who'd approached me, shouted "Do something!" and threw a napkin in the direction of the pan.

The pan growled and ate most of the napkin, letting a scrap fall to the floor where it blazed on the lino.

I went to the tap, wetted some more napkins and threw them onto the cooker, reserving the first one for the floor. I was encouraged by the sputtering sound of drowning flames and the lessening of smoke, and ended by covering the cooker and floor with wet towels that someone pushed at me. Then I went into the dining room, and the guests trooped in after me. "I don't think there'll be any breakfast served here this morning," I told them. "But there *is* a McDonald's, right by the square." There was some grumbling so, struck by inspiration, I said, "Hand your receipts in when you're checking out and you'll be reimbursed."

I couldn't find Dad, so I went straight up to the attic. There was an oily, twisted doughnut of cloth hung on a nail in the centre of the attic door, all knots and tails. I didn't want to touch it or the door, and I settled for kicking at the door with the toe of my trainer. No answer, so I kicked harder, said "Sade" a couple of times, then gave up and went downstairs. The guests had dispersed, though I'd passed a woman on the stairs who looked as if she was ready to go back to bed. Sade was in the kitchen. She was a vision in nuclear red and blue. She was scrubbing at the cooker with her elbow turned in awkwardly, as if it was hurting her.

"I am so very sorry," she said, with such force I felt I had to turn aside to deflect it.

"Where were you?"

"Here, I was here."

"No you weren't," I said, flatly.

When I moved past her I saw that she'd hurt her hands; she had a plaster wrapped around each fingertip. She looked at me looking at her hands. I got a stool, climbed up onto it and poked at the smoke alarm. There was nothing wrong with it, except that it had been switched off.

"Oh that was me," Sade said. "I was cooking last night and I didn't want to wake everyone up so I switched the thingie off just to make sure."

She gestured towards an array of lidded tubs she'd stacked up on the counter nearest the fridge.

I nodded to show that I understood, stuffed my letters into my back pocket and left the kitchen. I had an interview in London to get to. Sade called me back.

"What will you tell your father?"

"About what?"

She looked me over, and for a horrifying moment I thought she might touch me, fuss over me, lick her finger and wipe away something on my chin, or smooth my hair out of my eyes. She let me go, but called: "Eliot, do you have a girlfriend?" across the passageway.

I sighed and put my jacket on.

"Ah. You should get a girlfriend. It would cheer you up. You are gloomy. Miranda too."

"Our mother died," I explained, and wandered around

to the back for my bike. Miri was looking out of her window, a white white face with the darkness of her curtains behind her, and I don't know why, but I ducked out of her sight.

The interview was conducted in a cream-coloured room with a flip chart. It was an interview for an internship at a television production company based in Cape Town. Since Miri had left the video with the advertisements on a chair in the sitting room, I'd watched most of the adverts as soon as I'd woken up. I filled my parts of the interview conversation with references to the apprenticeship "work" I sometimes did for an ad agency. By the time I got back to Dover, it was already dark. I wrestled my bike off the train and rode home, keeping an eye out for the girls who had been out to get Miri. There was no sign of them, but the cliffs were wearing broad chains of snow, so I took out my camera and slowed down, elbows on the handlebars, pointing the lens upwards. I took photos. Too many, and I worked the shutter too fast, because I kept thinking someone would come and get in the way, people with shopping bags or something.

Dad had had Lily's Haiti photos developed, and (Taking the film out of *that* camera, closing the back up again, how much had that felt like blinding someone?) among them was a sunset miniatured in purple, birds with long wings swimming through it in curious Vs. There was a bucketful of live sand, no, crabs, at a market stall. A potted tree, or a green skeleton, stood in a darkened doorway.

Tiny robots churning in a grey fishing net. Looking at those last photos was like flipping through a book of silence, all the information conveyed with the certainty of a glimpse. There were people in the photos—the bored, teenaged market trader was there, the fisherwomen too, kings of their boats—but they were there minus everything that was absurd and ungainly about them. They were in the picture but their bodies weren't.

You can only take pictures like that if you're able to see ghosts. Lily could. Miri too. Why can't I?

On Sunday afternoon Sade washed the sitting-room windows from the inside, an expression of pure patience on her face as Miranda tried to teach her to whistle. She couldn't get the hang of it. Every time she got the right length of breath going, she looked nervous, opened her mouth fully and said *whoooooosh*.

"I grew up believing it's bad luck to whistle in the house," she explained, eventually. "It's just no good. It's too late."

"Why is it bad luck?"

"Well. I know of witches who whistle at different pitches, calling things that don't have names."

Miranda was pleased with the idea of a whistler as a witch, and she let out a long, unmusical whistle, relenting when Sade winced.

"I was only calling Eliot home," she said.

The front door banged.

"Eliot?" Sade called.

He announced, "It is but the shade of Eliot," as he went upstairs.

Sade and Miranda looked at each other significantly.

"Whistler," said Sade.

"Witch," said Miranda.

Then: "Is it bad luck if a builder whistles at you? And if it is, is it bad luck for you or for him? Because technically he's sort of indoors."

Sade wiped a wet cloth over the soap, inspected the window and wiped her hands on her apron. "I'll tell you later. What's the time . . . actually, never mind, you."

She went into the kitchen and checked the clock. Visiting hours at the Immigration Removal Centre had begun. "Help me get the food together." Together they packed a bag full of food wrapped in tin foil and cling-film until it was a solid block, like a building caught in plastic. The sun shone on the garden and made it seem warmer out than it was, and Miranda hummed to herself and looked out of the kitchen window.

The couple who had made her circle the Cinque Ports on a map for them, the couple she'd heard together in their room, were sitting under one of the trees, on a blanket. The woman wasn't wearing a coat, just a short-sleeved white dress. Her legs were bare and a big white flower shone from the midst of her plaits. The man was wearing his sweater slung across his shoulders, the arms tied around the front of him. They were talking earnestly and eating apples. It was far too cold for them to be sitting out there having a picnic. Miranda wanted to open the window and shout "It's January!" but she didn't, because there was something so lovely about their being out there, their faces turned towards each other, their gazes chained together. They had stayed for quite a while now, longer than most other guests stayed. She wondered what were they doing in Dover. She thought she should try to remember their names.

Sade turned up the volume on the kitchen radio. Up at the port, fifty-eight people had been found dead in the back of a truck. Chinese. They had suffocated. Miranda was a heartbeat away from putting her hands over her ears. What is wrong with Dover, she thought.

Eyes closed, Sade stroked the scars on her cheek.

"Didn't they call Dover the key to England?" she asked, slowly. "Key to a locked gate, throughout both world wars, and even before. It's still fighting." *political history*

She drew her scarf around her neck and wriggled into her coat, swinging the heavy carrier bag as if it was nothing. As she left, a gust of wind came through the hallway and the back door slammed. It was the couple who had been picnicking outside. Now they came into the warmth and looked around, and shivered. They were sweating. They passed Miranda and she was troubled. The woman smiled vaguely and gave Miranda the lily from her hair. The man followed the woman up the stairs without even glancing at Miranda.

"Is everything okay?" Miranda asked.

No reply. She tried to add up how many days the couple had booked in for; she should look in her father's book. The flower in her hand was so large and sweet smelling that she might have been carrying the frozen scent of a lily. She paused halfway up the staircase, looked up and listened to them.

"A tisket, a tasket," the man sang, off-key, outside the door of the couple's guest room. "A tisket, a tasket."

"Stop it," Miranda heard the woman say, just as she herself mouthed, "Stop it."

"Something's killing me." There was a static quality to their voices, as if they were people on the radio. Miranda's vision blurred until the staircase was the only thing she could see clearly. A helter-skelter of wood and carpet, a backbone.

"What is it?" the man asked.

"I don't know. Maybe it was the apple. Where did it come from?"

The woman began to choke. Miranda, who did not know CPR, ran up to the second floor, but the man had led the woman inside the bedroom, saying, "Sh, sh," and the horrible coughing was quieted somehow.

The doorbell rang.

"Er . . ."

Jalil had brought her a bunch of sunflowers. Miranda found sunflowers very ugly, and yellow made her so nervous that she suspected it was the cause of war. She was irritated with Jalil for bringing the sunflowers, and irritated with

herself for being ungrateful. She stood at the door, a barrier
between him and the house, sniffed at the brown florets that
spiralled at the centre of the petals. She couldn't smell anything, but she said, "Thank you. These are beautiful." Then
she closed the door, praying that no one else would come
up and ring the doorbell until he had gone. Jalil stood on
the doorstep for three seconds, smiling uncertainly, waiting
for her to open the door, but she said, "Goodbye! See you
at school!" through the letter box, and then he went off,
disconsolately dragging his feet against the gravel.

As soon as he was out of sight, she thought charitably of
him. It had been brave to bring the flowers. Once Eliot had
come in with a bunch of flowers he'd bought for someone,
then had thrown them into the almost-full bin on his way
out, slamming the lid again and again to crush the petals
farther down into the mass of eggshells and old bread.
When Eliot saw Jalil's sunflowers on the sitting-room man-
telpiece, he asked where they had come from. She told him.
A look of such extreme sarcasm crossed his face that
Miranda rushed to him and covered his mouth with both
hands before he could speak.

Monday was the day I got the letter from the South
African production company, offering me their
internship. The acceptance sank my heart. My dad knows
magazine people who wrote me glowing, if vague, references. I tried to remember if Lily had been in Cape Town—if

she had then I would have something to connect the words
to. Then I remembered that Lily had been there, and she'd
hated it. "It's that mountain . . . Table Mountain. It stands
there and glowers like some kind of club bouncer, and you
just can't get away from it—no matter what part of town
you look around and somehow the mountain is there. If it
doesn't block your light then you feel it."

Monday was also a day Miri said she'd stay at home. I
went out to the garden to get my bike and she emerged from
the shelter, looking vague. She said that she wanted to help
Sade take some snacks up to the Immigration Removal
Centre.

"Are you avoiding that brer?" I asked her.

"That . . . brer," she said after me, looking inquisitive.

"The fellow you pulled in the pub." I tried to stop, but
couldn't stop myself from adding: "The one who came yes-
terday, with the sunflowers."

"Jalil."

"Okay. Yes, him."

"His name is Jalil."

"I know."

"I'm not avoiding Jalil. Get the homework for me."

"Are you not planning to go in tomorrow either, then?"

"I don't think school suits me at the moment," Miri said.
She was holding on to the side of the shelter so hard that
her knuckles were white. She kept looking somewhere to
the left of me. Her concentration was unflickering. The

thing she was watching, whatever it was, moved from a point just behind my head to somewhere near my kneecaps, and by the time the thing (and her gaze) had reached the ground, I realised she wasn't watching anything, she'd lost consciousness. Almost as soon as she'd fallen, she opened her eyes again. "Don't worry, don't worry," she said. I picked her up and carried her inside the house, worried by how little effort it took to lift her. She laughed. "Oh, are you actually carrying me? Am I heavy? Eliot you are such a gentleman—"

She threw her head back as if on a ride.

"I'll drop you and see how you feel about that," I warned her.

She whispered in my ear, suddenly serious. "I'm scared of those girls. They're going to come after me."

I set her on her feet in the lift. "Get some sleep. I'll find out about the homework for you. And I'll sort the thing with Tijana out."

"Promise?"

"Er . . . I'm not in a boy band."

The lift door closed on her smile.

On my way back from lunch I saw Tijana standing at the school gate. She had her blazer thrown over her shoulders like a cape, and her hair was loose and sort of stumbling down her back in different stages of curl. She was talking to a boy, and their body language was interesting. They were talking loudly (and not in English) but the volume wasn't hostile and it seemed to increase and increase despite the fact that they were standing almost close enough to simply whisper. I should have realised just by that token that Tijana and the boy she was talking to were related. The boy sat on his bike, one foot on a pedal, as if ready to ride off at any second. He stared at me when I walked up to Tijana, and I stared back, then ended up having to look away because he looked so sick. He had big yellow rings around his eyes.

"I need to talk to you for a minute," I said to Tijana. Tijana raised her eyebrows. She looks like a fortune-teller. I'm not sure what I mean by that, but it's true.

"What is it?" she said.

The boy on the bike looked at me patiently, waiting for me to go away. He looked as if he hoped he wouldn't have to exert himself.

"I need to talk to you about the thing with Miranda," I said, and I moved away as an indication that she should step aside too. Tijana didn't move. She did something with her hair that made me realise what writers mean when they say "she tossed her head."

"Talk then. This is my cousin, the one who was attacked. Agim." He winced at her introduction; I was glad not to be the only one, except my wince stayed inside my face.

I turned to Tijana and got on with it. "Did you think it was clever to come after my sister with knives? Say you cut her, do you think you would have got away with that?"

Tijana didn't even open her mouth. She just rolled her eyes at me.

"No, they would not have got away with it," her cousin said. "It's only the other way around that nothing is done."

"You're pretty stupid. And you're lucky I didn't call the police when she told me," I said, simply.

"Why didn't you?" Tijana asked.

"Because there's obviously been a misunderstanding, and I'd rather sort it out between us."

"I wish you had called the police," Tijana said.

I sighed.

"She ran away before I could go and get Agim—"

"Because you were waving knives in her face," I finished.

"She ran away before I could go and get Agim to *confirm* that it was her," Tijana insisted.

To Tijana's cousin I said, "You really think you've met my sister?"

I had pulled a photo off the wall above my dad's desk. It was at least a year old, from a holiday in Cornwall with Dad and Lily. In the photo Miri and I are sitting on a fence at dusk with an eerily empty square of grass behind us. I took the photo out of my rucksack and showed it to him. "Are you sure?"

He looked at the photo, and I saw his relief.

"That's Miranda?"

I didn't answer, and he said, hastily, "Okay, well that's different. I don't know that girl. The girl I meant has short hair and smokes these weird red and white cigarettes, and she said her name was Anna. It's the same word backwards and forwards, the same word in a mirror, she said."

"Miranda has short hair now," Tijana said.

"She doesn't smoke though," I said. I didn't put the photo away. The sight of it seemed to calm him down.

Over Agim's shoulder I could see, through the gritty windowpanes of the Old Building, Martin furtively fetching a hammer out of his locker. Martin had been smoking a lot. It gave him these unrealisable ideas for arts and crafts. He was with Emma, and she was chatting blithely as he stowed the hammer in her bag. I think all my friends at school smoked too much. There really isn't much else you can do regularly if you're young and there's no one thing you're really into. Miri was the only friend I had who didn't smoke at all.

"Agim," Tijana said. "Just tell the truth if you recognise her. Don't be scared."

Agim turned to her. "I swear to you . . . this isn't the girl."

"But . . ." Tijana took the photo herself and looked at it closely. "I don't understand this."

I took the picture out of her hands. "Not interested. If either of you bother my sister again, I'm going to the police. Nothing long."

"He nearly died," Tijana said. Then she spat in my face.

I wiped my face and went in for the next lesson. The duty to speak when Miri couldn't, to make sense when she didn't. I checked that no one was around, then put my forehead to my locker and stood against it just like a plank, with all my weight in my head. I stood like that until I stopped feeling like breaking something. Otherwise I could snap the Biros in my pocket, go into the nearest empty classroom and spin the chairs into the bookshelves, then what? Go home and smash Lily's camera? Thank you, Lily, for leaving me in charge of someone I just can't be responsible for. She won't forget or recover, she is inconsolable.

There were protestors outside the Immigration Removal Centre. Miranda and Sade walked into a bristle of placards that tilted as people moved to let them through. "What's the matter, what's happening?" Miranda asked. She didn't notice how tightly she was clutching Sade's arm until Sade gently removed her hand. They were surrounded by grim faces and black print.

"Another inmate hung themselves." It was a wiry woman that had spoken; her sleeves were pushed elbow high. "No social visits today."

Sade made a short, low keening sound that seemed not to come from her mouth.

It was strange on the Western Heights, you could see both town and sea, one seeming to hold the other back with its split brick and glass. On the Heights you were high and not at all secure, you felt as if you could fall at any moment, and that gave the stones and water a vitality of colour—if these things were to be the last you saw while falling, then they belonged to you.

Miranda had known the address of the detention centre before she had come, she knew that the place was called The Citadel, but she had forgotten that it actually looked like a citadel. She had reimagined the building as white and similar to a hospital. But now she understood that that would have been silly. A building of this size would not blend on the Western Heights if it was

white

was a colour that Anna Good was afraid to wear. Her fear reflected her feeling that she was not clean. She had, of course, been baptised in white. As a child she had been buttoned into frilly white pinafores and had subsequently been too frightened to move. At school, her gymnastics class had been filmed for a programme on British sports and pastimes, and she'd been picked to wear a bronze-coloured helmet and a white gown and a blue sash and sit at the top of a chariot built of the other girls' bodies. She was Britannia, and her shield was a round tea tray covered with coloured crepe and ribbon. There was no lion, but some of the girls dug their fingernails into her thighs, and it was just like being bitten. She had still smiled, though, and waved her arms at the camera. Britannia had to have pluck. Anna never thought she would have a granddaughter who didn't know what Britannia meant; Lily said that patriotism was

embarrassing and dangerous. *Who gave you your mind?* Anna
would wonder, when Lily said such things. She couldn't
believe her ears. How had Britannia become embarrassing
and dangerous? It was the incomers. They had twisted it so
that anything they were not part of was bad.

When Anna met Andrew she was wearing a cream-
coloured dress, the material having been the cheapest she'd
seen on sale and easily slid beneath the needle of her sewing
machine. Anna smoothed the cloth of her dress over her lap
as he, Andrew, walked past the desk she shared with Alice
Williams at the newspaper office. Andrew was on his way
to see the editor; you could tell he was someone important
because of the way he wasn't afraid to be caught looking at
whatever interested him. He stopped and nodded at Liz
Welles, who had a little band of scarlet ribbon fixed around
a spare scroll on her typewriter. Was it a charm to help her
type faster, he wanted to know. His smile was charming,
but very dark somehow. Liz laughed shyly and said she
didn't know, her daughter had made it.

"He's stinking rich, that Andrew Silver," Alice Williams
whispered to Anna. "From an American merchant family, but
they had him schooled over here and he's almost English. Isn't
he handsome? It's just him in that big house on Barton Road."
"Stow it, will you, he's coming," Anna muttered desperately,
smiling hard at her typewriter as he passed.

His manners were strange. He didn't speak to her, but he
looked at her for longer than was polite, and she knew that
they had met now, that everything real that had ever been

going to happen to her would happen now. She inspected the
entire front of her dress once he was gone, convinced that
some vast stain had left her and entered the cloth. It was
summer. She was sweating slightly, but that was all.

White is for witching, a colour to be worn so that all
other colours can enter you, so that you may use them. At
a pinch, cream will do.

Four years later Anna Good put the cream dress on
again, and an expensive white coat that Andrew had bought
her, and she did some witching.

Andrew Silver was a Dover Queensman, one of the
"buffs," as they were called, a brave man in brown who flew
a plane to Africa to fight the Germans there. One morning
someone knocked on my door and gave Anna a telegram,
which said that her husband was dead. She looked at it and
then she wandered up and down my staircases, in and out
of my rooms, flinching, hearing bombs far away. I curved
myself into a deep cup, a safe container for her. I did not let
her take any harm to herself, I did not let her open the attic
window to jump. I was like a child with its mouth obsti-
nately closed, refusing speech, refusing air. She had bought
some rat poison the week before, and though she did not
turn to that, I shook the pellets so that they fell deep into
my recesses. Just in case. She was pregnant, you see. It was
two Silvers at stake. My poor Anna Good, my good lady.

"They killed him," she wept. I could not respond. Her
fear of her pica and the whispers and her fear of shrapnel
and fire and, yes, her fear of me, of being left all alone in a

big silent house. Her fear had crept out from the whites of her eyes and woven itself into my brick until I came to strength, until I became aware. I could keep Anna Good from killing herself and her child, but I had no other gift.

"I hate them," she said. She sat down on the kitchen floor, the telegram rumpled on her lap. A rat scampered past her, putting its feet on her white coat. Her hair fell from its pins. She was supposed to go to the newspaper office and type, but she would not that day. Instead she gave me my task.

"I hate them," she said. "Blackies, Germans, killers, dirty . . . dirty killers. He should have stayed here with me. Shouldn't have let him leave. Bring him back, bring him back, bring him back to me." She spoke from that part of her that was older than her. The part of her that will always tie me to her, to her daughter Jennifer, to Jennifer's stubborn daughter Lily, to Lily's even more stubborn daughter Miranda. I can only be as good as they are. We are on the inside, and we have to stay together, and we absolutely cannot have anyone else. It's Luc that keeps letting people in. To keep himself company, probably, because he knows he is not welcome (if he doesn't know this he is very stupid). They shouldn't be allowed in though, those others, so eventually I make them leave.

Since GrandAnna's washing machine was there, the ration-book larder became a mini-laundry, washing powder scattered over its tiles, its shelves stocked with small piles of clothes. If you were a guest and had booked in for three days or more, you got your clothes washed, dried and delivered back to you for free. "Just human kindness," Luc said. The clothes on the shelf were sorted according to whether they had been washed but not dried, or whether they had been both washed and dried and were ready to be returned to their owners. There were no tags or coloured dividers; Miranda had no idea how Sade managed to keep track, but she did it effortlessly.

From her place by the door, where she sat with her course-work notes spread over her knees, Miranda watched as Sade picked up a pair of Eliot's jeans and laid them over the ironing board. "Please, you mustn't iron Eliot's denim, he hates it."

Sade looked up from the ironing board with eyes like liquidized stars.

"Are you—are you alright?" Miranda stammered.

Sade seemed to laugh; at least, her shoulders shook.

"I'm thinking of the shame. To make a man hang him-self. That place is a prison. You come without papers because you have been unable to prove that you are useful to anyone, and then when you arrive they put you in prison, and if you are unable to prove that you have suffered, they send you back. That place up there is a prison. He didn't deserve that."

"Yes," said Miranda. She touched her own cheek, expect-ing it to be wet. It wasn't.

Sade laid her hands down on the ironing board and stared at the plasters on her fingers. "I hate them," she said, in a voice that seemed to include Miranda.

Miranda picked up her notes and said she was sorry from behind them. She left the larder quietly, walking backwards. She knew then that Sade had not personally known the dead man. Her grief was almost theoretical. It didn't mean any less, but it was a different sort of grief from Miranda's. It was the sort of grief you didn't have to suppress because letting it out made it smaller instead of bigger. The sort of grief you could say something about because you instinctively understood that it could not continue, rigid inside your breathing apparatus like a metal stem. Miranda made a face at herself in the hallway mirror. Deep thoughts. Why didn't she just draw a diagram of the different kinds of grief?

June was bread and nuts and berries. It was also uncharacteristically hot, but Eliot and Miranda didn't let thoughts of summer come until after exams. Before exams came limbo, spent on the roof, squinting at old notes through sunglasses. Neither of them tanned in the slightest, though the sun's heat brought into view messages they'd written to themselves in lemon juice on the margins of their pages. Miranda rotated her three halter-neck dresses. Eliot didn't stoop to shorts, but folded up the bottoms of his jeans and wore flip-flops.

He got through the exam period on the "brain bread" that Luc baked—the loaves were round and coarse and filled with all sorts of seeds that neither of the twins had heard of. It seemed that every time Miranda looked at Eliot he had some of that bread in his mouth—with Luc's champagne marmalade, or mackerel, or honey, or butter. Miranda tried not to judge him, but it was hard. In revision sessions at school, Eliot leaned forward and answered the teacher's questions around a wad of bread. The Sunday before their last set of exams, Miranda and Eliot tested each other on key dates and terms beneath a giant picnic umbrella in the garden. Miranda's last module was for her history paper; Eliot's was for politics. They answered so many of their practice questions correctly that it seemed like a jinx.

Sade sat at the other end of the garden, by the back door, in case she was called. For months she had been knitting something white that grew wider and longer. She didn't seem to have a final form in mind for it. It lathered her lap like beaten egg white, full of sun, and she paused to brush leaves off it. As she worked she lowered her head and hummed, smiling as if the work was for someone she thought tenderly of.

"What will you do when it's really summer?" Miranda asked Eliot.

When Sade glanced over, she picked up the thick smoothie that Sade had blended for her and pretended to drink. She let the fruit sit on her lips, then, when Sade looked away, she wiped it off. Her heart wasn't in the subterfuge. The summer before last, Eliot had refused to go on holiday without Lily and spent much of August up on the roof wearing a black balaclava and writing poetry, which he then balled up and threw as far and as hard as he could, in various directions. Lily, contacted in Mumbai, had said that he was clearly exploring the role of the poet as incendiary. When she came home she'd advised that Eliot cut his hair, unless he preferred cheaply acquired androgyny.

"Will you go to South Africa straight away?" Miranda asked.

Eliot drank from her glass and suddenly half her smoothie was gone.

"Thanks," she said.

"South Africa's not until October," Eliot told her. Perhaps he would spend summer on the roof again, then.

"What will *you* do when it's summer?" he asked.

Miranda had spent the previous weekend looking through her GrandAnna's prudent, economical knitting and sewing patterns, and she felt sorry for the old black Singer sewing machine, which seemed never to have had any fun.

"First I will knit you a scarf, as I've read that South Africa won't really get warm for you until November. Next I think I will make myself an overcoat, with a violently coloured lining."

After their last exam, Eliot vanished with a group of friends whose schoolbags clanked with bottles, while Miranda went straight home and returned the notes she'd taken to school to the bundle beneath her bed. She had not answered many of her exam questions completely—she had too much to tell the examiner, and everything she had to

say was of the greatest urgency. She'd been reduced to sum-
marising points for the final questions, to give illusions of
answers.

Miranda found Sade and they went down to London
together, in search of suitable scarf and coat fabrics at Petticoat Lane Market. Miranda liked the market very much.
It was steps away from a main street full of fast-food restaurants, a street that glowed with buses like wheeled danger
signs, but the market itself smelt like fried spice and flour
and the musk of cloth before it is ever worn.

Sade bought a brown bag full of peppers more wizened
and vicious-looking than chillies, tie-dyed fabric, and a pair
of square-toed silver shoes with diamanté buckles that
silenced Miranda for a full ten minutes. There was no time
or place or event fancy enough for those shoes. She knew
that Sade would have to wear them as house slippers.

Miranda bought plenty of purple thread and some unas-
suming polyester and viscose mix that fell well and warmly
when she held a sample length of it up against herself. She
decided that she wanted her overcoat to be a full frock coat,
and got some black petticoat gauze too. Then Sade persuaded
her to buy a big square of red and purple tie-dyed into shad-
owy mandalas. "For your violently coloured lining," Sade
said, as they held the cloth out between them and gaped at
it and then at each other. There was too much cloth, but that
was a good thing, as Miranda had not yet learnt to sew with
a machine and was bound to get it horribly wrong at first.

Sade and Miranda paid for the fabric and the silver shoes together, and the shop owner bantered with Sade while finding her change, peppering his talk with Yoruba words as he wrapped the cloth in tissue paper. He was Indian. He saw Miranda's surprise and laughed. "Why wouldn't I know some of this lady's language? My best customers are Yoruba . . ."

He also let them take, for only ten pounds, a mannequin that he no longer used because it was too old and he'd had too many complaints about its proportions from his mainly full-figured female customers. The mannequin had no hair, no face, was very white under a film of grime, and had a fifties waist and a nonexistent bust, which pleased Miranda because that way she would be able to see how the coat would look on her even as it was being made.

At home, she put the mannequin in the bath and washed it with a flannel, from face to torso to heels, until it was completely clean. The mannequin was taller than her, but as she pulled it out of the bath by its hands, she felt as if she was its mother. In her room she covered the mannequin's nakedness with one of the long T-shirts she slept in. The mannequin stood beside her wardrobe, arms at its sides, looking cowed somehow.

Miranda put a knitted hat on its head and started work on her coat. The lack of light in her room made it the coolest part of the house. She had her windows open beneath the closed curtains, and humidity drew the curtains and the window together, giving the impression of a gaunt head looking out of her wall. Its skin was loose, and it gasped vacantly.

An influx of new guests in search of the perfect beach-to-town balanced holiday meant that Sade couldn't help Miranda with her knitting for another three days, and it was four days before Miranda saw Eliot for longer than the time it took for him to stumble indoors in the early morning, toss food into his mouth, go to bed, then, in the late afternoon, rise from his bed, toss food into his mouth and leave the house again.

Eliot came and found her in the garden, where she sat beside Sade and her enormous crochet project, a book on her lap, her face turned up to meet a butterfly that flitted in place just above her nose.

"What the fuck is that in your room?"

The butterfly veered away.

"It's a mannequin," Miranda murmured. "Have you been having fun?"

"Yeah. But I start work tomorrow. What's the mannequin for?"

"Work?" Both Sade and Miranda looked at Eliot.

"Indeed. Junior reporter at *The Dover Post*. Probably just retyping memos from the council on their new initiatives or something. What's the mannequin for?"

"My coat," said Miranda.

"Oh." Eliot looked at the scarf she'd begun for him, nodded politely and grabbed his bike.

Agim died—it was in *The Dover Post*. Unexpected medical complications were cited—even Eliot was unable to explain what that was supposed to mean. Miranda hid the newspapers for that day under an armchair in the sitting room and resumed work on her coat. Her hands shook, and her stitches kept failing.

In the evening Sade took advantage of the empty sitting room and watched a Nigerian film. She put her feet up and divided her attention between a bowl of salted peanuts, some warm Guinness drunk from a glass she'd left to chill in the fridge all afternoon, and the film, which brought tears of silent laughter into her eyes. The film seemed not to be a film at all; rather it was a competition between a cast of actors to see who could shout and moan the loudest and show the greatest amount of agony at the death of a close relative.

Miranda got up and wandered out to the garden just as Sade called out to Luc—"Mr. Dufresne, Mr. Dufresne! This part you will love—Wole now knows that Yemisi is the one who poisoned Mama Atinuke's chin-chin."

Luc smiled at Miranda as he passed her. Sade had been teaching him how to make chin-chin, which was basically pastry, thickly folded and heavily buttered. Luc couldn't bear to bake anything as dense as the chin-chin Sade produced, and his version of the snack was closer to mini-palmiers than anything else. Sade disapproved, but she took some on her weekly trips to the detention centre and said that they had been declared passable.

Miranda moved Luc's spectacles and notebook onto a nearby deck chair and climbed into the hammock that Luc had set up between two of the trees. She rocked, but the moon wouldn't let her sleep. Its light was faint, yet, like the breeze that soothed her bare arms and legs, it kept moving. She had to watch the moon through the apple-tree branches. It was easier to watch through her fingers.

When she grew tired of watching and realised she couldn't drop her hand, she began to think it possible that in those months of her madness she had been supplanted by someone that she could only be vaguely aware of. Her nails locked into her forehead, but there was no pain. *Interesting, all is very interesting.*
She closed her eyes.

Heavy footsteps crossed the grass and stopped just behind her.

"Miranda," her GrandAnna whispered in her ear. Her words met the air with difficulty, as if there was something in her mouth she had to talk around. "You must eat."

Miranda said nothing. She had decided the key was to pretend as if she hadn't heard. Her hand came loose, the moon let her alone, and she tried to sleep on an empty stomach, which everyone says not to do.

After a while she pushed herself out of the hammock, rolled confusedly on the grass, then picked herself up, arms above her head in case the trees fell on her. The air was full of the smell of burning. There was screaming. It wasn't human, it was mechanical and without pause. There wasn't a house light on for miles and miles. She had to get into the shelter, they were calling her, they were waiting. She moved through the pitch-black house and she was the only thing that stirred. She came through the trapdoor, and Lily stood beside a table laid for four. Miranda put her arms around her mother, and they held each other for longer than a greeting took; the house shook as the ground outside was beaten—just one hit, but the vibrations went on for so long that Miranda realised it was only her ears refusing to forget the sound.

Over Lily's shoulder, Miranda counted—four places, four people—Lily made one, Miranda made two, for number three there was Jennifer, Lily's mother, and the fourth was her GrandAnna, her white hair gleaming. Jennifer and GrandAnna sat side by side with their elbows on the table. They leaned forward, anticipating a meal. They were naked except for corsets laced so tightly that their dessicated bodies dipped in and out like parchment scrolls bound around the middle. They stared at Miranda in numb agony. Padlocks were placed over their parted mouths, boring through the top lip and closing at the bottom. Miranda could see their tongues writhing.

"Who did this to them?" Miranda asked Lily, curling her arms around her mother's neck.

Lily turned her head away. "I did," she said. She sounded proud.

The long table was made of pearl, or very clean bone, and it was crowded with plates and dishes; there was fruit,

mother is serving Miranda food

and jugs of the spiced wine her father would make in a cauldron at the beginning of November. There were jugs of the pithy lemonade that her father made in the very same cauldron when May came. Miranda knew exactly what was on the table because she and Lily joined hands and walked up and down its length, looking for something, anything, that Miranda might like to eat. Food steamed and sizzled and swam in juices and sauces hot and cold and rich and sweet, there were even sticks of chalk and strips of plastic, but all they did was make Miranda hungrier for what was not there, so hungry that she released her mother's hand and held her own throat and gagged. Her hunger hardened her stomach, grew new teeth inside her.

"Miranda, you must eat something," Lily said, sorrowfully. "What will you eat? Tell me and I'll bring it to you." Miranda shook her head. She didn't know. No, that was wrong. She knew, but she couldn't say it.

Lily sat down at the table, opposite Jennifer and Grand-Anna. Lily played with a padlock. She looked angelic, too pure to be plainly seen. Her combat trousers and vest top were badly crumpled, the way they usually got when she took night flights and spent the hours squirming in her plane seat. Her hair was a little longer.

Miranda began to speak, but Lily raised a finger to her lips—there was a fifth in the room, someone listening. Miranda looked very carefully at each thing in the room, waiting for the fifth person to appear. She looked under the table—maybe the fifth person was there. They were not. As she straightened up, she met her GrandAnna's gaze. Her GrandAnna's eyes spoke to her; they said, *Eat for me.*

"Eat for us," Jennifer slurred through her padlock.

Another bomb struck, with such force that Miranda fell. She lifted herself up on her hands and crawled into the corner, feeling as if she'd broken her shoulder on the floor. None of the others had even moved. They were used to this.

WWII setting

"Will there be another one after this?" Miranda asked. No one answered her. "Oh my God," she said. She was shaking already, in anticipation of the next drop. "Please don't let there be any more."

"There's a war on," GrandAnna said, slowly, clearly, and with great severity.

"It's safe in here," Lily added. "Us Silver girls together." She sounded sarcastic, but looked sincere.

Miranda's fall had been cushioned by clothes. The clothes were familiar: jeans, a short-sleeved T-shirt, a hooded jacket, and a pair of trainers. The fifth person. Oh, she knew where he was; he was there, right beside her head. There were holes bored into the wall. She knew that they numbered ten when a finger inched out of each hole with a sluggishness that fascinated her. The way the fingers twitched, she got a sense that they weren't attached to a body, only to each other, and that she was watching ruptured nerve endings in denial. The hands were brown. Jalil's party trick hands, the hands he could turn in a full circle without putting stress on his wrist bone

(he should have kept away from her)

oh no oh no oh oh no oh

Miranda knew that she had done this, in a period of inattention. It was not unlike watching someone else take her hand and guide it and the pen it held into putting down a perfect copy of her signature.

More, Jennifer and GrandAnna said, but Lily came and ran a pitying hand over Miranda's hair and her face as she cowered in the corner, blood sticking her clothes to her body. Lily understood, she understood everything. Lily gave Miranda a padlock. Miranda gratefully kissed its cold loop. Jennifer and GrandAnna moaned and beat the table, pushing dishes and jugs off its edges as Miranda climbed back up into the main house. Miranda passed the hallway mirror and she was clean again. She looked at her reflection and saw a cube instead, four stiff faces in one. She went outside and climbed back into the hammock. The sun rose and that made it morning.

Her father was in the deck chair beside the hammock, his notebook on his lap. He'd fallen asleep with his glasses on. He looked happy in his sleep. Miranda ran her tongue around the inside of her mouth—*what can I taste, what can I taste, what can I*

Luc's head drooped and, in raising it with a guilty jerk, he woke himself up. He smiled at her.

Miranda was on the point of saying that she might need to go away again. Only she wasn't sure what good it would do. Hadn't it begun while she was away?

"You should have made me get out of the hammock," Miranda said.

Luc shook his head. "You looked far too peaceful for me to interrupt."

Miranda laughed emptily. She asked, "What are you writing?"

Luc took his glasses off and closed them back into their case. "A recipe book, I hope. Based around seasonality. Every other word seems to be 'Lily,' or 'my wife,' or 'the twins' *maman*.'"

"Father," Miranda said. She could only lie there and look at him.

"What if we sold the house?" Luc said. "What if I went back to food writing and we went back to London?"

Miranda held her hand out to him, even though she had no chance of touching him from where she was.

"I don't mind. I'm sure Eliot is the same. We'll do whatever you like," she told him, not really believing that they would be allowed to leave. They had never lived in London, they had always lived in her GrandAnna's house.

"Miranda," Luc said. "You look . . . so different, since . . . I don't think you understand how different you look."

"I cut my hair and lost some weight—which I'll put back on, really I will—that's all."

Luc put his glasses on again and looked her over. He shook his head.

"Something misgives me."

Miranda said nothing. What was there to say?

"What's your date of birth, daughter of mine?"

"Father."

"Well?"

"November 12th," she said, and laughed. Her father did too.

"And the year?" he asked.

And the year, and the year, and the year. There was no answer anywhere. She tried not to panic. Four numbers came to her, but they were upside down and she couldn't read them. She tried to count back from the year 2000. To do that successfully she would need to know how old she was, and she didn't know. Rather than make a wrong guess, she said, "Father," as scornfully as she could manage. He smiled.

"But seriously, Miranda. What if we left? I would not even sell the place, just rent it or something."

Miranda waited for more, but there wasn't any more.

"We've been happy here," she said, gently. "Moving here was a good thing. You're not to be a Calvinist about it—I promise you'll go to heaven. I'll even put it down in writing if you'd like."

"I like you," her father said, and got up to start seeing about breakfast orders.

Miranda went to her psychomantium and turned it upside down looking for her passport. She couldn't find it. She sat on the floor with her eyes closed and tried to recall the years before now. She tried to recall games, arguments, secrets, toys, trips, TV shows. Just like the night before she'd checked into the clinic, they had not happened. It was 11:00 AM in the place where Lily had died.

Miranda knocked on Eliot's door, and when he didn't reply, she went into his room and took his passport out of the top drawer of his desk. He slept so heavily that she felt no particular need to move quietly. Nineteen eighty-two. November 12, 1982. In her room, Miranda wrote 1982 large on a sheet of paper and blu-tacked it to the wall above her mirror. She didn't look into the mirror itself. She was becoming someone, it seemed. She had read somewhere that you only became a woman once your mother had died. But that wasn't what worried her. She worried about becoming as perfect as the person shown to her on paper in Lily's studio.

D ad packed all Lily's things up one day in the middle of August. Miri knew what he was doing, and she let herself out of the house quietly and just disappeared. If I hadn't caught Dad in the actual act of dragging bags full of her clothes over to the lift, no one would have said anything to him. I took a bag in each hand and asked him where he was taking it all. Suddenly there was the smell of rose attar all around us. I couldn't keep my grip on the bags—the way they bulged—in my mind I saw Lily in them, in clean pieces. *Put me back together and I'll stand up.* I nudged one of the bags with my foot. Soft. Just clothes.

"They're all going to charity," Dad said. "Miranda won't wear these things, use these things. It wouldn't be good for her if she did. These things are being wasted here." Something about the slow way he spoke made me think he hadn't known what he was going to do with Lily's things until he'd said it aloud. He walked past me and into the bedroom, brought out more bags, more boxes. I met him at the door and threw bags back into the room. One of them hit him, then sagged across the floor. Multicoloured scarves flowed out. Dad said: "Eliot. Eliot, I know. But it's got to be."
I thought briefly of pulling the door shut and locking him in somehow (how?). I thought, Don't take her away. "Just . . . don't give her stuff away, Dad. Not now. Alright?"

Dad opened his arms. The bare room seemed to settle around his shoulders like a cloak. It took me a moment to interpret the gesture as a request that I come across the room to him. I started to go, I really did, but in the time it took me to make a step he'd dropped his arms. He sat down on one of the boxes.

"Listen," he said. "I cannot endure that dream again."

"What dream," I said.

"The one where it's dark, and the house gets warm, warmer. Then it's hot and I'm all . . . dried out. I drink from the kitchen tap and go out into the garden to breathe. After a few moments I feel much better and I try to get back into the house, but my key won't work. I walk around to the back door and the key for that doesn't work either. The key breaks when I try to turn it in the lock, the handle breaks under my hand. It's pathetic, really, but I walk around to the front of the house and start pleading. Let me in! I don't know who I'm talking to. The house just stands there, dark, absolutely silent. I put a rock in my pocket and climb a tree in the garden, thinking I can open a window, and climb in. But I can't even touch the windowsill—it gives off a strange, feathered static that bites me. Back on the ground I shout out, Lily. I shout out, Lily can you let me back in? A light goes on in the house. It goes on on this floor. And each time I dream this, I try to work out what room the light goes on in, as if that matters. But I just can't work it out. It's not mine, not yours, it's not the light in the psychomantium. It's not the bathroom light. It's like there's an extra window, or an extra room I haven't seen before. Three figures come to the window. One is in the middle and has her arms around the other two. I can't see them, just their silhouettes through the blind. They're standing there watching, waiting for me to go away. They want me to go away. I know who they are; it's Lily and Miranda. I don't know who the other one is. But suddenly I'm glad that the blind is over the window, because I have this feeling that they look different, not the way I thought they did. I'm cold then, as cold as I was hot. Then I wake up."

I had nothing to say. I picked up a box and walked out to the lift with it. That's what I did instead of telling him that I had had that dream too, that exact same dream, only I had been calling Miri. Sometimes our subconscious is so transparent it's boring. I would have written that in my diary, but I'd stopped keeping one.

By the end of August, Eliot's scarf was ready, and the fat dove-grey band of wool took pride of place on the mannequin's neck. By then Miranda had moved the mannequin closer to her bed so that it didn't seem so lonely anymore. Sade's trips to the Immigration Removal Centre no longer included Miranda, who forgot even to be apologetic, enthralled as she was by her sewing machine, her courtier-like hovering around a still white figure, her hands smoothing cloth, and her mouth full of pins. At one point Miranda became convinced that she had hurt the mannequin. She carefully checked the material she'd draped over the mannequin, and she found a pin embedded in the right shoulder where she'd pressed too hard. She didn't say sorry aloud, but she was sorry.

Later, Eliot dragged her down to the beach to swim, but she wasn't strong enough, so he stayed on the sand with her and bought her ice cream. He mocked *The Dover Post*: "Remember how a guy hung himself at the Immigration Removal Centre months ago?"

"Yes," Miranda said.

"No one wrote in or said anything about it—not one letter," Eliot said. "I checked."

Miranda's ice cream was melting onto her hand.

"It's an über-local paper," she said, when Eliot wouldn't

let her get away with not responding. "The upstanding citizens probably saved their letters for *The Times* or something."

"Hm," said Eliot. "There were letters from people complaining about misanthropic parking attendants."

A boy who was building a sandcastle nearby looked over at them. Miranda pointed at his handiwork and held her head as if the sandcastle had given her a headache of admiration.

Gruffly, the boy called out: "You can kick it over if you like."

"You are very kind," Miranda said, and stayed where she was.

"Can I kick it over?" Eliot asked. The boy shook his head. His eyes were almost the same grey as theirs.

They opened each other's envelopes on results day, and Miranda felt that the rows of numbers and percentages that added up to three perfect A's beneath Eliot's name belonged to her. She smiled and nodded at them, as if the panic of the momentarily misplaced lucky Biro was hers, as if the five-minute amnesia regarding Gladstone and Disraeli was hers. Eliot ripped Miranda's envelope open so hurriedly that a corner of the paper inside fell off. He cast a glance over the page, seemed to make some quick calculations, then whooped and lifted her off her feet. Both their grades got tattered in the crush between them—Eliot spun her round with her results envelope fanned out against her back.

"Fuck you Cambridge fuck you Cambridge fuck you," he chanted.

Eliot and Miranda walked out of school with their arms around each other. They passed Jalil, standing by the results board and running a pensive finger down the list of names. Seeing him she felt her relief in her chest, as strong as if she had just won an impossible race, or a bet.

Tijana was nearby, with her mother. Tijana's mother was radiant with smiles, but Tijana's eyes were red and her wrists stuck out of her black sleeves with alarming scrawniness.

September ended. The night before Eliot was due to leave, Miranda was so cold in her bed that she knew she couldn't survive it and knocked on the wall between her and Eliot's rooms. With minimal grumbling, he came and climbed into bed with her and let her lie with her head on his breastbone, his arms around her a blanket beneath the blanket. She tried to tell him she would miss him, but he said: "I'm asleep, actually."

The next morning, his preparations were simple. He had one suitcase. He slung his satchel across his body, stuck his hands in his pockets, and he was ready to leave. Sade seemed anxious. She didn't say it, but she was. Luc patted her arm. "Only two guests booked in, and we're away for four hours, four and a half max. You and those silver shoes can handle anything."

Sade smiled, but said nothing. She appeared to be conserving energy.

All the way to the airport, Miranda and Eliot could not stop looking at each other. Luc let them sit in the back together and managed not to mention that he felt like a taxi driver. Miranda and Eliot slid low into their seats and considered each other completely. In November, Miranda and Eliot would be eighteen, and they would be apart. At Departures, Miranda put Eliot's scarf around his neck.

"Thanks," he said.

She took Luc's hand and walked away quickly.

The next day Miranda's overcoat was ready. She could barely believe that such a simple-looking coat could take so much work, so much staring at rumpled sewing-machine tracks on cloth, wondering what had gone wrong, wondering why the needle had stabbed that place instead of this. It looked so fine on

the mannequin

proved very useful for me when Miranda, Luc and Eliot left for the airport. Especially as I did not have much time. I could not, for example, use the looking people. Things progress quite slowly with them. And Luc's precision meant that when he said four hours he would most likely be away for a little less than that, even. It was very unlikely that he would be gone for more. Besides, the key thing was to have everything as it was, or almost as it was, by the time Miranda returned. I allowed three hours and forty-three minutes to pass without incident. I was confident. The forty-fourth minute before the fourth hour, began in Eliot's room.

Eliot had left his room painfully tidy, chair fitted into desk like a puzzle, his bed made (his bed made!), excess clothes folded into each drawer. But he had left his door open, trusting his sister to lock up after him. He had left his window open. His window is so close to some of the trees that, if the branches were safe, which they are not, he could climb out of his window and crawl straight along a branch. An apple fell in through Eliot's window. It was an all-season apple. I can make them grow. Do you know the all-season apples? They have a strange, dual colouring. If you pitied Snow White, then you know. One side of such an apple is always coma-white, and the other side is the waxiest red. The apple bounced and rolled across Eliot's floor, only a little bruised. It made a smooth track to the door of Miranda's room, where it stopped, because Miranda's door was closed.

A moment of utter silence throughout me, then the mannequin opened the door. It bent and picked the apple up. I very much enjoy the way that mannequin moves—it rejoices in its limbs, rearranging itself quickly and expertly, ending each sequence of movement with a flourish. It stood holding the apple high, offering it to no one, the empty hand slanted towards the full one, hips jutting jauntily. Then the mannequin skipped downstairs. It is not easy to explain how the mannequin skipped. Just that it was too fast for plastic, too slow for fabric. It sort of rippled. It met the African house-keeper in the garden, where she was quietly knitting. The woman saw the mannequin out of the corner of her eye. She said, "Miranda . . . ?"

When she saw what it was, she was so afraid that she became stupid and babbled senselessly. The mannequin stood over her, displaying its apple like a child proud of its prize. It had no lips, so it said nothing to her. The African woman looked at the apple and

(this had not at all been accounted for)

her heart stopped beating. It was some sort of trick, for I was certain that the woman was still alive. For one, she continued to blink. There was a dark, lean intelligence in her eyes, something that stirred yet did not know itself. Stillness, stillness. The mannequin bent over her and re-arranged the white wool on her lap, like a solicitous waiter preparing her for her meal. It seesawed forward so that its body was halved, seized her chin, opened her mouth with its fingers and pressed the white side of the apple, the bad side, against her mouth.

She bit at the white side—she bit! In my distraction I lost hold of the other black guests, the couple on the second floor who I had kept in their bed the past three days, curved around the bed like fitted sheets with their faces crusting over. The African with the silent chest chewed, swallowed and opened her mouth for more, while the couple picked up their cases and fled, leaving money on the hallway desk as payment for their stay. Then, precise as ever, Luc Dufresne's car pulled up outside, the car with my Miranda inside it, and there was nothing more to be done at that time.

The next day, the frock coat was the last thing Miranda took on her way out of her room; she pulled it off the mannequin, put it on and left for Cambridge.

PART TWO

And Curiouser

On the first day of Freshers Week the sunlight turned the stone buildings silver. Dad got so baffled by the one-way system that we ended up parking, walking up to my college and borrowing a luggage trolley from a porter to wheel my suitcases up to my room. Mum kept dabbing her eyes with a handkerchief, but when I asked her what she was sniffling about she said, "Ore, I'm fine." Each college we passed stood as taut and strong as a flexed arm and had its flag flying from a pennant. Both road and pavement were full of people on foot, laughing and calling out to each other. I thought it could be Camelot, or Lyonesse. I thought, I can't live here. I was relieved when it finally got dark and the town became more anonymous. By then people had started sharing their A-level results, and when they had exhausted that topic, they started on their GCSEs. You could tell who'd gotten 5 A's at A level because they'd ask the question, yet hold out on contributing their own answer until the last possible moment.

Everyone seemed upbeat, except for Tijana. I discovered her at matriculation dinner. She was sullen until tricked into smiling. Her accent was gentle, she had long, dark hair and the high forehead of a romantic heroine. She smelt of some sweet fruit, or a jam. She had put her arms through only one of the two pairs of slits in her college gown, but I decided not to offer her any advice about that—she probably knew already, also she looked very dignified sitting there with these enormous black sleeves that were too important for food. She drank her wine and she listened patiently to the rules of a game that a mockney guy from the year above us explained to her.

The game was to flip penny coins into each other's wineglasses. If you found a penny in your wine, then you had to drain the glass in one go. I listened in on what the guy was saying to Tijana, and I looked up and down the table (boys outnumbered girls by about three to one) and thought it was a cheap trick for getting girls drunk. But there was more. The guy explained that the rules were the same if a penny piece was dropped onto your dinner plate—if you were "up for it" then you ate the food on it as quickly as you could, and with your hands behind your back. Tijana's face was expressionless as she listened. Once he had finished explaining about the game, the guy dropped a penny into Tijana's glass. She didn't even wait half a second. She picked up her dessert spoon, fished out the penny and went to drench the guy in wine. I disliked his chat so much that I almost let her do it, but then a sense of responsibility kicked in. I took her glass from her and put it down on the table. "You don't have to play," I said, at the same time as the guy, who drew back from her (he was already quite drunk, so he nearly fell off his seat) and said, "Calm down, it's just a bit of fun."

Tijana turned to me and nodded. "Thanks," she said. "You're right. I was being unreasonable. The wine is not bad." She toasted me and took a small, deliberate sip, then looked about her uneasily. Like me, she seemed actually menaced by the faces that observed us from enormous frames arranged all around the candlelit hall. Apparently they were all former masters of the college, but aside from differences in weight and degree of facial-hair coverage, they could not be told apart. During lulls in the awkward conversation, I examined the portraits nearest to me but couldn't get past the sensation that here was the same man over and over, crouched in old boxes, readying himself to spit on my plate.

Tijana broke the silence by asking the question that sat between me and the others at our table. "Were those your parents who dropped you off?"

She meant the grey-haired couple with the Kentish-farmer accents who had hugged me golf club-shaped and cried when it was time for them to leave.

"Yeah," I said. "I'm adopted. Obviously. Neither of them went to university, so it's a big deal for them."

Across the table, a girl with a freshly scrubbed–looking face began telling a story about a friend of hers who was adopted. Tijana and I eyed each other, not sure which of us was supposed to respond to her, and in what order. I don't think either of us wanted to.

After dinner Tijana and I walked back to the foot of her staircase. Someone had said that our college had been built in the fourteenth century. Our bedrooms ate into the walls of the college buildings, small pockets lined with posters and printed fabric. But from the outside I could see we had made our beds in a tomb. I already knew that that night I would be afraid to fall asleep, almost as afraid as when I was a kid and no one could promise me that I would absolutely, definitely wake up. It took me about a minute to notice that Tijana was crying.

At first it just seemed as if her eyes were sparkling excessively. Aside from the wetness of her eyes, she seemed alright—she giggled and ran across the square of grass in the centre of New Court that we didn't have permission to walk on—she touched my hand lightly and pulled me along behind her by my fingertips.

The porter's lodge was lit up and I could make out the large shape of one of the porters behind his desk, pretending not to be able to see us. New Court was spiked with light, but I couldn't see its source. The sparkle in Tijana's eyes lengthened and slipped down her face. She simply wiped her cheeks and continued to talk as if nothing was happening to her. We sat down on the cold steps leading up to her room. She cried and talked about *Buffy the Vampire Slayer* for another ten minutes; that Tijana could really cry. Finally I offered to cry too, to keep her company.

"My cousin drank bleach and died this summer. He was all fucked up over something that happened to him. I don't know what happened to him. No I do, but I don't understand it. Why did it happen to him? No one can tell me why," she said.

"I'm sorry the summer was like that," I said.

She was drunker than she knew. Before I could say anything she'd convinced herself that she was being silly. She nodded. "I'll be fine tomorrow. I just wasn't . . . ready today."

"Ready for what?"

"I don't know. I feel looked at."

"You've been fine," I assured her. "Nothing out of the ordinary, I promise. I would have subtracted a point for dashing your wine at the guy next to you at dinner, but you didn't, so it's fine."

She smiled, a real smile. "Good night. I'll see you tomorrow?"

My room was almost opposite Tijana's. Walking back around New Court, I saw a girl struggling through the door-sized gap in the college gate. I remembered her from my interview. The one who wore a stopped watch. I noticed again how pale she was. In her black coat, she seemed to fade into the air behind her.

"So you got in," I called out to her.

She twirled so that her hair and the full skirt of her coat flew out around her, and then she curtseyed.

In my room at college, the walls have a strange relationship with the ceiling. The room feels as if it has more than four corners. I tried to sleep, but kept waking and walking to the window, looking down onto the cobbled street and wondering where I was. I ended up opening the present my mum had sneaked into my suitcase. She thought I hadn't seen her, but she's no good at hiding her intentions. She can't help tiptoeing around with a finger to her lips at key moments. The gift was a book of Caribbean legends "for storytellers," and she'd tucked a note in between the first two pages: *Tried to find a book of Nigerian ones but they all seemed to do with a tortoise! Have these and our love, we are so very proud of you—love, Mum (and Dad)*

I had already bought the book for myself, with pocket money years ago. I opened it (its cover was crowded with anachronistic woodcuts of nubile women carrying water jugs on their heads)

and read my favourite story again. I read about the soucouyant, the wicked old woman who flies from her body and at night consumes her food, the souls of others—soul food!—in a ball of flame. At dawn she returns to her body, which she has hidden in a safe place.

I read to the walls. "Kill the soucouyant." Dawn tore a rosy line through the clouds. "Find her skin and treat it with pepper and salt. How it burns her, how it scratches her. Only the night gives her her power, and if she is unable to reenter her body by sunrise, she cannot live. Kill the soucouyant, that unnatural old lady, and then all shall be as it should."

I folded that page over at the corner and read on, no longer aloud. As always, the soucouyant seemed more lonely than bad. Maybe that was her trick, her ability to make it so you couldn't decide if she was a monster. Still, I wondered if the salt and pepper were really necessary—they seemed too cruel when it would be easier to despatch her by blowing out her flame before it grew, or by holding a mirror up to her wrinkled face and saying, "I don't believe in you." But then, maybe "I don't believe in you" is the cruellest way to kill a monster.

My mum keeps worrying that she's not filling the space left by my birth mother. My dad was the same as well, forcing me to spend hours at the park with him and a football until he realised that, like him, I was much better at watching football than playing it, plus if I wanted to talk to him I'd do it without using sport as a crutch. But Mum . . . she keeps finding stuff in the African folklore section of the local library that she feels bound to tell me because she thinks my mother might have. Mum kept calling me Ore even though she really wanted a daughter called Rose. My name is not a big deal to me—if it was Rose it would've worked better with my surname and people would be able to spell it without that moment of uncertainty before putting pen to paper. Rose Lind is easily filed, she is a delight, she is Shakespearean, sort of. My birth mother was a legal immigrant. She and whoever my birth father was weren't together. Aside from that, all I know about her is that she suffered from quite serious postnatal depression and couldn't cope with me. Postnatal depression is common enough for me to assume that there were other factors that led to me being put in care. I'm assuming she hurt me, my birth mother. I wasn't even a year old. I'm glad I don't remember anything.

During the first few weeks, I saw Tijana every day. We went to the Freshers Fair together and debated buying membership to the union, finally deciding in favour when someone at the stall told us that not only was Ben and Jerry's sold at the union at cheaper prices than those at Sainsbury's, but it was sold there long after Sainsbury's closed, too. When students handing out flyers for the Assassin's Guild started circling us, an expression of distaste crossed Tijana's face and she was, quite suddenly, gone. I wasn't fast enough. One of them, a very large guy, and brooding, not unlike a manatee with matted hair, was wearing red-and-white-checked trousers and a top hat with a tag in it for ten shillings and sixpence. He started hovering across my path, his arm out, doing something very like cornering me, smiling and cajoling, saying I looked like the sort of girl who was really game. Game for what? Pretend murder. I smiled, took a flyer, then pretended I saw someone I knew and strolled away without looking back.

Someone else called out to me from a stall—their accent was African—"Hello my sister!" I knew he was only joking, but I bridled anyway. He was tall and shaven-headed, good-looking if you liked tall and shaven-headed, wearing a Harvard sweatshirt as a nice touch of irony. He waved his clipboard at me. "You should put down your e-mail address for the Nigeria Society mailing list," he said.

I frowned and said "No," and tried to pass him, but he pressed a leaflet into my hand anyway. I walked away with it, wanting to drop it on the floor, but I thought he might still be watching, then wondered why I cared if he was watching, then wondered why I was so upset. Because I was upset.

Tijana caught up with me, looking pleased with herself. "What were those strangely dressed people?" she asked. I told her, but she'd already lost interest and plucked at the leaflet in my hand. "What's that? The Nigeria Society? Did you sign up?"

"Nope."

"Why not?"

(I will really resent you if you persist with this)

"Too busy."

"For what? Don't you want to meet people? I think you should join."

"Yeah? And why don't you join the fucking refugee society?" I knew as soon as I said it that she would probably never speak to me again. If I were her I would never speak to me again. I walked away to spare her the trouble of having to get away from me. Wanker. I was such a wanker. I gritted my teeth and ran across Parker's Piece, slapping savagely at lampposts as I passed them. I was almost back at college when I noticed Tijana was walking silently behind me. She smiled when I looked at her.

"I didn't mean to say what I said," I said.

"I know," she said. "I could hear you calling yourself a wanker this whole time."

She tutted, hugged me and kissed my cheek. I hugged her back, harder.

In the first couple of weeks I only caught glimpses of Miranda—Miranda in the phone booth across from our college, dialling, waiting and hanging up, dialling, waiting and hanging up. I saw her leaving the college library one morning, her arms crammed with more books than we were allowed to take out.

"How's it going?" I asked her.

"I'm just trying to read everything I can," she said. She seemed out of breath.

"You've got all term," I said, and she nodded politely and wobbled away.

Miranda wasn't among us gowned girls in cocktail dresses at formal hall. She didn't come to the Freshers Week events, she didn't watch TV in the common room, she wasn't anywhere. I remembered something from a short story I'd read, about how the girl you want is the girl you see once and then she is nowhere to be found. The girl who does not appear in the crowded room.

Tijana and I got into the habit of 2:00 AM visits to the Van of Death. Apart from the men who worked the van, we were often the only sober people there. Everyone else was on their way back from a club or something. As we stood in queue, watching fat melt and resolidify between busy spatulas and the heat of the grills, I heard someone behind me, probably an English student at our college, mention the name Miranda Silver. I eavesdropped intently then, but all the guy said was that she was an affected little goose. "She almost didn't go to matric dinner, you know. She said she didn't care for dinners, and compared cutlery to cages."

He sounded indulgent of her, but that didn't change the fact that "affected little goose" was quite an affected thing to say in and of itself. We got to the top of the queue, and, as usual, Tijana ordered salad in a bap, which I continued to consider a pointless choice. She eyed me sternly, daring me to say anything as she opened the bap and splashed chilli sauce all over the inside of it. I talked. I touched on a variety of subjects unrelated to Miranda Silver—the parallels between hall food and the meals served in old people's homes, the fact that getting drunk was already boring, concerns surrounding my inability to actually answer either of the essay questions I'd been set so far.

Tijana took one of my chips and said, "Miranda was at my old school."

"Not friends?"

Tijana said, "No," and she smiled at her own seriousness.

At college, my inability to sleep became terrible. Very quickly I learnt to seek Tijana out late at night. There were other people that I had begun talking to, people on my course, people who lived on my staircase and swapped CDs with me, but no one I could legitimately ask to climb graveyard gates at 4:00 AM with me for Fortean experiments in spirit photography. No one but Tijana, who yanked her hair up out of her face in a Buffy-esque ponytail and said, "Let's go."

She trembled all over as the notched shadow of the church fell on her, but she kept her hands steady enough to set my tripod up properly. She insisted on setting the tripod up, as if my doing it would somehow skew the results. We drank sugared tea from flasks and talked and measured each other's Nosferatu-like shadows while the camera clicked serenely and independently.

Once I rolled her onto her back on the grass and looked into her face to learn her opinion about that. She laughed. I kissed her. She kissed me back, hard, and wrapped her legs around me as if she wanted to climb up me. Her skin was fever hot. When I kissed her neck I felt her breath catch in her throat. She rolled me over and sat up on top of me, and we kissed and fumbled with buttons and put hands and lips to bare skin until one or the other of us said, "I can't," and if it was me I don't know why because I wanted to. Maybe I'm just remembering it wrongly to help me get over the rejection.

Once before I have been the scared one, in a best friend-ship brought from primary school to secondary school. It was the hugest secret that Catriona and I had ever had. It had to be. Adorned with yin-yang "best friend forever" necklaces and whatever else glittered on the racks of Claire's Accessories we were, are, Faversham girls. By the time she and I were nine we were using the word "dyke" as a deep insult, even though our parents told us not to—we'd even use it on boys. There was something in the way my mum would say, "Don't *say* that," that let me know that calling someone a fat dyke wasn't as bad as swearing.

Cat had red hair and so did her brother, Paddy, who kept chatting me up. Red hair didn't work on Paddy. The first kiss with Cat might have been in a public place—at the cinema, I think. It's hard to say because I was so scared that it felt as if we were kissing in front of everyone every time. I let Cat go farther and farther with me, and I touched her as little as possible. She allowed that poor love of mine. It was the dread that comes about when you are allowed to have something that seems costly and yet you're not asked for payment.

In Narnia a girl might ring a bell in a deserted temple and feel the chime in her eyes, pure as the freeze that forces tears. Then when the sound dies out, the White Witch wakes. It was like, I want to touch you, and I can touch you, now what next, a dagger?

The thing with Cat took about a year to grow, and about a week to be finished. The whole thing was so intense, so full of hurt that when I look back at it I squint. I want it forgotten. Not the way she was—she brought her body to mine with this strange and shocking innocence, when she came the first time she said "I love you" into my ear, words convulsive and unintended, not needing a reply. It's the way that I was that needs forgetting. I behaved like a boy or something. The ending was clumsy and stupid and the friendship couldn't survive it.

Tijana and I stuck to Scrabble and neutral talk on the other nights. She worked at essays, her flashlight steady between the gravestones as she crashed through her reading list hundreds of pages at a time, marking significant lines with sticky index tabs. She was not easily distracted; when it was her turn at Scrabble, she looked up from her notes and I could feel the words she'd just read still migrating from the pages and into her.

The guy who'd sat on the other side of Tijana at matric dinner came up to me while I was in the computer room and started talking about this and that. I kept my answers brief and shrugged a lot. Finally, he came to his point.

"Tijana's probably got a boyfriend, hasn't she," he said. He still seemed like a fool to me. A low-key fool, but a fool all the same. So I said, "Yeah." Actually I didn't know. Did she? Maybe at home.

The University Library is a mouth shut tight, each tooth a book, each book growing over, under and behind the other. The writing desks are placed in front of bookshelves, some of them between bookshelves so that whoever is sitting at the desk gets a feeling of something dusty, intangible and unspeakably powerful, something like God, watching them through tiny gaps in the shelves. People kept trooping past the desk I'd chosen, in search of books and free seats, and within half an hour I'd stopped looking up when someone passed. I wanted to read about the soucouyant. I wanted to write about her, I still do. What do I want to write? Just a book, probably, another tooth for the UL's mouth. Something that explores the meaning of the old woman whose only interaction with other people was consumption. The soucouyant who is not content with her self. She is a double danger—there is the danger of meeting her, and the danger of becoming her. Does the nightmare of her belong to everyone, or just to me?

After a listless half hour flipping through critical essays on *Dracula*, I went in search of the likeliest-looking soucouyant-related titles that came up on the computer. I found Miranda at a desk beside a staircase on one of the wings. She had her head down, and her hair blackened the pages of her opened book. I thought she was sleeping, but as I came closer I saw that her eyes were open and she was looking sideways at me. I said, "Whoa," before I could check myself.

"Hello Ore." She didn't sit up. Maybe she couldn't actually bring herself to. She hadn't even taken her coat off.

"How's it going," I said. She was much too thin. She was serene, like someone accustomed to sickness, someone who lay back to back with it in bed. For a second her face made no sense to me. Her enormous eyes, the curve of her lips, they locked me out. I couldn't imagine ever touching her.

She smiled with a scary energy, as if she had been told to at gunpoint. She said she wished she could sleep more.

I looked around for a seat, so I wouldn't have to stand up and crick my own neck in order to see her properly. *She's unreal, she's an affected little goose*

The nearest empty seat was two bookshelves away. I tucked the three books I had under my arm (I looked too studious just holding them) and stayed standing.

"I haven't been sleeping that well either," I told her.

She didn't say anything and I racked my brains to fill the silence, but before I could add to what I'd said, she said, "I think it is the moon." She said the words softly, to some tune of her own devising, and she drew the word "moon" out for a long moment. It was so odd and unnecessary that something told me that I had to proceed carefully.

"The moon?"

"What do you do when you can't sleep?"

"Walk about," I said.

We looked at each other for a decade, or at least eight months.

"Let's walk about tonight," she said. She gave her night away so easily that it was almost impersonal—this conversation could have happened between her and anyone who'd come up the stairs and said they had trouble sleeping. But it wasn't like that somehow. It was like at the interview, when I was so panicked that I heard myself singing "Frère Jacques" under my breath and sat feeling detached from my mouth while my voice got louder and louder and I had to get up and take the song home, locked up under my temples. I had known that I was going to apply to Cambridge since I was fourteen. I have always tried to do more than anyone else, crouched over essays carefully ticking boxes I'd drawn on a separate sheet of paper to remind myself of all the key points so I would drop as few marks as possible. I type everything, and if typing is impossible I write in block capitals, so safe in the perfect spaces formed inside my *O*'s and *P*'s and *Q*'s that I could step into one of them and throw it around me like a hula hoop. I may be adopted, but I know exactly who I am. I am desperately trying to earn my keep. No one told me I had to, but in a way that's why I'm trying. Other people's parents expect things from their futures, but mine say nothing, as if, after the fact of my childhood rescue, I don't need any future. I suppose they think they're helping by not putting any pressure on me. *Frère Jacques, Frère Jacques, Suis-je mort? Am I dead? Sonnez les matines! Sonnez les matines!* Miranda had come and looked at me and stopped "Frère Jacques" up with her soft, light voice, and she'd known she could do it before she did.

After my lecture that afternoon I phoned home. I called to see if I missed home more than for any other reason. My mum answered, and I knew I did. It was like being kicked in the chest. That first term—every term, in fact—I was constantly negotiating reprieve from execution. Everything, every essay, every conversation, even casual ones in the bar, seemed so final. Everything rested on being right, or at least insisting that I was not incorrect. I was taking the whole thing too seriously. Or I was taking steps to blindfold myself so that when I came out of the door of my college room this morning I didn't see the glass windows glaring at me out of the fourteenth-century walls. Walls and windows forbade me. They pulled at me and said, *You don't belong here*. Again and again, over textbooks and plates of mush in hall, I gritted my teeth and said, Yes I *do*. Everyone else seemed to blend into the architecture. Even Tijana had already lost her perturbed look. My mum wanted to know whether I'd met my future husband yet, and my dad wanted to know if I'd met any snobs, whether I'd run into anyone who was "being funny" with me. I said no. I wondered what he would have said if I'd told him yes.

I went and knocked on Tijana's door just before dinner, to see if she was going to come to hall.

"Come in," she said. She was in bed with a big book and a multitude of pens. She didn't look as if she'd be going anywhere for days.

"How's it going," I said.

"Fine. I can't come to dinner. I probably won't be around later, either." I was about to ask her what she'd do for dinner, but she gestured towards a box of Nutri-Grain bars and a sandwich on the floor by her bed.

"Cool," I said. "See you . . . later, then." It wasn't just the work. I knew she was retreating from me.

"Wait," she said. "I have something for you."

"Yeah?"

She put her pen behind her ear and pulled distractedly at her ponytail, looking around, trying to remember where she'd put the thing she'd just mentioned. She pointed. "There. On the table. Beside my pencil case . . . the bottle."

There was a photograph on her desk; Tijana in the midst of
a crew of girls, all wearing variations of the same hairstyle,
lots of ringlets and clips. The loose, tousled way Tijana wore
her hair at college suited her better. The girls in the photo
with Tijana were a tangle of arms thrown round each other,
mischievous, warm. They looked like the sort of girls who
started trouble just so they got the chance to stick up for
each other.

I picked the bottle up—it was see-through plastic, and
filled with purple water. "Nice," I said. Tijana threw a pillow
at me. It bounced off my head, but I picked it up and
advanced on her with it. She was about to learn not to start
what she couldn't finish.

"What's in the bottle?" I asked, pillow held high.

"A light when all other lights go out," Tijana whispered
dramatically. She had a sexy whisper, even when she was
being stupid.

I whacked her with the pillow. "What?"

"Oh God," she cried. "You're so violent."

I bopped her again, gentler than the first time, but she
dropped flat beneath her covers as if I'd dropped a slab of
rock on her.

"Bitch! It's exorcism water."

"Ah," I said. I put the pillow back on her bed and carefully moved her head so that it rested on the pillow. I patted
her neck. She burst out laughing.

"Where did you get it from? Is it *meant* to be purple?" I

asked. Tijana tapped the side of her nose and winked. I picked the bottle up and told her I'd use it as bubble bath.

In hall, I gave up on trying to eat my dinner. It had been listed on the menu as shepherd's pie, but the description seemed inaccurate. Miranda came in carrying a tray. Everyone in hall looked at her, then went back to their conversations, some of them adding "Who is she?" to their cluster of topics. I nodded at Miranda and she sat opposite me. The others said hello to her and introduced themselves, but she didn't answer them, or even look at them. She looked at me, and she smiled at me, and I looked back, and smiled back. It got awkward. Neither of us was eating anything.

I looked down and felt Miranda smile at me, but when I looked up again she was thoughtfully regarding the ceiling.

"Come on," I said. "Eat your dinner."

She dropped a napkin over her plate. "It's gone."

That seemed a sound idea to me, so I did the same and we left.

"Would you like some tea?" she asked. I had to be honest; I don't like tea.

"Would you like to watch me drink some tea?" she asked. "It's a very ordinary sight, but ordinary in a way that's good because then you could use it as part of a representative sample in a study on the habits of the English tea-drinker, a dying breed."

Her room was much bigger than mine. Its darkness was softened by scent—it reminded me of a nature documentary,

a simulation of the inside of a flower that had closed its
petals for the night. She had a piece of cloth hung over the
mirror on her wardrobe. She took her coat off, pointed out
a chair I could sit on and sat opposite me, stuffing tea filters
with dried leaves from a bowl beside her chair. Neither of
us said anything for a moment. Then she started talking
about the blend she was making, a mix of jasmine tea, black
tea and rose petals. She said her father always drank it in
the colder months. I nodded and looked around. Her bookshelf was quite good—*Grimm's Fairy Tales*. Perrault, Andersen, Le Fanu, Wilkie Collins, E. T. A. Hoffmann. No Poe,
which surprised me, considering the presence of the others.

[handwritten margin note: Gothic influences]

There was a small cluster of images on the wall above her
desk. A white-haired woman in a dark-red dress, a school
photo of a girl with a sleek ponytail and eyes like smoke
fixed in ovals, a short-haired woman who looked as if she
was trying very hard not to burst out laughing. Beside that
was a photo of a girl and a boy sitting on a fence, cousins of
hers, I assumed. I nodded towards them. "Who are the
pictures of?"

The kettle boiled. She attended to her teapot, then said,
"Me, mostly."

I took the tea she offered me. It wasn't bad. I tasted the
smell of the rose petals more than anything else.

"Do you like them?" She pressed some rose petals into
my hand. "Smell them on their own."

I did, then reached over and sprinkled petals over her
head. The withered pink clung to her hair, and she wrinkled

her nose, but didn't brush it away. She crossed her ankles and sipped at her tea.

I fought the impulse to tilt the chair I was sitting on onto its rear legs. I'd only fall over and look like an idiot.

"Tell me about that woman," Miranda said. "The woman with the covered face?" She put a hand over her face and spread her fingers so that only her eyes shone through. "Is she *your* mother?" she asked.

Something told me that Miranda was talking about the soucouyant, that this girl looked at me and saw the soucouyant at my shoulder. I became very aware of the purple water in the pocket of my coat. I don't know whether I was thinking about dousing myself in it or dousing Miranda. I thought, I've got to get out, but she stood up too and tapped my sleeve.

"Please don't be cross," she said. "I was just being silly."

"I'm not cross," I said. I sat down again and let her tell me about the project on her wall. The white-haired woman was Miranda's great-grandmother, who had raised the short-haired laughing woman, who was Miranda's mother. The girl in the old school photo was Miranda's absentee grandmother. They were all dead.

"My mother had a condition called pica. She ate lady-birds and things," Miranda said, reflectively. She glanced at me, then back at the picture of her mother. "I only just remembered that recently. And I'm forgetting all sorts of other things of my own."

I tapped the photo of the boy and the girl. "And these two?" The boy looked out of place in his T-shirt and jeans—he had costume-drama looks, the whole dark wind-swept hair and scornfully curled lip thing. As if he belonged in a topcoat and tails, menacingly tapping a silver-topped cane. The girl was one of those Gothic victims, the child-woman who is too pretty and good for this world and ends up dying of tuberculosis or grief—a sweet heart-shaped face and a river of blue-black hair.

"That's my twin brother," Miranda said, touching the guy's face. "He's in South Africa."

"And who's she?"

Miranda sighed. "Very funny," she said. She picked up her teacup. "That's me. I suppose it's quite an old picture. It was taken nearly two years ago."

I stared at her, and when she didn't smile to show she was joking, I looked at the picture again. I suppose I could have drawn an association from the black dress that the girl was wearing. But otherwise the girl in the picture was not the girl who stood in the room with me; I can unequivocally say that it wasn't her. The eye colour matched, the hair colour matched, but that was all.

I found myself nodding uncontrollably

(get away from this girl and do not go near her again)

"You've . . . changed a lot," I said.

She said, "Let's go for that walk."

I nodded again. Maybe it was just that I needed air. We

stopped at the kitchen on my staircase while I filled a bag with food—bread, brazil nuts, Brie, half of a dented pork pie, a six-pack of Cadbury Creme Eggs that I'd been saving since Easter for a special occasion and should probably have poisoned us. I wanted it to be a long picnic; if necessary, as long as we might have slept. Miranda sat on the kitchen counter and suggested fruit, so I added two of someone else's apples and two of someone else's oranges.

I didn't have any particular direction in mind, and we ended up wandering towards Newnham Village, passing through the hedge corridor that led to Midsummer Common. It was around midnight and the passage was pitch-black; it ticked over with the sound of our footsteps on the leaves, and insects hissed above. Miranda was carrying the food, her steps were sure and she didn't put her arms out to feel ahead. Not once. We didn't really speak. Walking in the dark behind her there was a thing I noticed that can't be true. It's this:

[Occasionally, to tease her for walking slowly, I'd put a hand to the small of her back and gently push her forward. Whenever I did, her hair swished over my fingers like torn silk. I felt this more than once, but I can't explain it. Her hair only came down to her shoulders, but when I couldn't see her clearly, her hair was very long.]

When we came out of the hedge, we faced each other. In her stilettos she was taller than me. She asked, "So how is this going to work, are you going to kiss me?"

"No," I said. I had been thinking about kissing her.

She seemed amused. "Why not?"

All I could give her was an "Um."

She didn't take her eyes from mine. "I'm not saying I'm amazing or anything, but I'm decent-looking. Why shouldn't a decent-looking girl expect to be kissed?"

She sounded bold, but there was so much terror in her eyes. She thought I didn't want her.

Walking over Midsummer Common at night on minimal sleep is like trying to cross a place-between without a map. You suspect that you might be walking back in the very direction that you came from. It doesn't feel like Cambridge. It doesn't feel like anywhere. The ground is suspended and the sky pins it down on one corner, like an elbow. You can hear the river, and feel how close the running water is. We knelt down on our coats, nibbling at olives—now I remember there were olives—then sat cross-legged for the sandwiches and pie, then lay down with the chocolate and the apples. I'd never been so hungry—it tied in to my tiredness somehow, the tautness I felt in my arms and back. We were both very rude. We lay facing each other, eating like mad, each stuffing cheese fast and hard, as if to prevent the other from getting more than their share.

"Hall food really is rubbish," Miranda said. She had finished everything and was eating the peel of her orange.

I picked up a piece of my own orange peel and considered it lazily. "Are you sure that's alright to eat?"

"It's just a bit harder to digest, that's all."

"If you say so, Miranda."

"Tell a story," she said. She scratched the ground and began eating earth. I began to think I was dreaming.

"What are you doing? You'll get sick."

She looked quizzical, but let me take her hands and wipe them on the grass. The mud around her mouth. She ate without smudging her lipstick.

"I'm already sick," she said. She held up her arm and closed her thumb and second finger around her elbow. Which she shouldn't have been able to do. I didn't wince, but it was close. "You can see exactly how sick I am. That's why you don't want to touch me."

I said, "Miranda."

"For a year I've been trying and trying to fill out the dresses I wore before I got ill. And I just can't," she said. "Please tell a story about a girl who gets away."

I would, even if I had to adapt one, even if I had to make one up just for her. "Gets away from what, though?"

"From her fairy godmother. From the happy ending that isn't really happy at all. Please have her get out and run off the page altogether, to somewhere secret where words like 'happy' and 'good' will never find her."

"You don't want her to be happy and good?"

"I'm not sure what's really meant by happy and good. I would like her to be free. Now. Please begin."

I was silent. I couldn't think of a single story she would want to hear.

Finally she sighed and said, "Alright. What's your favourite story?"

Our hands were joined across our coats. I hadn't seen it happen, but since it had I drew her closer and told her, very quietly, about the soucouyant. The night didn't listen to us—it had a noise of its own, wind murmuring in the branches. I told Miranda about the girl who killed the soucouyant.

That girl had grown up friends with her shadow, grown up hugging herself and singing to herself, so happy alone that everyone in her village thought that she was retarded. While they slept the girl took herself out dancing, put her arms around the moon and travelled to see things no one else in the village would ever see, not even if they lived to be a thousand. She saw the wicked soucouyant feast on the girls and boys in her village and the next. She saw where the soucouyant slept, and was bold enough to follow her there. She saw where the soucouyant put her skin when she walked in her true form. Her lover the moon told her: "If you cared to, you could kill the soucouyant. Treat her skin with pepper and salt. How it burns her, how it scratches her. Only the night gives her her power, and if she is unable to reenter her body by sunrise, she cannot live." The girl cared to protect the lives of the young in her village, and she knew you cannot bargain with a thing inhuman. So the girl reached right inside the old-woman skin and rubbed salt and pepper all along it; she stretched past bone and sinew because she was herself entire, and knew she could not be consumed. She hid and watched as the ball of flame returned to its tree hollow at dawn, searching for its skin. She watched as it filled the old-woman skin, watched as the body rose and bulged with life, then screamed and fell deflated. She watched as the soucouyant, having no other option, rushed to join her flame with that of the rising sun.

I stammered finishing the story, because of Miranda's gaze, her eyes like swords. We were nose to nose.

"Thank you," she said. "That was just the thing."

"The girl doesn't get away. It's not a story about her getting away. She was born free."

"The soucouyant gets away though. Doesn't she count as a girl?"

I drew back. "No, she doesn't," I said. "She is a monster. She dies."

"Does she?"

"All monsters deserve to die."

Miranda didn't say anything.

"Miranda," I said. "Come on. The soucouyant is bad. She sucks the life out of people."

"That is true." She smiled in a way that undid every knot in me. There was no way I could be afraid to kiss her when she smiled like that, so I kissed her, and she kissed me back and we were like that until we gasped for air and laughed at each other, her eyelashes scraping my cheek so when I blinked they felt like my own.

. . .

Miranda woke to find Ore smiling at her from a cushioned window seat across the room. The curtains were wide open. It was more sun than Miranda could tolerate. She threw the covers over her head, then changed her mind and got out of bed, reaching for her bag, which she'd spotted on top of Ore's bookshelf.

Ore said: "Do you never go a day without that red stuff?"

Miranda dropped her rouge back into her purse without opening it.

Ore saw her expression and put her books down. She drew Miranda to the window seat. There wasn't room for the two of them and their legs were happily entangled.

Miranda looked down. "Is it alright to say how much I like this?"

Ore kissed her forehead. "What?"

"The way our skin looks together."

Ore's beautiful lips. Before she could reply, Miranda kissed her mouth, first the top lip, then the bottom, then both together, then a tiny bite on the bottom lip for good measure. There. So this was kissing, a thing she could probably do forever. Decent sleep after so long made her feel elastic. Even when she'd left Ore's room and sat through two lectures and muttered her contribution to a supervision on an essay question about *The Tempest*, a song called "Earth Angel" played in her head all morning—also three trumpets and a piano.

Miranda's father came to visit her—they went to Browns and he scoffed languidly when the baked camembert arrived at their table. Miranda counted out the acceptable number of bites of food she'd agreed with Lily, then doubled them to please him. He didn't notice. He only noticed the food that she didn't manage.

Everything was fine at home, he said, but he missed the sound of her sewing machine and doo-wop CDs, and he even missed the badly disguised smell of Eliot's marijuana.

"*Où le marché est?*" Miranda asked, smiling.

Luc sighed.

"Have you spoken to Eliot?"

"Yes, some days ago."

"Oh," Miranda said. She had been trying to call Eliot from pay phones nearly every day, shivering as she dialled, her gloves slipping around her fingertips as she pressed the numbers that Eliot had written on her hand on the way to the airport. He hadn't answered once.

Luc scanned Miranda's face. "I think he only called because he needed a certain sum of money, half of which I allowed him."

As a diversion Luc spread some of the illustrations for his cookbook out onto the restaurant table. The cookbook was to be published, and the final plan was to combine photographs of each dish with little ink drawings done by a friend of a friend who had already read parts of the man-uscript. In the illustrations, the chef was a round-faced stick man in a puffy chef's hat—his face was free of all features except a neatly curled moustache, which twitched when he was moderately excited by his work and spun around like a windmill when he was extremely pleased. When Luc packed the drawings up, Miranda, at a loss for things to do, offered to show him the Botanical Gardens, or to take him around her college.

"Has it changed since you moved in?"

Miranda's college "aunt" was a pigtailed girl from the year above that Miranda had not spoken to again after the first day. The college aunt had given Luc and Miranda a tour of college. Miranda confessed that nothing had changed.

"Then I'll be off," her father said. His glance skipped sternly off her three-quarters-full plate as he stood up from the table.

She wrote an essay in her room until evening, tossing her responses to what she'd read onto paper without even checking it for sense. She followed Eliot's rule of always making recourse to the essay question at the beginning and end of every paragraph, no matter how obvious the connection. He had sworn to her that teachers loved it, and it seemed to be true. She didn't know how it could be that she hadn't spoken to Eliot properly for weeks. She felt she had done something wrong, but what?

Ore was so stark in her mind that Miranda bypassed her name; she didn't so much think of Ore as think her. On days before this one Miranda had lingered on her way back from the post room and looked at Ore in the common room, reading *Varsity* over someone else's shoulder; it seemed Ore never saw fit to pick up her own copy, even though there were plenty of each recent issue stacked under the snooker people. Ore read the student newspaper without a smile or a snigger—everything she read seemed very grave to her. But sometimes Ore read things aloud and the person whose shoulder she was reading over would laugh. Ore had a gap between her front teeth and wore her jumpers too big so that the neck slipped down on one side and bared her shoulder and the strap of her vest. Now Ore had kissed her. She had tasted Ore's mouth. *A tisket, a tasket* . . . momentarily, she wondered what the goodlady would have to say about that, then forced herself to knit meanings out of the words in the book before her. Don't concentrate on Ore. Don't witch her to death, Miranda.

first sign that things aren't going right

She took a stick of chalk from her cigarette box, but before she could raise it to her mouth it broke in her hand. Her palms were clammy. She licked her lips and asked Lily a question; she asked Jennifer and her GrandAnna the same question: *How is consumption managed?*

She heard stones rattle against her window and pushed it open. Down on the street, Ore closed her hand over her remaining pebbles and stepped out of the path of a cyclist. She was wearing a blue dress over her jeans, and at least four belts around her waist. Her eyelashes were neon blue. It was complicated just to look at her.

"Can I come in?"

They tried to cook dinner for themselves, something with

rice and dried beans and fresh tomatoes and nutritional value, but the water in the pot shrank much faster than expected and everything burnt black while they kissed and kissed and kissed on Miranda's sofa. The food burnt even though they'd left the door open so they would smell an emergency.

Ore rose, her lips stinging, to turn the cooker off before anyone else on the staircase complained, and while she was gone Miranda crossed her arms over her body and watched, out of the corner of her eye, the perfect Miranda, who had taken Ore's place on the sofa and crossed her arms too. She was giddy with hunger.

Ore came back and said, "So much for nutrition. Let's go and fatten our calves."

They went arm in arm and kissed in the street, bumping into people because they couldn't keep an eye on where they were going and kiss at the same time. Boys thought they were drunk and whistled at them. Ore's skin was hot, and her lips were dry. She touched Miranda's face and said: "You're burning up."

There was a chip shop just off Market Square that displayed photos of its customers on one of its walls. Hardly anyone looked good in these photos. These were photos taken at the end of nights out—the featured subjects had spent hours rising in sweaty heat and then blithely collapsed, like soufflés. There was a photo of Tijana near the bottom. She was with two girls and a guy, none of whom Miranda knew. There was glitter in Tijana's hair and the photo seemed to have been taken while she was in the middle of saying "What?" Miranda was surprised. But then what had she expected Tijana to do when they got here; evaporate?

They bounced down from the shop doorstep, and Ore commanded: "Now you tell me a story." She held the paper cone full of chips between them as reverently as if it had been a ring to bind them. Miranda took a chip.

"Once upon a time, there was a woman who kept dreaming about a little girl called Eden. She knew exactly what Eden looked like, how tall she was, what her voice sounded like, how she smelt, all sweet and powdery. Everything. But she had never met a little girl called Eden."

Already Ore had nearly finished the chips; Miranda stopped and gave her a reproachful look while she made up for the time she'd lost talking.

"Go on," Ore said, after a few seconds, raising the cone up above Miranda's head and out of her reach.

"Well . . . she didn't know how she'd get to meet Eden," Miranda improvised. "So one day she stood outside the gate of her local primary school at home time and called out: 'Eden, Eden,' in a motherly sort of voice as all the kids ran out."

"And?"

"Well. One girl stopped and looked at her, and smiled mysteriously."

Ore frowned. "*And*?"

"Well, it was Eden."

"What, just like that? What's the twist?"

"There is no twist, it was Eden. The little girl the woman had been dreaming about."

"So what then?"

"Er . . . well, then the woman took Eden's hand and they went home together."

Ore looked disgusted as she threw the last few chips into her mouth. "And lived happily ever after, I suppose," she said.

Miranda smiled. "In a way. As they walked home the woman began to remember why she had been dreaming about Eden, and why Eden had been sent to her."

"Oh?"

"Yes. As soon as they got home she strangled Eden and cooked her for supper. Then she went to bed all drowsy and full and she settled in to get ready for the next dream. The dreams were like a menu, you see, only someone else chose the courses for her."

Ore laughed, but she seemed aghast. "You just made that up on the spot I suppose," she said.

"Indeed no, it's a very old story. Older than the one about the soucouyant," Miranda teased. "Now. Your turn again."

Ore thought.

"Okay, this one is true and, I suppose, more boring because of that. For a couple of years I had a birthday every other month. If I wanted my mum to make me a cake I'd just say that I felt as if it was my birthday. My mum would say, It's not your birthday yet, wait a bit. And I'd be like . . . I'm not even asking for presents, just some *cake* to show you're glad I was born, and Mum would get flustered and say, But it's not your birthday! And then I'd pull out the silencer, which was: 'How would you know? You weren't there, man.' She'd bake the cake after that. But one day my dad took me aside and said that I couldn't keep doing it, that I was worrying her. He said my mum thought I was trying to tell her that I didn't like her. I went through the whole *how do you know when my birthday is, you weren't even there* thing with him and he put his hand on my shoulder and said, 'Let me show you something.' He showed me my birth certificate. It was just like he'd showed me a gun— suddenly I was looking at something that had no life of its own but was stronger than me. I was eight. I hadn't known that everyone had a bit of paper that proved the date and place of their birth and all that stuff. I was trapped. And embarrassed. Yeah, so I stopped doing the frequent-birthday thing—"

Miranda interrupted her: "What are you doing?"

"What?" Ore said. "You mean why are my eyes closed? I was trying to see it while I said it. To make sure it *was* true."

"And did you?"

"Yes."

"You might want to keep your eyes open whilst walking," Miranda said.

"You wouldn't let me walk into anything," Ore said.

Miranda took her hand.

Sade

puts the kettle on.
Sade puts the kettle on,
Sade puts the kettle on and sparks fly out. Electric shocks
say it's time to leave, bye bye. They get inside your head and
hurt you so you can't speak you can only tremble and for
some time the will to open your eyes escapes you, bye bye.
A word that you believe in jangles in your head until it no
longer has meaning.
Courage, cabbage, cuttage, cottage.
What was the first word?
Cabbage?
Very good.
Juju is not enough to protect you. Everything you have I
will turn against you. I'll turn sugar bitter for you. I'll take
your very shield and crack it on your head. White is for
witching, *so ti gbo*? Do you understand now? *White* is for
witching, Sade goodbye.

The Midnight

I woke up and Miranda was on top of me, clinging to me, I knew she would be lost. Her head was thrown back, and her mind was gone from her eyes. When I tried to move, she clung tighter, her thighs locked over and around mine. Her head was up; her eyes looked down but didn't follow me. She wasn't awake. I rolled off the bed and she came down with me. I had to prise her fingers from around my neck one by one. I heard her bones click. That broke the spell, and she came to, weeping.

"I can't stay here," she said, and got up, hurrying around the room, gathering things and dropping them. "I'm to go home. The house wants me," she cried. The moonlight made her look blue. It made her look as if she was dead. She opened my window and sat herself on the ledge; she dangled her bare legs over it. We were four floors up.

I approached her carefully. "Miranda. You can go home in the morning. There aren't any footholds down this wall—you can't climb down it. If you try you'll fall and you'll . . . you'll be hurt. The house doesn't want that. It wants you back in one piece." Her back was to me; I couldn't see her face.

"She doesn't. She doesn't care how I come back. You can't hear how we . . . how they're calling me," she said. She bent forward

(did she mean to fall headfirst?)

wobbled and almost toppled from the sill, but I grabbed her shoulder and dragged her off the ledge with a sharp jerk, sharper than I meant it to be, but I was scared. I lay spread-eagled over her, pinning her to the floor until her struggling turned into giggles. "What are you doing?" I heard her ask, in her usual voice, her waking voice. I let her crawl out from under me, watched her walk up to the window and close it. She got back into bed, but I stayed where I was. The floor felt secure.

Ore spent afternoons reading to Miranda. Miranda liked hearing *The Arabian Nights* best, because then Ore used all her voice, changing accents and tone and speed—when she was a djinn, she threw her voice so that it towered. Miranda was awed by the strange sorceress who could force men to become birds and mules by throwing dust into their faces and commanding: "Wretch, quit thy form!" On the very rare occasion that her necromancy failed and the man stood before her unchanged, the sorceress would laugh coyly and say that she had only been playing.

Miranda lay on her side in her bed, or in Ore's, and she heard Ore and dreamed with her eyes open. She grew to find a sunlit room bearable; she no longer feared a change of light that she couldn't control. She stopped taking the pills she'd been prescribed. She washed them down the drain, ripped the labels off the bottles and threw them away. There wouldn't be any of those doctors' letters reminding her to make another appointment until after Christmas.

She felt fine, but she began to feel followed. When she passed through the back gate of her college, it took an age until she heard the gate close behind her. But as she turned the corner into New Court, no one else came through the arch. Clare College had prettier grounds than her college, and she took big detours so that she could pass through them on her way to and from supervisions, fanning herself with a rolled-up essay and catching falling leaves in the skirt of her coat. And there came moments when she knew that there was someone behind her, remaining out of sight by taking one step for every five that she took. Other people moved past her over the bridge between the gardens; they carried books and bags and musical instruments, they were on their way to places. But not the person she felt hovering up in the air behind her, doubling the path she'd walked from Ore's room to her supervision, or from her supervision to hall. She paid attention to the sense of surveillance because it seemed unconnected to the night. She never felt followed at night, and that made this feeling she had less likely to be paranoia. Probably. She was afraid. Afraid that she was imagining the surveillance, afraid that it was real. When she entered a room she tried to look at everyone in it individually, trying to catch the person who had just been looking at her.

For at least ten minutes most evenings I'd taken to waiting outside a phone box on King's Parade while Miranda tried to call her brother. I watched her stiffen expectantly and then slump, and it made me dislike her brother. There was no way that he was so busy that he couldn't answer the phone just one of the times that she called. There was no way he couldn't find five minutes to e-mail her or something. When Miranda came out of the phone box I'd get her a hot chocolate in the yellow-tinged gloom of a vaulted underground café on Market Square. She'd make excuses for him.

I said, "I think he is probably just self-absorbed."

She kicked me in the shin. It's no joke being kicked in the shin by a chick wearing stilettos. I was in pain.

Miranda found out about a rock 'n' roll dance night at Fisher Hall, and she fetched a flared skirt with a poodle embroidered on it from her wardrobe. The skirt was pink, and she tied a pastel-pink scarf around her neck in a jaunty bow. I think that was the only time I saw her wearing a colour other than black. I couldn't find anything similar, so

I settled for wearing a crinoline under a strapless polka-dot dress that already had a big skirt. She tied pink ribbons to the ends of my plaits. I left my room with her kisses tingling on my shoulder blades.

When we got to Fisher Hall, I found out that Miranda could *jive*. She grabbed my hand and shimmied in circles, flicking her heels and flapping her hands as if the music the Elchords were making was mowing her down. She said she had learnt the style from a videotape. I just shuffled and two-stepped and let her use me as a prop. I couldn't get five minutes' rest, either—the other dancers stayed away. They cast admiring glances but stuck with their partners.

At the end of the dance Miranda was so exhausted that she lay flat on the floor by the emptied drinks table, unable to move even to minimise the effort of the people who laughed nervously and stepped over her. I made her drink lemonade through a straw, and got her back to her room on a sugar rush, singing *too lay too lay peppermint stick*. I wanted to say something to her, something like "Hey I like you," or "You're so so pretty. You're actually gorgeous." She had a black sash tied around her head; it drove stray strands of hair behind her ears and suddenly even her ears were beautiful.

"Why don't you take a picture," she said, flapping her hand at me. "It'll last longer."

I climbed onto her bed and tucked myself around her, my knees against the backs of her knees, my stomach against her back. We were both trembling.

"Nice ears," I said.

Our bodies struck like matches; she changed form under my hands, I went slowly, slowly,

(only do as much as we both want)

her nipples hard under my lips, her stomach downy with the fuzz that kept it warm, the soft hollows of her inner thighs. She said, "Please stop."

I flopped down beside her, turning her face towards me, stroking her hair. Her hair felt endless in the dark. "Are you okay?"

"Yes." Then, surprisingly, she asked me if I was okay.

"Not really, not if I've upset you. Did it feel weird?"

"No. Well, a little, perhaps. It was . . . I don't know. Too much, probably. I've never . . . not even with a boy."

I know I said something, but whatever I said made no sense. She was so worried that there was no way for me to assure her that I was no marauder out to feast on the shattered remains of her hymen or something. My fingers snagged in her hair and her head jerked on the pillow. She got up and got dressed and I did too, trying to think of a way to stop this becoming a crisis.

I caught up with her at the college gate. "I'm sorry," I said. "I'm sorry," she said.

We both smiled, embarrassed, not at each other, in different directions. "What are you sorry for?" we said.

I felt every vein in me move closer to the surface of my skin, all veins plucked in one direction as if I was a stringed instrument.

She opened the college gate with her key and stepped out onto the street. I followed her; she hadn't said that I couldn't. It was full moon. No one was out, and it was so cold that our breath stained the air around our heads. Birds chirped. I don't know what kind of bird chirps at night. We walked towards the mill pond.

"My mental health is questionable anyway," she said, not looking at me. She told me she'd been in a clinic for just over five months because she'd had a breakdown and forgotten who she was. I sat down on a low wall; the river was at my back. She sat down too.

"What, the breakdown came just all of a sudden?"

"No. There was this one night when something went wrong. Some kind of splinter swerved in my brain or something."

"What happened on splinter night?" I asked.

"Splinter night?"

"The night everything went wrong."

She paused. "I can't remember."

"Can't you?"

She took a deep breath and rested her chin on her hand. "I have a theory," she said. I nodded at her to continue and she said, "There's this fireplace downstairs. I think I went down there for some reason. To hide, maybe. I thought it was all my fault my mother died. And I hit my head on the marble. My brain bled. I died."

She watched me.

"Right," I said. "I don't think that's possible."

"Why don't you think it's possible?" she asked. "Because everyone can see me?"

"It's not that. It's just that it seems to me that the dead only return for love or for revenge. Who did you come back for?"

Neither of us smiled. I felt light-headed. I couldn't believe that we were discussing this.

"Love or revenge," she sighed. "Neither."

"Miranda," I said. "You're not dead. Okay?"

"Ore," she said. "I'm not alive."

I had found the bottle of purple water that Tijana had given me; I ran my thumb over its lid in my pocket.

"Let's suppose that what I say is true," she said. "Just as a thought experiment. Let's say I'm not alive anymore. What would be helping me to maintain the appearance of life? That's the baffling thing."

"That rouge of yours," I said, giving in. I touched the dip between her collarbones, it was like touching thin paper as breath shifted through it.

"You should run," she said, mournfully.

"No, you should," I said. I pulled the bottle out of my pocket and shook it.

"What is that," she said. Her pupils were huge satin cavities. There was no curiosity in them.

"Run," I said, and threw some water at her. It didn't touch her, but she blenched, turned and ran away between the trees.

I followed her. For someone with so little energy, she ran fast. She was really and truly running from me. She crossed

the mill pond bridge, sprang right and headed back towards
college. I tossed the exorcism water into a bin a second
before I caught up with her and grabbed her arm. She slowed
down immediately. She was crying angry tears.

"If you don't believe me just say you don't believe me.
Don't go along with me and then make fun," she said. She
shrugged my hand off her arm and collapsed onto the zebra
crossing. There were no cars coming. I sat down beside her.

"I wasn't taking the piss out of you," I said, unsure
whether I was lying. "I just wanted to give you some way of
knowing for certain. It was an experiment. That was exorcism water."

She sniffed. When I dared to look at her, she was smiling.

"Why was it purple?" She wore her tears like tiny crystals
that tipped her lashes.

"Because . . . I don't know." I didn't have the heart to
make anything up.

"It's so quiet," she said. Three AM and as usual, the town
was dead. She lay down with zebra stripes stacked behind
her, and she pulled me down beside her. "Don't you care
where you come from? Don't you wonder why you do the
things you do and like the things you like?"

"Er . . . not really," I said.

"Do you think it is her fault," she said, without inflection.
"Whose?"

She didn't repeat herself.

We looked at the moon and the moon looked at us. I
had thought we would be able to hear when a car was

coming, or feel the rumble of its wheels through the tarmac, but headlights were the only warning, and even then I noticed them so late that when we scrambled up from the road the car's driver took fright and blared his horn at us as he went past.

We went back to college. I went to my room and Miranda went to hers.

I wanted to ask her something. I wanted to say, "If you're dead, then why did you get up when the car came? Why bother?" But I didn't want her to run from me again. And, I suppose, having died once there is no reason to die again.

I went home on the last weekend of term. I left most of my things in my college room, so all I had to take to the train station with me was a Reebok bag filled with dirty clothes. The last thing I did before leaving college was check my pigeonhole in the post room. Tijana was in there, checking for post herself. The mockney guy from the year above us, the one who'd wondered aloud whether Tijana had a boyfriend, was holding her hand and whispering in her ear while she giggled and read a letter. I was amazed. I shook my head. The mockney guy saw someone he wanted to speak to out of the post room window and bounded out of the door like a badly made puppy. As soon as he'd left, Tijana turned to me and said, "What are you all shaking your head for?"

"Well," I said. "Are you with him?"

"What if I am?"

"Nothing. I just wouldn't have thought you'd go for that type."

"That type?"

I pointed at him. He was standing in New Court with another guy who looked just like him, laughing from only one side of his mouth. Couldn't she see what he was?

"Tijana. He's public-school wanker."

"How can you say that? You don't even know him."

"Have a good Christmas, Tijana."

"Not knowing people doesn't bother you, does it? That's why you have this thing with the girl who hardly even exists. I mean, do you want to be with her, or is it that you want to be her?"

I wanted to wither her with a look followed by a superbly dismissive comment, but instead I said, "What?"

Tijana said, "Look at yourself. You're disappearing."

It wasn't as dramatic as Tijana had put it. But that day I was wearing the jeans that I usually reserved for thinner days, and even though I'd belted them up as tightly as I could, they still slipped down over the spiky new angles of my hips. I couldn't acknowledge it, though. The trick was not to think about the shrinkage, or how tired I was. I could not say aloud how draining it was to share a bed every night, how it became so difficult to breathe together, because if I said it aloud it would sound like a complaint and then it would become a complaint. I could not say anything against Miranda. There wasn't anything bad to say, she did nothing wrong. I deferred thinking about the fact that for most of the term I had been eating and eating in my room with the door closed, crisps and chocolate and sausage rolls in the hours when Miranda's lectures overlapped with my free time. I had never eaten so much, I had never wanted to eat so much. But my clothes kept getting looser. I would think about all this once I'd spent enough time unconscious in my own bed at home, beneath my poster of Malcolm X. "By any means possible" . . . first I would sleep alone, later I would look for wounds.

A way from my sister it became more and more difficult to tell whether I was alright. Before it had been simple: I could look at her, or think of her at the clinic and then there I was, paper-clipped to my flesh, tidy where she wasn't. But when her term started . . .

I was sharing a flat with another guy and a girl. Both of them were in radio production. Both of them laughed too heartily. The guy's room was next to mine, and at nights he'd knock on the wall between us and ask me what the fuck I was doing in there: feng shui? And every time I'd be about to say something about his mum or how he should fuck his own furniture I'd look, and, yes, my bed had moved from north to west, or my table had moved from beneath the window to beside the door. And it had been me that had moved it without thinking—I could still feel the work of it in my hands. I'd sit on the floor with my back against the bed and my laptop on my knees, trying to send words to Miri, my frail and feather-like problem, to whom I couldn't write "I love you" because I meant it angrily and she would know. Not just that though; it wasn't safe to say something like that without Lily between us. Lily was always very careful to pull us apart, to make Miri and I understand that we were not each other, that my pressing my lips to Miri's nine-year-old heartbeat was not the same as feeling the blood move in myself. Once Miri jumped me in the Andersen shelter, pinned my arms behind my back and kissed my dick through my boxer shorts, so quickly I felt the damp and the presence of spiders more than I felt what she'd done. But Lily still knew somehow—she must have. Why else would she have pinched Miri so hard after dinner? So hard the bruise rose, as if the pain of it had put yeast in her skin. I e-mailed Miri about it; subject line: Do you remember . . .

I didn't send it.

Neither did I send the messages to Miri that said: Can you help me, I do miss her, you are the only one who knows where to find her, I think you talk to each other when I can't hear.

So what did I do while Miri fed her intellect amongst the greatest minds in the country?
I drank coffee.
I moved the furniture in the place I slept in
(moved it and moved it and moved it),
I walked down alleyways with a camera stuck to my face as if I couldn't see without it.

I got good at cooking Mormon funeral potatoes. They're basically just potatoes fried in a batter made extra crunchy with cornflakes. The trick is to get the proportion of corn-flake to batter right. Mormon funeral potatoes are the sort of thing that would pain Dad to serve. They're the sort of thing Miri would beg to be excused from having to eat.

I got back the day before Miri came home. Dad had offered to pick me up, but I told him not to worry about it. There was a Christmas tree in the hallway, a giant, pointy witch's hat quivering with red-and-silver ribbons and lights, scraping the ceiling like something out of *The Nutcracker Suite*. We'd never had a Christmas tree before. I half expected Dad to spring out from behind the tree dressed as Santa.

Sade was by the telephone table, and I was about to make a comment about the tree, but she was standing with the receiver in her hand, listening, looking huge and sad. Her eyes were just pinpricks above her cheeks. I said hello, and she didn't answer me. I was halfway up the stairs before I realised that when I'd walked past her I hadn't heard any-thing but the dial tone.

Dad found me in Lily's studio, trying to see what I could make from the film I'd transferred from the bottom shelf of the fridge in the flat to a mini-cooler for the journey. I was wearing one of Lily's aprons, and my gloves were doused with solution. I was well aware that the goggles on my face only added to my look of idiocy.

"Welcome home," Dad said. Red light met daylight.

"Can you come in or stay out, Dad?"

He came in. I told him about Sade and the phone, and he nodded thoughtfully.

"Is that all? Nod nod? She's . . . mad."

It was too late to tell him how she'd nearly burnt the house down. I said again: "She's mad."

"She's taking medication," Dad said, abruptly.

"What?"

"Her problem isn't anything dangerous, just a perception thing—visions, voices since childhood. Information supplementary to life, assurances of an afterlife, that sort of thing. She didn't hide it from me when she was applying. Think of her as a modern-day St. Bernadette."

"St. Bernadette would've made a brilliant housekeeper, wouldn't she," I said.

Dad said very seriously, "I don't know about that, but Sade is very good."

I asked, "Does Miri know?"

He said he'd had no reason to tell her.

About an hour before Dad went to pick Miri up, I heard hammering in Miri's room and put down the photography book I was reading next door. Dad was in the psychomantium with the light on, nailing Miri's drawers shut, fixing the closed compartments in her wardrobe so that they wouldn't open again. I waited for a break in the hammering, then asked Dad if he needed a hand nailing any other cupboard doors in the house shut. It would stop the guests from stealing clothes hangers, I suggested.

He gestured towards Miri's bed. An array of chalk pack-
ets were heaped on the bedspread, alongside a mass of
plastic, which I poked and watched fall into separate
components—it seemed they were the remains of spoons,
curved with tooth marks. I felt vaguely nauseous. It was like
looking at leftover bones in a KFC bargain bucket.

"She's been hiding them all over her room," Dad said. "The
whole time she's been saying, yes, yes, I'll eat properly, yes,
I'll get better, and she's been doing this."

He stood, still holding the hammer, and stared at me. His
pupils looked black.

"Did you know about this?"

I looked back at him steadily. I shook my head.

"She won't do this anymore," he vowed.

"I don't see how this is going to work. She'll just find
new hiding places. And, Dad . . . she's going to be pissed
off that you went through her stuff."

He turned to her desk drawer and swung the hammer
with much more force than he needed to. He didn't even
hit any of the nails he'd already embedded in the wood.

"It's got to work," he said. His voice as he said it made
me respond immediately: "I know."

"While you've been gone I've been working on"—he laid
the hammer on the table, inhaled deeply—"new recipes for
her. Appetizing things. I know what to do. It'll work, Eliot."

"Okay," I said.

"It'll work," he said. "It's not going to be easy, but I know
she wants to stop all this. I know she wants to get better."

"No one likes being sick," I agreed, and walked backwards, softly, into my room. After a moment the hammering began again.

Miranda and her father sat in the Dean's office with the Dean himself, nodding and smiling soberly at each other, taking turns to talk and to listen. All three of them had expressed their sorrow at the fact that Miranda's change of environment had worsened her condition. Miranda watched the Dean's goatee beard move as he explained that, if she continued as she was for the next two terms, she would fail her first year and be sent down.

Everything in the room was quietly powerful; leather-bound books, an antique globe, near-black wooden chairs and surfaces, stiff, richly coloured drapes. The window cases swooped into domes, like those of a chapel. There might as well have been stained glass, but it seemed someone had thought that would be too much. Outside the Dean's windows, people yelled goodbye to each other across New Court, luggage wheels chattered on cobblestones.

Miranda took out her notebook despite the fact that the discussion was still ongoing. She began writing. Luc's and the Dean's eyes followed her pen with astonishment, but neither of them asked her what she was scribbling. To calm herself she scrawled:

I am lucky, in her GrandAnna's mountainous hand. She was lucky. Had it been the fifties, her father wouldn't be taking her home from here, he'd be dropping her off at a clinic that specialised in electroshock therapy. She'd be on her way to the gag and ball.

Behave yourself, she wrote. *Eat.*

How had Lily managed it? It was like dancing with a mask that was attached to a stick—she dared not lower it, no matter how tiring it was to hold the mask up. She was the ugly girl at the ball, hungry but plastic was nothing anymore.

Last night had been the fifth, perhaps the sixth night that Miranda had lain by Ore, smelling her, running her nose over the other girl's body, turning the beginning of a bite into a kiss whenever Ore stirred, laying a trail of glossy red lip prints. Ore's smell was raw and fungal as it tangled in the hair between her legs. It turned into a blandly sweet smell, like milk, at her navel, melted into spice in the creases of her elbows, then cocoa at her neck. Miranda had needed Ore open. Her head had spun with the desire to taste. She lay her head against Ore's chest and heard Ore's heart. The beat was ponderous. Like an oyster, living quietly in its serving-dish shell, this heart barely moved. Miranda could have taken it, she knew she could. Ore would hardly have felt it.

The watch had ticked loudly, with the sound of a tongue slapped disapprovingly against the roof of a mouth. Then came the recoil—would I really?

and she'd bitten her own wrist, to test the idea of Ore not feeling a thing. Beneath her teeth the skin of her wrist bulged, trying to move the veins away from the pressure, trying to protect them.

In her seat in the Dean's office, Miranda crossed her ankles. *Manage your consumption*, she noted, beneath *I am lucky, Behave yourself,* and *Eat.* Then she took a new line whilst nodding agreement to some words the Dean addressed to her (she had no idea what) and wrote in her own handwriting:

Ore is not food. I think I am a monster.

She looked at the last thing she had written and she felt calm. Then she crossed the words out vehemently, scribbling until even the shape of the sentence was destroyed.

Miranda wouldn't be returning to college next term. She wasn't well enough, the Dean said, her father said, she said. She would rest at home and undergo some cognitive therapy and return when she was ready, they agreed. She would retake first year if that proved necessary. None of this was her fault and it would be a pity for her potential to be wasted just because of her health. There were papers to sign. Miranda and her father signed them.

"Let me tell Eliot about this myself," she told Luc, and he nodded. If he was relieved, he hid it well. He listened to her with his head cocked slightly, and his expression was serious and attentive, as if she was speaking to him from a great distance and he was making sure to catch every word. When Miranda and Luc walked out of the Dean's office together, she stumbled, and he steadied her without changing his expression.

I know they said it could never be love, but I wonder . . .

My Miranda came home from college and her change had almost come full circle. She looked so beautiful. Tiny. Immaculately carved; an ivory wand. Her eyes were oracle's eyes, set deep, deep in the smooth planes of her face. She had six and a half ulcers on the insides of her mouth (one was not yet complete), jewels formed by the acid her stomach had hopefully, uselessly produced. She was no longer able to eat comfortably, even if she wanted to. When she kissed her brother hello she had to close her throat for a second, to stop herself from wincing aloud. The layers between her inner and outer cheek were not thick enough.

She had been finding it difficult to see, and as she came in on her father's arm and hesitantly turned her head from side to side, I saw how heavily she was relying on her hearing—I felt her struggle to perceive shapes. The exact dimensions of doorways seemed dim to her, and they slid around uneasily in the shapes she fixed them in, like magnets repelled by their poles. I depressed my floors for her, made angles of descent that led her across the hallway and through my rooms and up my stairs with the decisiveness of someone who could see properly.

Once Eliot and Luc had left her alone, she set to feeling around her room for me, looking for me. Her fingers trailed across her chair, her desk, her shelves, the back wall of her wardrobe. What's mine is hers. She noticed the nails, frowned momentarily as she checked for her stash of chalk and found no way to access it, but it didn't matter. She moved on, even touching her mirror. Searching.

"I'm sorry it took so long," she told me. "I'm back."

Only I knew how unwell she was. Really she should have been hospitalised. But what would have become of her beauty then?

I was—there is no correct word to place here—shy. I wanted to show myself to her, in a way she would understand. I wasn't worried about frightening her. It was not possible for her to be frightened. When she was little I did not allow anyone or anything to do it, and now that she was older, fright was not a thing she understood.

She tucked herself into bed, drawing the blankets up over her head, smoothing them around her so that she was completely covered, as she liked to be.

"I'm in love," Miranda whispered, once she was hidden.

We saw who she meant. The squashed nose, the pillow lips, fist-sized breasts, the reek of fluids from the seam between her legs. The skin. The skin.

(is it alright to say how much I like this

the way our skin looks together)

Anna was shocked. Jennifer was shocked. Lily was impassive.

Disgusting. These are the things that happen while you're not looking, when you're not keeping careful watch. When clear water moves unseen a taint creeps into it—moss, or algae, salt, even. It becomes foul, undrinkable. It joins the sea.

I would save Miranda even if I had to break her.

Miranda slept. How easy to peel the covers back and pinch her mouth shut with one unyielding hand, to close the nostrils with the other. How easy to suffocate. Her heart and lungs were already weak. It would not have taken much to kill Miranda. That moment passed. In the next moment my thought was to let her die. If she continued as she was, that would be soon. Then in the moment after that I resolved to take her away.

For a lullaby that afternoon I played her Vera Lynn's *Greatest Hits*—*there'll be bluebirds over/ the white cliffs of Dover . . .*

It was my little joke.

L uc and Eliot brought Miranda dinner in bed; the tray was silver and a single white rose flowed through the slim glass vase balanced in its corner. The food wasn't troublesome: poached egg and a bright jumble of peppers and tomatoes and lettuce that stood for salad. Luc had carefully served the meal onto a saucer. On another saucer he'd placed a single chocolate-covered ganache, cut open with a knife so that she could see and smell the creamy paste inside.

She allowed Eliot to turn on her bedside lamp and sat up to eat with the tray on her lap, laughing as Luc pretended to covet her chocolate, stabbing a fork at it but always missing. This time it was easy to please him, easy to make the food disappear—it was so light and there was so little of it.

Eliot read aloud from Luc's manuscript. The project, it seemed, had changed, from a book themed around seasonality to a cookbook for reluctant eaters. She recognised meals she'd pretended to like and struggled through as Eliot read them out, and she suppressed a smile. Before each recipe Luc included some small remark or anecdote. Before caramel ice cream he'd written: "Eliot's first word was 'mummy'—" Eliot broke off and sighed, "I can't believe you're doing this to me, Dad," then returned to the text: "and Miranda's first word, said very firmly a couple of seconds later, was 'yummy.' Eliot spent quite some time babbling 'Mummy, Mummy, Mummy,' and looking very pleased with himself, but Miranda maintained a stately silence, as if she felt she had said enough."

Miranda laughed. She kept forgetting that her father was capable of making her laugh.

Surprised, Eliot looked up from where he was sprawled on the floor with the manuscript, and Luc, seated on a chair he'd drawn up beside her bed, raised a hand as if to touch her face. He began to explain about the drawers he'd nailed shut, but before he finished she said she understood.

That night Miranda's dreams were of the drawers that had been nailed shut, the ugly grey worms that stuck their twisted heads out of the wood. When she had slept enough, Miranda stumbled downstairs to turn the milky light of her torch on the shelves in the larder cupboard, looking for a screwdriver to undo her father's work. When she found the screwdriver, she ran the torch beam along it, the bevelled silver of its tip, then she held it to her throat. Just to feel the chill of it. Her drumming pulse.

She heard and felt the life of the house; there was light and a smell of candle smoke outside the half-open larder door. There was music upstairs. Her GrandAnna laughed at something Lily said. They were in a good mood, like guests sipping on aperitifs before a main meal. Jennifer Silver danced a few steps of a song that came on and Miranda heard their feet on the ceiling and thought, What if I push this point in? She wondered if the house would come down this time.

A pair of hands slipped over her eyes and rested there, heavy and warm. The screwdriver fell.

"Hello, Gretel," her brother said in her ear. She heard the screwdriver roll across the floor and knew he had kicked it. No more music, and Lily and her GrandAnna stopped talking. Their silence had breath in it, though, as if they were simply waiting.

"Hello, Hansel." She laid her own hands on his wrists; he kissed the tip of her ear.

"So we're in a fairy tale . . . I knew it," she said, as he led her out of the laundry room, steering her into the sitting room, switching the light on with his elbow. "You weren't in South Africa, you were in a gingerbread house, getting fattened up, weren't you? And there weren't any telephones in there."

He uncovered her eyes, sat her down on the sofa and handed her a stick of chalk. She held it and looked up at him, blinking at the sudden rush of light. He rubbed his head and left flecks of chalk in his hair. "I'm sorry," he said. "I'm just really shit."

"You are a bit," she said, and tried to look at him as if she forgave him everything.

"Dad's just trying to help you," he said, and as he continued speaking she found she could tune him out, swap his words for the conversation between Lily and GrandAnna. They were talking about her. She licked the chalk and their voices filled the room; she kept looking at Eliot to see if he heard. Lily and GrandAnna were on her side. "Luc shouldn't have nailed Miranda's drawers shut," Lily was saying. "That was the wrong thing to do. Miranda didn't deserve that. She has always tried to be good."

Whenever Eliot paused in his speech, Miranda nodded politely. Eventually he fell asleep with his head on her shoulder, their hair mixing together. She made no move to disturb him.

I *am* good, Miranda thought. I am good, I am.

Mum was in Dad's minicab and parked, probably illegally, outside the station at Faversham. I started to get into the car, but she got out first. "What's this?" She picked up one of my arms and let it drop. She tapped my wrist, pinched my cheek, poked me in the stomach. "Did you leave the rest of you in Cambridge?"

Her hair was greyer. I forgot to look at her eyes. Instead I could see the smiling and the frowning she'd done while

I was gone, her face quietly folding itself away into some scary distance. I couldn't think of anything to say. I hugged her. She smelt of flour and vanilla.

"I made you a birthday cake," she said. "In case you decided to have a birthday today. Remember that, eh?"

Inside the car I buckled up my seat belt, wanting to wrestle the tip of my tongue out of my mouth with my hands, to see if that would encourage sound. She didn't seem to notice that I hadn't said anything, not even hello. She looked over at me as she started up. She said, "You probably won't be having any cake, though, by the looks of you. Cambridge has turned you bougie, hasn't it. I'll make you a nice cup of tea instead."

At last: "*Bougie?* Are you really calling me bourgeois? What are you on about, Mum?"

Mum grinned. "Your figure's all boyish now. You know, like one of those girls with skin from a makeup ad who goes off to a lovely house in Italy and has the most beautiful breakdown because the philosophy books she's reading are too much for her brain."

"Oh one of *those* girls," I said. "And she lounges around in a lace nightie and a silk dressing gown all day. She is also called Cecily."

"Or . . . *Laura*. Our poor darling Cecily-Laura couldn't put away so common a thing as a piece of cake. It would . . . hurt her."

Mum's "posh" accent was hilarious. She was laughing at it before she'd even finished speaking.

"Oi," I said. "I'm going to hurt that cake."

"Hm," said Mum.

"Jam and cream, yeah?"

" 'Course."

The cake was Mum's best yet, but I ate more of it than I wanted to. I couldn't have Dad shaking his head and thinking I'd changed. I sat cross-legged in front of the TV with Mum and Dad on the sofa behind me, watching *EastEnders* and eating so much cake I couldn't taste it, licking cream off my fork to let them know I was still theirs.

"Mel's coming round later. Leave some for her, will you," Mum said, astonished.

We had a crowd at Christmas dinner, because Mum insisted that everyone come over even though there wasn't that much room. Me, Dad, Mum, aunts and uncles (three of the former and two of the latter), and my cousins, Melanie, Sean, Adam and Abbie.

Abbie was eleven and kept saying that everything was "so weird." We had rare roast beef and potatoes because none of us really liked turkey, and Abbie said, "It's so weird to be having beef for Christmas dinner." She also said, "It's so weird not to have the fairy on top of the tree this year," and "If you think about it, gravy is so weird."

Sean's and Adam's dogs chased each other around the room—Sean and Adam said that the dogs weren't allowed to have names, so when they were in earshot we just identified them by colour—the black one was Sean's and the brown one was Adam's.

When Adam and Sean weren't around I whispered the dogs' names into their ears. The black one was Puck and the brown one was Marco-Polo, because he had knowing eyes, as if he'd been around. I knew that Mel called Puck "Melchior" and she called Marco-Polo "Monty." I don't even know what Abbie called them. Without being sure why, Abbie, Mel and I agreed that nothing can live without a name. The dogs were confused, but patient, on the whole unusually sweet-tempered for Staffordshire terriers. Uncle Terry had brought them home to give my boy cousins something to keep them out of trouble. What Uncle Terry didn't know was that Sean and Adam were trying to train their dogs to viciousness so that they could be taken to late-night dogfights in Gillingham. Apparently good money changed hands those nights. Sean and Adam kicked their dogs and subjected them to periods of hunger that were unpredictable in length and frequency. Sean and Adam set their dogs on each other round the back of Sean's house and acted confused when Aunt Jan came out and asked what on earth was going on.

I'd known that they'd do these things even before Uncle Terry gave them the dogs—Sean and Adam were just like that somehow. If they'd lived in Victorian England they would have been the guys shouldering their way to the front of the crowd to get the best view at a public hanging. If you had to pay to see public hangings, they would pay.

Sean's my age, and Adam's two years older. I swear they've been skinheads since birth. Mel's a year younger than me and is probably the only cousin of mine that I would even have contemplated introducing to Miranda. Mel is unflappable. She got her nose pierced because I dared her to, and almost immediately after that she became so sexy that her parents are all worried about her and are constantly asking where she is and where she's going and who she's with. Nothing tawdry, she just sits there and quietly smoulders, as if she'd quite like to be undressed. Dark blonde hair and narrow brown eyes. She sticks up for me when Sean gets stupid.

Some local British National Party bright spark had spent the week before Christmas posting leaflets into every accessible letter box in Faversham, and Sean had kept one to piss me off. So far I hadn't given him a reaction, but in front of the TV after dinner, his tactic was working. It might have been because there was so little room—he, Mel and I were squashed together on the sofa while Abbie and Adam arm-wrestled each other for the remote in the space between their armchairs. Adam was clearly torn between exercising his obviously greater strength in order to watch the show he wanted to watch and the nobler option of letting Abbie win. He won, and Abbie jeered, "Do you feel like a big man now, beating an eleven-year-old at arm-wrestling, eh?"

"Do you know how many immigrants are living in the UK at present?" Sean read, for the fifth, sixth or seventh time. The leaflet featured clip art of a bulldog and a British flag on it. He was practically poking me in the eye with a corner of it.

"Sean, you're so weird," Abbie said. She fed the brown dog, Marco-Polo, with bits of beef she'd kept in her napkin. "Don't, that meat is bloody. He'll run wild," I told her. I'd read about it in an article on keeping pet tigers, and it probably only applied to tigers, but I wanted to be sure that Abbie didn't aid Sean and Adam in their pointless mission.

"We don't know either," Sean continued. "Neither does the UK government. The government lost track of immigration figures years ago."

"Oh help," Melanie said. "They'll take all our jobs. Shut your face, will you, Sean." She crumpled the leaflet up and threw it on the floor.

"Alright, Margaret Thatcher," Sean said. He grinned at me. "You don't take me seriously about that, do you, Ore?" I shook his head. His ears move when he grins. He's my cousin and I don't dislike him.

The phone rang. No one moved. We don't answer the landline after twelve noon. After twelve noon, that's our parents' job. Mel and I reason that anyone we really want to talk to calls before noon, or will call us on our mobiles.

Mum came in and said to me, "It's for you, lazybones. Your friend Miranda. What if I never answered the phone? You would've missed it."

I muttered that she would have called back and took the phone.

"Hi," I said.

"Hi," she said. Then: "Are you cross?"

"No," I said. "But couldn't you have called me on my mobile?"

"I lost it. I had to look you up in the phone book. I've phoned four other Linds asking for Ore."

I laughed.

"I miss you," she said.

I had to let a moment pass for credibility before I said I missed her too. I did. I wasn't tired of sleeping alone yet. But I'd been having that feeling again. The one that came that night outside college when I thought I'd lost her, the force that worked against my marrow. So scared I had to hold on to her to stay upright. I still can't sort out how I feel about Miranda. Even worse, I can't sort out how much any of what I feel about her has to do with her.

"That one of your Cambridge chums?" Mel asked amiably, when I went back into the sitting room.

It wasn't worth making a retort, so I just said, "Yup."

"What's she saying?"

"She wants me to visit her."

"Where? In Buckinghamshiiiiiiiire?" Sean said, suddenly, without taking his eyes off the TV.

"Is she fit?" Adam wanted to know. I ignored him.

"Piss off, Sean. Dover, actually," I said.

Adam leaned forward. "*Is it* . . . Dover is a fucking mess. Bare refugees pissing off the locals. A short piece ago some Kosovan brer and his landlady got stoned. On the actual doorstep of the landlady's house! That's dark, man. You'd better take care of yourself in Dover, or they'll fucking bury ya. You can take my dog down there with you, if you like."

I could tell his offer was only half a joke.

"Take mine too, if you like," Sean said, not to be out-done. Mel laughed until she was too weak to sit up.

Tijana had told me about a good half hour spent on a bench in Dover's main square while some old black guy had explained to her that refugees were a drain on the resources provided by the taxpayer, so I don't know exactly what I thought Dover would be.

Three days later Miranda met me at Dover Priory and tucked her arm through mine. The town wasn't that different from the Kent I knew. More shops and cars than Selling, more height and dizzying views than Faversham, but the people were pretty much the same. A group of white girls in their early teens, chains clanking from their baggy jeans as the music from the boom box one of them was carrying inspired them to make the street they walked on into an impromptu mosh pit. Women with Sainsbury's bags and kids in prams, lost in the tight-lipped silence of the deeply annoyed. Granddads going into and coming out of a grand-dad pub. These didn't look like people who'd stone refugees. If I didn't see the refugee-stoners as I walked from the station to Miranda's house with Miranda beside me, then where were they, the baddies? Did they ("They") spring up at night like toadstools? It was hard to believe in their existence.

Miranda rummaged in her handbag for her door keys, then she said, "Oh!"

I thought we were locked out, but, keys in hand, she raised her wrist to her ear and listened. "The watch has stopped."

She'd explained to me about Haitian time; now she meant that the watch really wasn't telling any time at all. She turned the tiny dial on its side over and over. "It was my mother's," she said.

She wouldn't let me handle the watch, but it looked alright to me. Undented. "It probably just needs a new battery."

She didn't reply. She looked stiff, as if in shock.

When we got indoors, Miranda said, "I'm going to go and wake Eliot up—wait and we'll come and find you," and disappeared. Her dad led me upstairs—he'd kept a guest room unbooked so I could stay over. He looked like a model or something—he was wearing an impossibly white shirt with the collar and sleeves unbuttoned, jeans and pristine navy-coloured Nikes. I followed him up the stairs.

"What are you studying?" he asked.

"Arch and anth," I said.

A woman with an armful of leaflets came down the stairs—she wove between Miranda's dad and me. She brushed against me. I automatically said, "Sorry," and walked closer to the wall so as not to jog her. The leaflets were red, blue and white. The woman winked at me.

"Any good?" Miranda's dad asked.

"What?"

"Arch and anth?"

"Oh. I recommend it."

My room was the first door after the staircase on the second floor.

"Are you vegetarian?" he asked, showing me in. "Have you any allergies? What foods disgust you?"

His voice was endearingly melancholy. "No, no, and I can't think of any off the top of my head," I told him.

He turned to me, smiled and pressed my hand. I thought perhaps he had some kind of mental checklist—friends Miranda brings home are alright if they a) like their studies and b) aren't fussy eaters. He said, "See you at dinner," and left.

The room I'd been put in had big windows that looked out onto the road. Across the road was a bank of grass and some trees. The view was a winter view, grey and dispirited. But it wasn't just the season. All the light in the house was subterranean, as if the place had been built out of mildew. I switched on the light and drew the curtains in the room open as far as I could, to little effect. I dropped my bag onto the bed.

There was an apple on my pillow.

It was white.

The apple had not been there when I came into the room with Miranda's dad. I am certain that it hadn't been there. It had arrived while my back was turned, while I had been at the window. My first instinct was to look up. It must have fallen from somewhere. The ceiling looked innocent and ordinary. I touched the apple; it was very cold, so cold that it was hard to run my fingers over it in a single smooth line. It was only white on one side. The other side was red. Paint? I scratched at the white on one side; there was plain fruit flesh underneath.

I dropped the apple into the bin on my way out of the room.

I don't have a lift phobia, but the lift in that house daunted me from the first. It was a steel cage with lots of ornamental coils in the metal. It rattles as it arrives at the floor you're standing on, but the doors open smoothly and silently. I took the stairs—Miranda had told me that it was only a flight up to hers and Eliot's rooms. It seemed more like four. But in an unfamiliar house, when you're uncertain where you're going, every movement is prolonged by the sense that you're going to try the wrong door or get in some- one's way and bother someone. It doesn't matter how big or small the space—if you don't know it, you get lost in it. Somehow I was at the top of the house, looking at a door with a twist of rancid-smelling cloth nailed to it. I turned away to try my luck with the staircase again, but turned back when I heard whispering. It was as soft as snowfall, but it took over all my hearing. I couldn't hear what exactly was being said, but the murmuring glowed in my skull and didn't stop, not even when I covered my head with both hands. There was more than one voice.

Who is it?

Bent double trying to find a place in the air where the whispering was not, I opened the attic door.

She was in there alone, kneeling by her bed, a woman dressed entirely in silver and fire-engine red. She didn't look at me, but a strength stood behind her—I'm thinking of the tarot card with the image of the smiling woman subduing a lion at the jaw with nothing but a gleaming hand. *La force.*

"What was happening in here?"

She looked at me then. Her face was notched with scars, but her gaze was soft. "What are you doing here? Go home."

"I'm Ore," I said, lamely. "Miranda's friend."

"I'm Sade," she said. "Please go home." She got up and closed the door in my face.

I almost walked into Miranda's brother on the landing outside his room. Miranda came out behind him. They were holding hands. When Miranda introduced us, Eliot turned the handshake into a complicated back-patting and finger-snapping thing he'd picked up in Cape Town. He did it with enough irony for me not to dread him. He was milder than I'd expected. Like Miranda, he smiled a lot, but more as if he was amused than as if he was trying to fend off the anger of the person he was speaking to. By the end of an hour's lolling around in the sitting room I'd decided that he was alright. The sitting room was severe and full of space—the chairs were arranged a respectful distance away from the television screen—you could sit and converse in the armchairs by the window, or sit in the chairs in the middle of the room and switch the TV off so it wasn't part of the conversation. It wasn't the sort of room where you sat and ate snacks or meals while watching *Neighbours*. For example there were no cushions. My family uses cushions to protect our laps from hot plates.

I sat on the sofa beside Eliot and Miranda took an armchair miles away and began turning her watch dial. I smiled at her and she smiled back, nervously. We watched a film from their dad's collection—a German film in black and white, about a serial killer who abducted only children, I think.

Eliot kept making comments and asking questions, which I welcomed, because after the first ten minutes the film became very slow. Eliot was obviously a stoner and collector of trivia—you could probably sit in companionable silence with him for half an hour and then he'd mention something about a rare toad or a semi-plausible conspiracy theory and then shut up for another half hour, or longer. For some reason he decided to address me by my surname only.

"Now look here, Lind . . . are you a Kentish maid, or a maid of Kent?"

"What's the difference?"

"Well. Where do you live?"

"Faversham."

He reached across and went through the whole jazzy handshake thing again; I was better at it the second time.

"Maid of Kent, maid of Kent!" he and Miranda shouted. "What?"

"You're a Kentish man or maid if your home is west of the Medway—so places like Orpington are Kentish. You're a man or maid of Kent if your home is east of the Medway, like Dover is, and Faversham is," Miranda told me.

"Oh," I said. So she and her brother carried maps of Kent in their heads. "But why?"

Eliot shrugged. "Ancient distinctions, man. Ever since the Angles and the Saxons . . . "

"What happened to them," Miranda sighed. "The Angles and the Saxons and the Druids and the Celts and the Picts and the . . . who else?"

"Jutes," I supplied, bored.

Miranda's question was rhetorical, but Sade came in and answered with a great deal of satisfaction: "They died out oh."

Sade bossed me into the kitchen, her hand on my elbow as she murmured, "Sorry about earlier," and she poured me a drink. The drink looked like beer and it was bottled like beer, but it tasted of sugared vomit. I smiled politely at her over the top of the glass, but she tutted. "You are feeling like you can't ask for what you want," she said, and got a Guinness out of the fridge for me.

I pointed at the first drink she'd offered me. "What is that stuff?"

Sade raised an eyebrow. "Come on, get out. You don't know Power Malt?"

"Never had it."

"Never had malt? Heyeyeye." She looked at me even more closely than before and washed her hands with invisible water. "Well. It happens sometimes."

"So you live here?"

Sade snorted. "I keep house. As far as it can be kept."

I looked out at the garden through the kitchen window. The sun was setting into storm clouds; there was smoky brightness outside, as if the world was being inspected by candlelight. I saw the woman who'd brushed me on the stairs the first time I'd gone up them. This time when I saw her I knew she wasn't a houseguest. She was standing under one of the trees, standing so deep in the ground that the earth levelled around her ankles. As if she had no feet, as if she was growing. Her presence made the branches behind her jerk and contract, like hands trying to close around her but not quite daring to. She had her hand spread over her face. She was looking at me through her fingers. Miranda knew her. It was Miranda who had said: "Tell me about that woman, the woman with the covered face? Is she *your* mother?"

My hand moved to the window latch, making sure the window was locked, making sure the window was really there, keeping her out. More than anything else, I wished she couldn't see me. I forced the need to blink into a second of something like prayer—go away, with my eyes squeezed shut—and when my eyes opened, she was gone. It took minutes for the trees to recover from their shivering fit.

"Sade," I said. "Did you see—?"

Sade put her hand over my mouth. She had seen, but she seemed untroubled.

"Better don't, it's bad luck," she said. "But . . . if anything, come to me."

Her eyes begged me not to make a fuss. "Okay," I said, but I scanned the entire garden all over again. Then I sat down. Sade had a book on the counter. When I asked her what she was reading she held up the cover so I could see. It was a Mills and Boon romance; a white nurse swooned in the arms of a white doctor. I told her about the soucouyant. While telling her I realised that the story of her is much more to do with how she is ended than how she began. We know that the soucouyant has preyed on younger souls for years and years, longer than anyone can remember. It's as if she's so wrong that even in the mind of the storyteller she must be killed immediately.

"That's a good one," Sade said. "I had not heard that before." Then she asked: "Will you tell Miranda?" She wasn't talking about the story I'd just told her.

"Why shouldn't I?" I said.

"She wouldn't understand. She's different from us."

I resented the "us."

"Different from us how? As in, we are clairvoyant and she is not?"

"I'm sorry," Sade said, eyeing me. "You are a maid of Kent, are you not?"

I didn't say anything.

"I'm not mocking you," she continued. "I believe it. But does she believe it?"

"Who are you talking about, Miranda, or the soucouyant?"

"Maid of Kent, do you want to know what your name means?"

"No, thank you."

"It means . . . "

I put my hands over my ears and growled, but I still heard. She said my name meant "friend."

"I heard those . . . voices in your room," I said. "I almost thought there were other people in there with you."

"Yes there are," said Sade. "They're always there." She held up three fingers.
"Two of them tell me: You have no one. Jump. Open the window and jump. Join your old ones. It would be so easy. Jump, you have no one. On and on and on."

I eyed her. "Do you ever think you'll jump?"

Sade sipped at her Power Malt, her gaze distant. "It's true that I have no one, you know. But the third one says, 'Wait.' Her voice is so kind. I don't know who she is, I don't know who any of them are, but all this other one ever says is 'Wait.' So I don't even try to jump."

"Sade," I said. "Does this job pay well?"

She seemed amused at that.

"Then why do it? Do you have a British passport?"

She produced it from the pocket of her cardigan; it was bound in plastic, and inside the pages were as crisp as if she had only just received it.

"Five years," she said, proudly.

"Then why do this job? You've got choices. Get a job that pays better. Go somewhere else. Don't stay anywhere where people tell you to jump and die."

"Normally you would be right," said Sade, "but the other one says, 'Wait.'"

I stared at the tribal marks on Sade's face. She took my hand and drew it across the scar tissue, her expression matter-of-fact. "Only the men are marked, usually. It would be the men who go to war, I suppose. But I wanted marks. So I copied my father's."

"You did these yourself?" I had to touch them again after that.

Sade pressed her hand over mine and smiled into both our hands. "Salt keeps the cuts open until they learn to stay open by themselves."

"Ouch."

"Yes, much more than I can say."

I thought, there is absolutely no one even a bit like you anywhere else.

"Sade, I want to ask you something," I said. "If you say yes, I'll believe you. Just tell me. There's something wrong with this house, isn't there?"

"It is a monster," Sade said, simply.

While she had been talking, I'd taken the saltshaker that sat between us, and I'd poured small hills of salt into the pockets of my skirt. Sade made no comment, but when

Miranda called me from the sitting room and I got up to go, she grabbed my arm and said, "Wait a second."

She went to the kitchen drawers and took out some chillies in a plastic bag to give to me. They looked like crooked twigs—brown, but splashed with dark red where autumn had bled on them. She opened the bag and the smell made me cough. You didn't season food with this kind of pepper, you destroyed nerve endings. I said thank you and attempted a hug. She waved me away.

Miranda showed me the fireplace, the white cave she'd thought she might have lost her life in. She stared at the marble, rubbed its dust onto her fingertips. I tried to get her to look at me without actually saying "look at me." It didn't work. Miranda showed me her psychomantium—the place was almost friendly, like being carried on salt water towards yourself. The mirror seemed to cause the darkness. We silently agreed not to raise the matter of the nailheads glinting from her sealed desk drawer, the fact that everything she had seemed to be on view, her underwear folded and stacked beside the heater, even her pens and pencils tied round with a rubber band and placed on her desk amongst papers and tubes of lipstick. I think Miranda was sad that she didn't have more to show me. A fireplace and a black room were the only places in the whole house that she seemed sure of. In her bed we pulled her covers up to our chins and lay quietly, careful not to bump each other with the sharp parts of ourselves, the elbows and the knees, until our bodies had warmed each other. Then Miranda shifted and opened my mouth with her own. As we kissed I became aware of something leaving me. It left me in a solid stream, heavy as rope. It left from a hurt in my side, and it went into Miranda, it went into the same place in her. I tried hard to breathe, harder than I have ever tried at anything. I tried so very hard that I felt the strain on the blood vessels in my eyes. But I couldn't. There was so much air passing between our lips but I couldn't use any of it. It was like having my mouth blown into while my nostrils were pinched together. When I pulled away from Miranda she looked at me with eyes of puzzled slate.

I showered before dinner. I ran the water too hot as usual; I saw my face in the glass of the shower door and I concentrated on it as if it was a talisman or charm. A tune came unbidden, it was "Frère Jacques," so I was clearly terrified. *Hello monster, hello monster*, I sang, *Dormez-vous? Dormez-vous?* When I opened the shower door, tiny hooks of steam sank into the lino. There were huge white towels, hotel towels, draped over the towel rack and I took one and dried myself, keeping my eyes on my face. The towel the girl in the mirror was drying herself with—I frowned and looked at my towel. Where it had touched me it was striped with

black liquid, as dense as paint

(don't scream)

there were shreds of hard skin in it. There was hair suspended in it

"The black's coming off," someone outside the bathroom door commented. Then

they whistled "Rule Britannia!" and laughed.

Bri-tons never-never-never, shall be slaves

My skin stung. Where to put this towel? I grew ugly in my need to make sure no one ever saw it, my face collapsing in on itself as I hand-washed the towel in the sink. I dressed slowly and carefully, and by the time I'd put the towel on the rack to dry and opened the door, the passageway was empty.

Some other guests were booked in, so they ate earlier and Luc, Miranda, Eliot and I ate later. Candles flickered on the table. Miranda's dad produced a fat thug of a winter stew, full of meat and turnip and other vegetables that crunched. There was red wine in it, too. It looked so rich on the plate that I balked.

"Is everything alright?" Miranda's dad asked. He was at the head of the table, and Eliot and Miranda were opposite me. Suddenly everyone was looking at me. Eliot and Miranda were so alike. In photographs their twinhood was underwhelming, but in person, when they both had their eyes on you, you couldn't sort one from the other—or you could, but not quickly enough to stop yourself saying the wrong name by mistake.

"It looks lovely," I said. I added "sir," in case I was supposed to call him "sir" and also because he reminded me of a teacher I'd had. I was careful not to let any food or water touch my lips—I tilted my glass and swallowed air, I lifted the fork to my mouth, spoke and rearranged the forkful of

food on my plate whilst speaking. I wiped my mouth with
a napkin, left red smudges on it, stared and tried to reason
the colour away. Was my lip torn? Surreptitiously I lay a
finger across my bottom lip; the skin was whole, but there
was more red on my fingertip. After about five minutes I
remembered what this was: lipstick. Miranda's lipstick, the
imprint of her kisses on my lips. And there we all were,
Miranda, her father, her brother and I, sharing oxygen
around a dinner table. I scrubbed at my lips as hard as I
could without it looking pathological. I don't know what
kind of lipstick Miranda wore but it just wouldn't come off.
At best the smudges on the napkin lightened in shade until
they were a decayed pink.

I wanted to hide, or to sleep. I thought if I just slept
the discomfort off, the place would make sense to me in the
morning. Miranda wanted me to read to her, and I did, the
book on the pillow before her so that I had to curl my arm
around her to turn the pages. It was a Hans Christian
Andersen story about the disadvantages of a mechanical
nightingale when compared to the real thing, and towards
the end I got quieter and quieter until I was whispering the
story into her ear. She was asleep almost before I'd even
finished. I turned off the lamp and lay so that there was a
small gap between us.

"Ore," Miranda whispered. "Ore. Are you awake?"
I felt the heat rising from her skin. I ran my hands

over her arms, her breasts, her stomach; they were covered
with sweat. She said she was thirsty. She kissed me and said
again that she was thirsty. I said I'd go and get her some
water, grabbed a glass from her desk and ran into the bathroom, shaking all over. I jumped when the cold water from
the tap hit me; I was trying to fill the glass as quickly as
possible. If I brought her water she would be well.

I tried to take the water to her, but I couldn't find her.

I walked out of the bathroom door and, I don't know
how, found myself still in the bathroom. The room hadn't
grown any longer; the door was still in front of me; I didn't
feel any change in the ground beneath my feet. But when I
tried to pass through the door again I was in the bathroom
again, and my neck cricked, as if I'd turned my head too
fast. I tried one more time, and came through into the passageway, which was meant to be arranged into an L, with
the staircase completing the rectangle. I was on the longest
part of the L—the bathroom was meant to be in between
Eliot's room and their dad's room. But the doors had
changed positions. All four doors on that floor were now
ranged along one wall, and the rest of the "L" was blank.
None of the doors would open. The stairs were still there,
and I inched down them carefully, one by one, afraid that
they would change too, unsure where they would take me.
The staircase ended in the kitchen, every surface heavy
in the moonlight.

There was a long shadow behind me. It wasn't my
shadow. From the corner of my eye I saw it grow like a syrup

stain, called from nowhere. I went to the counter, spilled salt all over it and ran the flat of a knife through the salt, on both sides. I turned before I could lose my nerve; or more, the knife turned and took me with it.

Kill the soucouyant.

"Ore," Miranda said. I had her by the throat. It was the principle of knife and fork. You had to hold something down before you could stab it.

She was holding a pair of dressmaker's scissors to my chest, opened into a stark V. I didn't feel them there until I looked down. There was a rip in my pajama top. She let the scissors drop onto the counter, and I dropped the knife.

"I thought you were the soucouyant," I said.

She said, "I thought you were."

We touched each other's faces in the dark, trying to be sure.

"Did I look different?"

"I just couldn't . . . see you."

"You're shaking."

"The soucouyant—"

"The goodlady—"

We were talking at the same time; until she said "goodlady" I couldn't tell which of us was saying what.

"The goodlady?" I said.

Miranda fetched a cloth and a newspaper and wiped all the salt off the counter. She didn't answer.

"I'm off home," I said.

"You can't, it's two AM."

She drank noisily from the tap, then wiped her forehead. "God. That's better."

Miranda led the way through the house's unlit core. I wished I could see her face.

"Miranda," I said, but not loudly enough, because she didn't answer me. "She's not good," I said, once we were in her bed, her legs wrapped around mine.

Miranda put a hand on my backbone. Lately it had been starting to show.

"No. I don't think she is after all. Are you scared?" she asked.

"Aren't you?"

Very softly she said into my shoulder, "Please under-stand. We are the goodlady."

"You and I?" I asked. *Aware that the goodlady isn't good*

"No. The house and I."

I lay very still. I didn't know what would happen to me if I moved, if I tried to run. For some time I was aware of her talking to me, but I was concentrating so hard on being quiet and still that I couldn't understand her. When I finally tuned in, she was sleepy. She had been saying the same thing for minutes, it seemed.

"Miranda can't get away," she murmured. "She can let you go, but it will be bad for her because then they will be angry."

She slept, but I didn't. I tried to understand her. With my eyes closed, I touched her hair with both hands, found the place just below the curve of her shoulders where her

hair continued as a soft phantom, impossible when my eyes
were open. I wrapped this hair around my fingers and
sought faith in her goodness. When I couldn't find it I
slipped out from under the covers, away from her, and I
looked at her as she lay, weak but made of wire. I fought the
impulse to part her lips with my fingers, to check her teeth.
You have seen her teeth before
I told myself that no matter what Miranda said, the soucouyant was the old lady. That was the rule. It was the young
girl that defeated the soucouyant. The two did not enter the
story in each other's bodies; the two did not share one body,
such a thing was a great violation. Of what? I didn't know.

   The moon-coloured mannequin halfway across the room
had its arms out, as if it would smoothly and calmly murder
me if I moved for the door. Finally, I reached out and
switched on the bedside lamp, which didn't seem to disturb
Miranda's sleep. The light was sickly, but at least everything
in the room appeared as it was.

It's hard to believe that there are girls as straightforwardly
sexy as Ore Lind who also get into Cambridge. It's even
harder for me to believe that girls that looked like her got into
Cambridge and befriended my sister. Ore is almost as tall as
me. Plaits and ribbons and a scent of coconut. Big, bright eyes.
She had this constantly benevolent expression, somewhere
between a smile and a look of preoccupation. She'd brought

Miri a lollipop and spent the afternoon in an armchair in front of the TV, languidly licking both her lollipop and Miri's rejected one, the shoulder of her jumper dress slipping down, her knees drawn up so that her feet didn't touch the ground. Her legs were long and slim and she'd dressed them in stockings that travelled up and up, marked by a strip of lace where they stopped—I only caught glimpses of those stocking tops, and couldn't look too long without being blatant.

I kept wanting to ask her if she was cold. I kept wanting to run a finger along the seam of those stockings. I caught Miri catching me looking at Ore, and decided to dub our visitor Lind in the hope that I could inspire gentlemanly feeling in myself. Still, she must have had a reason for wearing stockings and a short dress in winter. Girls who dress for themselves dress like Miri.

I went to Martin's after dinner—he'd seen Miri and Ore walking over from the station and said, jokingly, that I should "get in there." Most of our sixth-form posse was there too, sitting and lying on beanbags, drinking beer and chatting breeze, soaking up the last week or so of holiday before trekking back to their essays at Durham, UCL, Kings, Bristol, Oxford, Edinburgh. People kept asking me about South Africa and then pitching in with their accounts of Freshers Week before I could complete a sentence. Dan was proud to have been appointed "the naked fresher" for 2001. I told him I thought that was mighty gay, and he said, "You wish it was, Silver, but I don't like you like that." So that was the quality of the evening's conversation. Emma was there, laboriously making Cosmopolitans for the girls with a cocktail shaker she'd got for Christmas. She'd grown her hair out and dyed it blond. She looked good. She tried to get a game of chess going but no one was interested. All in all that night was intolerable.

The house was dead when I got home, except for a couple watching Sky News in the sitting room. Not Americans then, otherwise they'd have been watching BBC news and loving the Britishness of it. I heard Ore and Miri talking in Miri's room, and thumped suddenly on my bedroom wall, to scare them. They fell silent. Haha.

I found a box of the Gauloises Dad had given me. As I lit one it came to me that my GrandAnna's husband, the RAF man, had called them golliwogs. A serviceman was smoking a golliwog in one of his cartoons and when I'd asked Lily what it meant to smoke a golliwog she'd just stared and crooked her finger at me and didn't relax until I brought her the cartoon.

I stuck my head out of the window and breathed smoke at the half moon. It snagged in the tree branches. I heard Miri's window opening, and a couple of metres away from me, Ore stuck her head out of the window too. She had a haughty profile, her hair like a ruffled crown. She wasn't wearing much—I saw a bit of silk and lots of skin. I hoped that, beneath the sill, she was wearing the stockings too. She turned and waved at me, I nodded back.

"Listen," she whispered across the window ledges. "I could do with a smoke."

I shook ash into the garden. It was good for the plants. "I'm afraid I can't help you; this is my last one."

"Liar. You look like a boy with a pocketful of smokes."

"Do you even smoke?"

"No. But it looks so relaxing."

"Alright. But it'll cost you."

Ore smiled. "Look at you, all brave when there's a room between us."

She ducked back into Miri's room and I opened my bedroom door.

She'd wrapped up in Miri's dressing gown. She wrinkled her nose and said, "Smells like pure tar," but accepted the cigarette I handed her. She made herself at home on my window seat, wadding a pillow under her knees. I didn't stare at her. I didn't talk about Mormon funeral potatoes or the fact that golliwog was just one slang term for Gauloises. I maintained a cool silence. I lit her cigarette for her, looked away when she gave an astonished cough, held her cigarette while she bent double and tried to thump herself on the back.

"Okay, you can put my one out," she said, when she'd recovered. I didn't for a while—I smoked both our gollies, with narrowed eyes and nervous intensity, like a Beat poet facing out his typewriter at dawn. Maybe. I hoped. The girl was making me reveal idiocy even in my silence.

"Insomniac?" I ventured.

She nodded. "Tonight, yes. Miranda's sleeping like a baby for once."

"So she wasn't sleeping well at college either."

"No."

"Do people talk about her at college? Do they talk about the way she looks?"

Ore said, "What do you mean?"

"Come on. Look at her. She's starving."

Ore leaned back against the pillows. "Oh, so you can see that, can you? And what about this lovely house you live in?"

I stubbed out the cigarettes and dropped them out of the window. "What about it?" I was wary, thinking she was going to give me some kind of Marxist chat. Miri had told me and Dad that Ore's dad drove minicabs and her mum was a dinner lady, that they had fostered her until they could adopt her. The information was interesting but of no significance; we hadn't even asked after it. And if Ore was going to make some sort of point based on her history I didn't want to hear it.

She started to speak, then shook her head and looked at the ground. I reached out and followed the line of her jaw with my finger. She looked at me then, with that strange half smile that said she'd forgive me if I kissed her. I kissed her and she let me. I kissed her again and she let me. By the third time it was ridiculous and really sort of painful, that she was just letting me and letting me, her lips slightly parted but not kissing back.

"I don't think I fancy boys," she explained, when I'd given up.

"You're . . . you only like girls?"

"Well. Never say never."

I reached for another cigarette, then changed my mind. I asked, "So do you fancy my sister?"

She shot back: "Why did you lock Miranda off all term?"

"I doubt you'll win Miri round," I told her.

She studied me. "Were you trying to punish her for getting in? Or was it brotherly concern, like you thought ignoring her was a way to help her out of her whole starving thing?"

"Not a chance," I said, knowing I sounded dogged and not caring.

"I know," she said. I watched her walk to the door; her legs. Mild agony, if such a thing is possible. And embarrassment at my clumsiness.

It took me a long time to get to sleep.

What was the rule to observe? What offering could I make?

By the time Miranda woke up I'd consulted the yellow pages and been to Deal, fifteen minutes' train ride there, fifteen minutes back and half an hour of waiting at the watch shop on the high street while a guy with white sideburns replaced Miranda's watch battery. I'd asked him, possibly more urgently than normal, not to set the watch to "the right time" and bought her two more batteries, just in case; each one was only a little larger than a five-penny piece, but each battery held five years bunched into increments of sixty seconds.

I was by Miranda's bed, trying to hold my breath because it seemed too loud, when she woke up. She looked at me uncomprehendingly for a long moment, her eyes dark through the hair tumbled over her face. She closed one eye, then the other, then opened them both again.

"I dreamt you were the soucouyant," she said, finally, then giggled. "Silly." A dream, she said.

I knew I would have to go home. I dropped the watch onto the pillow beside her head, then added the batteries. I watched her pick up the watch, stroke it, hold it to her ear. I watched her listen to the ticking of the watch. Tears rolled down her face. She looked at the watch, not at me.

"This is my mother's watch," she said.

After breakfast we walked up to Dover Castle and skipped the medieval court reconstructions, moved more slowly through the displays in First and Second World War army barracks, the caps and medals and coloured card in glass boxes bigger than us. From the grass behind the ramparts the sea was mossy peace—the weather had almost frozen it, and there was so much mist that you couldn't see where it led. Miranda sat on a heap of rock and tapped it. "Chalk," she said. The mist hung in her hair.

"Of course," I said, shivering. If either of us smoked cigarettes we'd have been warmer in some small way.

"My train leaves in half an hour," I told her.

She looked up at me. She smiled with her red lips.

"So you're running away," she said.

My eyes were watering and my nose was running. It was the cold, but I knew it would look as if I was crying.

"I'll see you at college," I said.

She didn't say anything. She sucked chalk from out under her fingernails. She looked tired.

Who Do You Believe?

Well? Is it the black girl? Or Eliot? Or me? Our talk depends upon the fact that you weren't there and you don't know what happened. At the very least I hope you take Eliot with a pinch of salt. He is a terrible liar. For example, he doesn't even need reading glasses. He just wanted something that differentiated him from Miranda, some way to get back at her for her pica. His lenses are plain and untreated, an indulgence earned from his mother when he confided in her at a trip to the opticians when they were ten. And to keep it up so long when he can see perfectly well . . . what a liar he is. I can't think how many times he's squinted and scrunched his face up, struggling to follow the print when Miranda has handed him a sheet of paper and his reading glasses aren't to hand. She would have found him out eventually. Besides the boy is strange, very strange. You couldn't guess what he has between his mattress and his bedstead—or could you?

It's a single A4 envelope, full of photographs of a girl in black. There she is, leaning over Kings College Bridge, hand raised to greet someone on a punt passing below. There she is again, the same girl, a dark figure passing geometrically laid flower beds and hedgerow so hazy green it's as if she's dreaming it. The girl again, at the barred back gate of a college, strands of her hair whipping the air as she watches for her watcher. Lack of variety in subject aside, the photographs aren't bad.

Where was Eliot from September to December? Africa? Really? How funny.

They are better off apart now.

Someone had been in my room—I mean that someone had been in the guest room that I'd been put in. My bag, which had hardly had anything in it anyway, had been emptied onto the floor, and the bed and dressing table were covered with leaflets. The disorder was so blatant that I already knew nothing had been taken. I wasn't as bothered as I could have been. I had my wallet and phone on me, this was my own fault for not locking the door, and besides, I was leaving. I stuffed my books and my spare pair of jeans back into my bag. The leaflets were BNP flyers with helpful tips for citizens, the same as the leaflet Sean had kept to piss me off.

Do you know how many immigrants are in the UK? Neither does the UK government . . .

There were so many leaflets that it took me nearly fifteen minutes just to gather them into the guest-room bin, which I dragged to the centre of the room when I could no longer bear to have my back to the door.

When I stepped out of the room with my bag over my shoulder, the corridor mixed twilight and green and I could hear a whistling sound from upstairs, like air gliding around something of great mass. I could have been inside a cannon. But I did not run. I took a deep breath and set myself a march—*I'm get-ting out I'm get-ting out, no mat-ter what, I'm get-ting out.* The lift doors were open. I walked past them, then backtracked. There was a little girl in the lift. I can't describe her; she was unexpected. She stood on tiptoe in the corner of the lift, and she had something cupped in her hands—she gazed and gazed at it, amazed.

"Are you okay?" I asked.

The thing in her hands was covered in flies. It was bloody and she seemed to have brought it out from inside her. There was a gap in her nightgown, at the stomach.

I pressed the lift button to go down

(take her down, she belongs in a grave)

but nothing happened.

"What is it?"

The girl's eyes were plaintive. She held the thing out to me. It wobbled in her hands like dirty jelly. I was very sorry for her.

"Please stay," she said. "Or I'll get into trouble. You've got to stay. You'll hardly feel it."

I'm not brave. I remembered the salt I had in both pockets, and the pepper of the wickedest kind wrapped in plastic. I coated my hands in salt. I crumbled pepper in my palms. I stepped into the lift and, expecting to touch nothing, I tore at the little girl's face until Miranda's came through.

Miranda struck at me, spitting and hissing. I said, "Oh God, oh my God, sorry, I'm sorry, oh my God," over and over, but kept her pinned against the back of the lift, both my hands around her throat.

The doors closed and the lift went up. She stopped struggling. She licked the back of my hand, slowly, making tracks in the salt. I screamed, but made no sound. I couldn't turn the volume up. I screamed and didn't let go. I concentrated on making myself colourfast, on not changing under her tongue. I know what I look like. The Ore I signed onto paper in the letters of my name, the idea of a girl that I woke into each morning. Arms, stay with me. Stomach, hold your inner twists.

The lift doors opened onto a floor of the house I hadn't seen. The walls were bare, and nails stuck out of the floorboards, so many, scattered but with an order to them, like ants in a crazed game of hopscotch. The corridor only stayed empty for a second—the next moment it was flooded with people who stared and said nothing. Their eyes were perfect circles. I didn't see them move, yet every second they were closer to the lift.

Miranda politely flicked my hands away from her and sashayed out among them. They all looked at her and smiled slavishly. When she had passed through them, they looked at me again. They were alabaster white, every one of them. I went after her. They looked at me, crowded so close, murder in their eyes. If I didn't believe in the salt I would be lost. Believe, believe. Salt is true. Salt is true. Kill the soucouyant, salt and pepper.

I closed their eyes. "Be blind," I said, rubbing salt on their eyelids. It was like stirring melted wax. "Don't look. Don't see me."

I looked behind me and there they stood, eyes closed, lips pursed in consternation, their arms out in front them.

I walked into a shuttered room full of the sound of a sewing machine. The machine was set on a stand and juddered away, sewing at nothing. There was a dirty white coat hung on a hook on the wall, newspapers, and other things that made me think it was a room belonging to someone small and sad.

Miranda was in the corner with her arms folded around her knees. She looked blissful, like one of the lotus-eaters, someone hearing comforting voices. When she saw me she looked astonished.

"What's this?" she said.

I didn't speak to her. If I was going to help her I shouldn't speak to her. I knelt beside her and rested my hands on her head. She tensed, and I cracked her open like a bad nut with a glutinous shell. She split, and cleanly, from head to toe.

There was another girl inside her, the girl from the photograph, all long straight hair and pretty pearlescence. This other girl wailed. "No, no, why did you do this? Put me back in." She gathered the halves of her shed skin and tried to fit them back together across herself. I fell down and watched her, amazed, from where I sat.

"I don't want to come out. Put me back in," the girl insisted. "Please. I can't . . . cope."

"Who are you?" I asked.

She stopped for a moment. "I'm Miranda Silver. Who are you?"

I didn't answer her, but I pointed at the rubbery skin she clutched so desperately. "Who is that?"

"It's the goodlady," she said. "Please help me get back in. I need her."

I got up.

"Don't become her," I said. I knew she wouldn't listen. This new Miranda's gaze was weak. She seemed soft in the head. Before I'd even walked out of the room, she was lying under the sewing machine, trying to sew herself back into the skin. Outside the room, the floor had gone

(where is the floor?)

I fell down into a pickled-lime smell that had frightened me as a child when we visited the plague graves in Deptford. My friend and I, we thought that that was how rotten marrow smelt. The blind faces

(I felt them nuzzle at me as I passed, their sucking and sly biting), even with no light to see them by, I know they looked at me.

Below someone threw their hands out and white flew from their fingertips. Someone red and silver, the spirit in the flame. I bounced. I couldn't see anything. Then I could, through white squares. I was in a net. Tens of feet of white cotton bunched around me. I was crying like a newborn: "Don't let me die."

When I opened my eyes I was in the room that had nothing in it but the white fireplace. I saw, through gauze, a figure walking towards me. It frowned and bent closer to me. Sade. I didn't move. With my eyes I told her that I might not survive this after all.

"Oh, lazy," she said. She put a hand to my forehead, rumpling the net against it, then she put a hand to my chest, then she put a hand to my stomach.

I sat up, still in the net. It was knotted at the top, but I couldn't see how. I sat in a huge white bag, like a stork's delivery.

Sade looked at me through the net.

"How—" I began, but she tutted. "Don't talk about it. It's bad luck, eh."

She checked her watch. "Alright, I'm leaving now."

"Where are you going?"

She rolled her eyes. "Better pull yourself together, Ore. You think I belong to you?"

"But the net—"

"Stand up and it will unravel. Goodbye."

She bustled away. I didn't feel like testing what she had

said yet; I felt so safe in the net. I put my hands against it and rocked myself. It was late afternoon. Sunset turned the room crystal and orange, like sugared fruit peel. I stood and the net fell around me with such sudden weight that I nearly lost my footing.

M iranda followed me to the train station. I didn't know it until the conductor blew his whistle and I looked out of the window—as a reflex, I always do this, the whistle blows and I check the window—and I saw the tall girl in black, swaying on the platform as if her newly stitched knees were failing her. That's all I know. Now I have said all that I know.

What is the Season?

Miranda almost didn't go home. She had run so hard and she had come to the end of her strength, and none of it mattered because she was too late. Ore had gone and a new rawness on the insides of her eyelids made her see what that meant. Miranda Silver was not, could not be herself plus all her mothers. She was just some girl on a bench on a train station platform, crying because something stood between her and another girl and said, no. The goodlady said it couldn't be. Who was the goodlady to say that? How did she dare?

If she could get free, if she could get well—

It would take a long time, she knew. She couldn't just pull the Silver out of her like a tooth or a hair. If she did she would concertina, bones knocking against each other. No, it would take a long time to get free, longer than Ore could wait. She thought of the inscription Lily and Luc had had engraved around the insides of their wedding bands alongside the date of the ceremony, the letters were as deep in the gold as if they had been written on the very ore: NOW IS FOREVER. That was how lovers saw time. No, Ore would not wait, she would not be able to.

Miranda turned in the opposite direction of home. At the post office she bought a postcard with Dover Castle on it, borrowed a Biro from the bored-looking woman behind the counter and addressed the postcard to Ore.

I'm sorry for everything, she wrote.

I am going down against her.

She bought a single stamp to post the card with. The woman behind the counter clacked gum and looked at her suspiciously. Miranda posted the card on her way back to Barton Road. She stopped at Bridge Street and skimmed pebbles off the water below it. She thought of Eliot. He anchored her mind, a troublesome weight, reassuring.

When she got home, all-season apples were heaped on one of the counters—the sheer number of them constituted a warning. Some kind of warning to her. The temperature in the kitchen felt well below zero, and the apples were turned so that their white sides were hidden and their red sides glowed like false fire.

Her father couldn't have brought them in. He would not pick such apples, especially if he had seen that they had grown outside the house in December. Her father was in his room, drafting an advertisement for a new housekeeper on his laptop. Miranda could see the words "minimum of six months' experience in a similar position (plus references) required" on the screen as she came in. Luc's hair was wet and he had a towel around his neck. The note that Sade had written him was at the top of his paper pile. He kept looking at it as he typed. Miranda sat in his armchair, and when he registered her presence he frowned and motioned towards Sade's letter. "She says I should stop trying to keep this place open, that it just won't work. That it's . . . ill favoured."

"Perhaps she's right," Miranda said, gently.

Her father switched his laptop off without saving the file.

She tried to hold eye contact with him, but he seemed unable to manage it for long. "Father, I'm stuck," she said. "I'm trying to think of next year and there's no place for me in it. Isn't that strange?"

"Don't say such things," he said. His helplessness. He was supposed to know what to do. How was it that he did not?

"Do you think I'll get to be thirty years old? Do you think I'll end up living anywhere but here?" She smiled at him. It was a slow-spreading smile, and after a few seconds it contorted her face; she felt it happening.

He was on his feet before her smile reached its most strained point—he walked away, rubbing his head with his towel. Miranda left after him
(briefly she thought of shadowing him down the stairs, sharing this smile with him every time he turned, but after all, what had he done to deserve it? The smile stopped.)

she turned towards her own room, but Eliot called her.

"Where's Lind?" he asked. He was sitting cross-legged on his bed. He dropped his headphones down around his neck and placed his book facedown, preparing for some kind of talk. Miranda eyed him without emotion.

"She went home."

"You're okay," he said. The hint of a question in his voice was an offering, and she refused it.

"I'm sorry," he said, crestfallen.

"What for?"

"That stupid thing I said before Lily died. I don't think you'll ever forgive me. Will you."

("Don't fall asleep Miri, I fucking mean it.")

She smiled politely and went into the psychomantium. She locked the door and put a chair against it.

Are you happy? She asked the walls, the ceiling, the floor. *Are you happy that we have no one but each other? Are you happy are you happy.* She locked her tongue between her teeth and drummed her hands and head against the wall by her bed until she lay motionless and everything she saw peeled back into whiteness, like a shelled egg from the centre out.

Lily Silver looked her eyeball to eyeball and said, "Hm . . . now you've hurt yourself."

"Don't expect us to help you," Jennifer said, reprovingly. She smelt of tree sap.

"You did this to yourself," her GrandAnna finished. "Why did you let the black girl leave?"

They looked the same now, all four of them. It was

tiresome to see herself repeated so exactly, without even the thin mediator that was a mirror.

I am going down *against* her

I am going *down* against her

She had meant something by that. They were waiting for her where they always waited, even when she hadn't known they were there.

It was night-time when she was able to stand up without her head spinning. She ripped her curtains open. There was a cloud on the moon, and two slick punctures in her lips. A pain as if her mouth had been stapled. She looked in the mirror and blood was drying on her chin. When she opened her mouth her teeth lifted, then sliced her bottom lip again. She couldn't see the teeth, only the cuts they made. But she felt the teeth. Her features couldn't accommodate the length of them, they were her skeleton extended.

What am I?

She strapped Lily's watch to her wrist. She swallowed her friend's gift of ten years, or two small watch batteries, as if they were pills. She had heard that people died from accidentally swallowing these. She wished she could be sure of it. Miranda went down barefoot, like Eurydice. She walked with her fingers spread over her face, because no one must see. Luc was asleep behind his door.

The ground floor of the house was the only part that was lit. She turned to trapdoor-room, but Eliot intercepted her at the kitchen door. He pulled off his oven gloves.

"I made you something."

She smelt baked apple. She gagged. The pie looked impressive, like a crisp brown basket. Even Luc couldn't have been critical of the lattices that Eliot had worked across the top. It was a sign that Eliot observed more than he admitted.

"I even made the pastry myself," he said.

The kitchen light was so bright she couldn't see him properly. But she saw the winter apples—their pile had shrunk. He offered her a slice of pie, saying something about it being an attempt to replace Lind, that he knew she was feeling down about that.

She took the slice he offered her and tossed it into the bin, saucer and all. She peered at him. Why couldn't she see him properly? It was hard to talk to him without opening her mouth fully. If she stood at a distance and in the dark, he would not notice. She stepped out into the passage and switched off the light. The air was crowded with droplets of rose attar and loomed behind her.

"I can't see you properly," she said to him. "Come out here."

He meant something by the pie. He meant to poison her in some way, to disable her. Or, misguidedly, he meant to cure her.

"Why did you use the winter apples?" she asked. He wouldn't come into the dark.

"What are you talking about?"

She beckoned him frantically, but he stayed where he was.

"Why did you use the winter apples?"

"Miri," he said. His eyes were wet. Or maybe not, it wasn't clear.

The goodlady called to her. She should not have to go to trapdoor-room alone.

"Bad. You are bad." They were the only words she could fit her astonishment inside.

He said something, but she could no longer bear his voice. When he left her and went upstairs, she followed him, silent and intent, delaying her steps until he was safely in his room. Bob Dylan crooned scratchily. Her breath on the wood of his closed door. She could see him, her thoughts bent against him, if she wanted to she could strip him down to true red, the thing hinted at in rouge and roses
(no he's eliot eliot is me we were once one cell)
he would be sour.

She ran downstairs, away from him. There was someone strange at the front door. They stood where the Christmas tree had stood until the day after Boxing Day, when Sade had dismantled it for fear of bad luck. The stranger wore a big black hat and she didn't dare to pass them. Their back was to her, and they stood very straight, with a shapeless coat draped over them in such a way as to put the existence of limbs in doubt. And yet they stood. It was in trapdoor-room that she fell, and the house caught her. She had thought she would find the goodlady below, or Lily, or Jennifer, or her GrandAnna, but there was no one there but her. In trapdoor-room her lungs knocked against her stomach and she lay down on the white net that had saved Ore but would not save her. Two tiny moons flew up her throat. She squeezed them, one in each hand, until they were two silver kidneys. Acid seeped through her.

It's July. I've been listening to one song by the Shirelles over and over. *Will you still love me tomorrow?* It's July and the low-growing plants in the garden are choked with humidity, but I've caught a cold in my head. It might be the song. I think this is the song that Miri liked to play, but I'm not sure, I just can't be sure. Her favourite songs sounded just like each other—she stuck to one musical era, twelve years in a row, holding hands like shy sisters going out into the world.

Dad has closed the bed-and-breakfast. That was three weeks ago. He couldn't run the place without help, and I haven't been any help. I'd push the Hoover down hallways with my foot, wishing the sound it made was quieter. What if the phone rang? What if it had news to tell? Miri may have been found drowned, washed up at the foot of the cliff with tiny seashells in her ears. Dad was aware of the phone too, of its power. When he answered a call he'd twist the wire between his fingers, moving down as far as he could, as if checking and double-checking that all was as it should be, that the line was in order and the phone was actually connected.

We couldn't find a recent photo of Miri to give to the

police, so her missing person's poster features a girl with long hair and dreamy eyes that don't see the fracture coming. I tried to explain to the police officer who visited, but she nodded and said, "We'll mention that she wears a shorter hairstyle now." She was right to say that, there was nothing else she could say. *Shadadapsha, shadadapsha.*

I didn't even know Dad was going to close the bed-and-breakfast until I saw him unscrewing the sign that said THE SILVER HOUSE from the gate. He made me set an answer-machine message saying that reservations are no longer being accepted. At first I said I wouldn't do it. Why should I? He was the one closing the place down. He picked up the receiver and slammed it into my chest. He didn't do it angrily; he did it as if he'd seen a groove in my chest that fitted the shape of the receiver. He wrote the message on some notepaper and I said the words, stumbling, for no real reason, over the last part: "We regret any inconvenience caused."

Sylvie and The Paul came to stay for the fifth time since Miri left, even though Dad told them not to come this time. I was glad to see The Paul. Every day we got *The Times* and *The Daily Telegraph*, because there was more in them to read than in tabloids. I think Sylvie expected that by now she would have to cook for us and take care of us, but Dad made three meals a day in the kitchen, chopping and whisking with a grim energy that pushed her out, pushed all of us out. Sylvie kept looking at us with doe-eyed shock, as if she

couldn't believe that Dad and I hadn't died of grief. Sylvie
phoned Lind. To ask if Miri had been upset by a boy. "Why
else would a young girl run away? It must be love."

"She'll come back," The Paul said to me, over the top of
The Guardian. "All the best people run away from home
when they're young. I ran away when I was just twelve years
old, and I came back when I was bored of it." Sylvie and The
Paul only ended up staying for a week. Dad spent most of
his time blatantly avoiding them (I mean ducking into
rooms and stepping hastily around corners when he saw
them, as if he was regressing into boyhood) and it was getting tense.

"Telephone if you want anything, or if you want to come
to us," Sylvie said.
She kissed my cheek and then dabbed at it with her perfumed handkerchief.

"Take care of your father," The Paul said.

Dad and Lily would never have this, they would never
be old together and think inside each other's clockwork.

Sylvie and The Paul went back to Paris, and Dad moved
around the house normally again.

The Shirelles block my nose. I breathe with my mouth
open and my mouth is dry. Headaches mean that from my
seat on the roof I mistake the cliffs for Table Mountain. The
headache that comes with this cold is invisible assault,
like being thrown into a sack and pummelled with rocks.

Sometimes Dad comes and stands in the garden while
I'm on the roof. We don't address each other, but we're aware

of each other. I look at the top of his head while he looks out in the direction of the road behind our house. He tries to find it, whatever it is he wants to say, then he gives up and goes back inside.

In the past couple of weeks he's been to London and Brighton, Liverpool, also Manchester, I think, to eat at restaurants. He comes back to write about what he's eaten. When he's away I eat refried beans cold out of the tin, sometimes with lettuce for nutrition. I'm glad when he's away because he keeps asking me questions. He thinks he's Inspector Morse. For some time it was the apples.

"Where did the apples come from?"

"They were on the kitchen table when I came down."

"Fresh apples? I didn't put them there."

"Maybe Sade did, before she went."

"Why would she? She knows that in winter I use preserves."

"Okay."

"Why did you use them?"

How was I supposed to answer that one? "For a change?" I said.

My head ached so fiercely that I actually gasped, and he looked at me expectantly, waiting for me to reveal what I'd just remembered. I hobbled to my room but he followed me.

"What did you say to her when she said she couldn't trust you anymore?"

"Nothing. Not a single thing, Dad, I swear."

I couldn't lie down and groan in front of him, so I sat up

straight at my desk. He stood with his hands behind his back, mulling my words over as if this was the first time I'd said them.

"And she didn't say anything else after that, she just left?"

"Yes," through gritted teeth.

Dad's questions make me think that there may be some large omission that my memory has made out of ignorance and confusion. For example, did my sister wound her foot? Am I trying to remind myself of that? And if she did cut her foot, is it a clue to something?

I ask this because of her shoes. They keep filling with a substance that's only identifiable to one side of my brain. The other side will only say no to it. I first noticed it the night I slept in Miri's bed instead of mine. Something was moving in the branches outside my window with a flinty rattle; probably a squirrel, but it sounded as if someone hoarse-voiced was laughing at me. Dad was away and I found that the possibility of the phone ringing was too big for me alone, or the house was too small. The phone rang a lot, and each time it did I fell through rooms towards it as if yanked on a leash. Miri's room was the only one safe from the phone. The psychomantium is detached from the house, even more so than Lily's studio. I smelt roses stronger than I ever had in my life. Miri's shoes were lined up at the feet of her coat mannequin. Six neatly polished size 6s with mad heels. The smell came from the shoes.

The shoes were soaked through with

(I didn't make a sound but stood away, tried to think and
looked again)

red water. Water that was red and smelt of roses. It was
thick, though. Some of it gathered in viscous lumps.
Between the sight of the shoes and my head cold I had to
throw up. Then I had to hide the shoes. They had to be
hidden or they would expose the omission in my memory
so bulky and strange. Miri left the house barefoot so she
was supposed to come back. My chalk-sickened sister, shhh.
Miri left the house barefoot . . . it would be stupid to hide
the shoes or get rid of them. I emptied them and cleaned
them as best I could. But would that colour stick to the inside?
The smell stuck, but I got rid of the thick water. The next
day there was more. I am chained to the shoes. There is
nothing to be done. Sometimes, if you sit still beside them,
you can watch them filling up, like rain puddles forming
before your eyes. I can't stop the shoes from filling, but I
can't ignore them, either. I have to keep emptying them into
the bathroom sink, then rinsing and scrubbing hard with
Jif and Dettol, then replacing the shoes exactly where they
were so that Dad never knows. What happened that night?
I can't tell anyone. I don't know. I didn't see.

There is no one in Dover who looks like my sister. I tour
the town walking and on my bike, shaken by the ratio of
water to land. Martin and Emma are together and are
spending the summer teaching English somewhere in the
Third World. The others don't come around and only ask

me over halfheartedly—I don't talk and my silences are not mysterious.

Dad doesn't notice, but chairs are moved in the house. You leave a room and when you return the chair is scraped back from the table. Doors you leave closed are opened behind your back. And every day, the shoes.

I will write this down now, before I decide not to:

This morning I had just put the shoes back in their usual place when I heard someone walking in the attic. They walked slowly, as if weak. Their tread was light.

I said, "Miri?" It felt as if I hadn't spoken aloud for days. The walker stood still as soon as I spoke. But she was there, I knew it. If she was there she'd step again.

Once for no, twice for yes

Once for no, twice for yes

hear me

I whispered, "Miri, are you alive?"

My question wasn't loud enough to be heard outside of the room, but two creaks came from above, paired with deliberation.

I had to hold on to the wall. I've read that madness is present when everything you see and hear takes on an equal significance. A dead bird makes you cry, and so does a doorknob. This morning I was not mad. The only thing significant to me in all the world was the creaking upstairs.

"Where are you? In the house? Where in the house?"

No sound.

"Miri. Are you coming back?"

Step, step, halt.

I asked, "When?"

Three creaks. She stepped three times.

What is the meaning of it? Three creaks, three weeks? If she comes back for her shoes in three days, then I only need to empty them another three times. If it really is three weeks that were meant, what then. If three months, what then. Three years. That's why I had to write it down now. By then I may no longer believe I heard anything in Miri's room.

Acknowledgments

thank you:

stan medland, boogie, tophe, leo, ali, bolaji, tracy, jin, choop, car, hazel, ray, chretien, loa.

HELEN OYEYEMI is the author of the short story collection *What Is Not Yours Is Not Yours*, as well as five novels, including *Boy, Snow, Bird*, which was a finalist for the 2014 *Los Angeles Times* Book Prize. She received a 2010 Somerset Maugham Award and a 2012 Hurston/Wright Legacy Award. In 2013, she was named one of *Granta's* Best Young British Novelists.

Anchored by her concern with fluid identities and narrative layers, Helen Oyeyemi's fictions take us through the past and present and across continents, with language that is as strikingly playful as it is poetic and beguiling. Oyeyemi has been compared to an eclectic array of literary geniuses—including Toni Morrison, Emily Dickinson, Jeanette Winterson, Neruda, and Rimbaud—but it's difficult to think of a writer who is more purely herself. Named one of *Granta*'s Best Young British Novelists in 2013, she has won the Hurston/Wright Legacy Award and the Somerset Maugham Award and has been nominated for the Shirley Jackson Award, the BBC National Short Story Award, and James Tiptree, Jr. Award, among others.

Oyeyemi's novels and stories are exuberantly intellectual and highly readable, wildly inventive and classically resonant. It's no wonder she has been widely recognized as one of the most gifted and consistently surprising writers of her generation.

T359-1214

MR. FOX

Fairy-tale romances end
with a wedding. The
fairy tales that don't get
more complicated. In
this book, celebrated
writer Mr. Fox can't
stop himself from killing
off the heroines of his
novels, and neither
can his wife, Daphne.
It's not until Mary, his
muse, comes to life and
transforms him from
author into subject that
his real story begins
to unfold. Meanwhile,
Daphne becomes
convinced that her

husband is having an affair, and finds her way into Mary and
Mr. Fox's game. And so Mr. Fox is offered a choice: Will it be
a life with the girl of his dreams, or a life with an all-too-real
woman who delights him more than he cares to admit?

"Oyeyemi's writing is gorgeous and resonant and fresh...
a shimmering landscape pulsing with life."

—Aimee Bender, *The New York Times Book Review*

BOY, SNOW, BIRD

In the winter of 1953, Boy Novak arrives by chance in a small town in Massachusetts, looking, she believes, for beauty—the opposite of the life she's left behind in New York. She marries a local widower and becomes stepmother to his winsome daughter, Snow Whitman.

A wicked stepmother is a creature Boy never imagined she'd become, but elements of the familiar tale of aesthetic obsession begin to play

themselves out when the birth of Boy's daughter Bird, who is dark-skinned, exposes the Whitmans as light-skinned African Americans passing for white. Among them, Boy, Snow, and Bird confront the tyranny of the mirror to ask how much power surfaces really hold.

"Oyeyemi breathes life into ideas like nobody else." —*The Guardian*

WHAT IS NOT YOURS IS NOT YOURS

Playful, ambitious, and exquisitely imagined, *What Is Not Yours Is Not Yours* is cleverly built around the idea of keys, literal and metaphorical. The key to a house, the key to a heart, the key to a secret—Oyeyemi's keys not only unlock elements of her characters' lives, they promise further labyrinths on the other side. In "Books and Roses" one special key opens a library, a garden, and

clues to at least two lovers' fates. In "Is Your Blood as Red as This?" an unlikely key opens the heart of a student at a puppeteering school. "'Sorry' Doesn't Sweeten Her Tea" involves a "house of locks," where doors can be closed only with a key—with surprising, unobservable developments. And in "If a Book Is Locked There's Probably a Good Reason for That Don't You Think," a key keeps a mystical diary locked (for good reason).

"Dreamy, spellbinding, and unlike just about anything you can imagine. It's a book that resists comparisons; Oyeyemi's talent is as unique as it is formidable." —**NPR**

GINGERBREAD

Perdita Lee may appear to be your average British schoolgirl; Harriet Lee may seem just a working mother, but there are signs that they might not be as normal as they think they are. For one thing, there's the gingerbread they make. Londoners may find themselves able to take or leave it, but it's very popular in Druhástrana, the far-away (or, according to many sources, non-existent) land of Harriet Lee's early youth. The world's truest lover of the Lee family gingerbread, however, is Harriet's charismatic childhood friend Gretel—a figure who seems to have had a hand in everything (good or bad) that has happened to Harriet since they met.

As the book follows the Lees through encounters with jealousy, ambition, family grudges, work, wealth, and real estate, gingerbread seems to be the only thing that reliably holds a constant value.

"The outline of Oyeyemi's remarkable career glimmers with pixie dust." –*The Washington Post*